D1985089

SABU

SHUGORO YAMAMOTO

Translated by
SHELLEY MARSHALL

SHELLEY MARSHALL

Copyright © 2023 by Shelley Marshall

All rights reserved.

ISBN 978-1-959002-05-5

No part of this book may be reproduced in any form or by any electronic or mechanical means, including information storage and retrieval systems, without written permission from the translator, except for the use of brief quotations in a book review.

Created with Vellum

CONTENTS

CHAPTER 1

1.1

One evening, misty rain billowed like haze. Sabu was crying as he crossed from west to east over Ryōgoku Bridge. He was drenched from the top of his head. Water drops fell from the thin Kokura sash and the faded black apron he wore over his Futagojima kimono. From time to time, his palm slid over his face soaked by rain and tears leaving dark blotches around his eyes and cheeks.

Sabu was a short and stocky youth with a round face and pointy head.

When he crossed the bridge, Eiji trailed after him. His thin build looked agile. The thick eyebrows and small tight lips on his long face reflected intelligence and a strong will.

Eiji caught up and blocked his way. Sabu kept his head down and tried to dodge him, but Eiji grabbed Sabu's shoulder.

Eiji said, "Please stop. Let's go home."

Sabu's hand wiped his eyes. He was choking up.

"It's all right. We'll go home," said Eiji. "Are you listening to me?"

"No. I'm going back home to Kasai. The proprietress told me to get out. This was the third time."

Eiji jerked his chin to the left and said, "Stop walking. People are staring."

The two youths turned at the foot of the bridge. The rain flowed nearly soundlessly at a constant rhythm.

"Honestly, I didn't know," said Sabu. "Last evening sacks of flour were in the cupboard, the proprietress told me to take one out to use in the kitchen. Only one was on the shelf, and one was left out. After she used it, I put the flour sack back, but she said I forgot."

"But hasn't she always been like that?" said Eiji.

"The flour got damp so she said I'm the apprentice who bungles everything," said Sabu, stopping short, crying as his palms rubbed his eyes. "She didn't give it back to me. I don't remember that. I didn't know."

"That's her habit. She doesn't think."

"No, I'm bad. No good. A fool. A dimwit. Even I know this wasn't going to work out. I've had enough." Sabu's throat choked up then he said, "That's what I think. It'd be better for me to go home to Kasai and become a farmer."

A samurai's mansion stood on the right side of the broad street along the river. A little further down the river on the left was Yokoami.

Two shabby-looking men, who looked middle-aged and may have been manservants or laborers, carried umbrellas with holes. They passed by while engaged in a lively conversation. Eiji shivered at the sight of their bare shins below their short winter coats.

For three years, Sabu had been a live-in apprentice at Hōko-dō in Kobuna-chō. He talked about never getting time off, always being scolded, ridiculed, and slapped. It was not a strong complaint, but a weak, monotonous echo resembling a baby's whine. As he remembered, the waters of the big river occasionally hit the stone wall and growled.

Eiji said, "An apprentice's life is hard anywhere you look. The proprietress's sharp tongue is her way." He nearly stumbled over his words. "And by nature you and women ... Watch it, a cart's coming."

Eiji touched Sabu's arm, and they stopped and moved toward

the river. A man came from behind pulling an empty cart and overtook them.

"Learning a trade is tough," Eiji said. "Think about it, won't everyone say you went back home to Kasai to become a farmer and get a kick out of that. They'll die laughing from morning to night? ... And at home in Kasai, won't they tell you to get out? Don't you think so?"

Sabu said nothing, but Eiji didn't expect an answer. Sabu seemed to be thinking about his family in Kasai: his grandfather stooped over and sick with asthma; his timid father; his strong-willed and quick-to-slap mother; his older brother's wife and her nonstop nagging and arguing with his mother that began each morning; his three younger siblings; his hard-drinking older brother; his five nephews and nieces; the old, cramped house with a thin coating of soot and leaning to one side; and the field little more than an acre. Sabu was distraught and sobbed as he started walking again.

Eiji said, "You gotta hometown. It's nice to have any kind of home to go back to. I'm alone and don't have parents, brothers, sisters, or other relatives. Last spring, I thought I was gonna get kicked out of the shop. Would they kick me out? Or would I have to leave? One or both would have been horrible."

Sabu turned around for a moment to look at Eiji's face. He didn't look back out of curiosity but bewilderment. Eiji was talking like he was upset and angry.

He had stolen coins from the reception desk several times last year and was caught by Yoshi, the proprietress, and confessed.

Eiji said, "A food cart selling eel broiled in soy sauce was set up at the canal beside Wakoku Bridge. I couldn't resist the aroma."

When he passed by and smelled the aroma, his stomach would not be satisfied until he enjoyed a meal of eel. He felt sickly, even his limbs trembled. He grabbed coins from the cash box at the reception desk twelve, maybe, thirteen times. He didn't think it was wrong because he wanted to eat eel so badly. In February, the proprietress Yoshi summoned him to her room.

"The proprietress didn't yell at me," said Eiji like he was chewing mud. She frowned and said, "On August 5 of last year and yesterday, I saw you do something at the reception desk. Don't do that again. If you want something, I will give it to you. Come to me and ask. That was it."

Was Yoshi only certain about seeing him steal twice? Did she deliberately try to not know? In either case, Eiji was so ashamed he could die and didn't think he could stay at the shop.

He didn't even think of himself as a thief. His grabbing coins from the cash box was disgraceful and embarrassing. He no longer wished to stay at the shop.

Eiji said, "If I fled the shop, where would I go? When I was eight years old, I was caught in the summer fire at Ōnoko-chō. My parents and younger sister burned to death. Only I was saved because I went fishing at Shiraogashi. Not one of my relatives' homes survived. My old man said he came from Ise, but I couldn't remember where. Even if I remembered, I wouldn't have gone there for help. My dark self at that time didn't grieve not having a home."

"I never knew. I didn't know anything about that," Sabu mumbled. "Ei-chan, that's why you never give up."

"I never stole again."

The pair came to the riverbank at Yokoami. Sabu stopped and stared at the ground. He scraped the toes of his zori sandals heavy with moisture back and forth over the earth.

"I've been thinking," he said, not sounding too sure. "I was thumped by my mother when I was little. My younger brother played a trick. She thought I did it and smacked me. While I was crying and saying it wasn't me, she figured out my brother did it. She didn't seem to care and said, 'Well then, this is for one of the times you didn't get smacked for all the things you've done before.'"

Eiji said, "Women are like that. They pinch you with the stroking hand and stroke you with the pinching hand. Either way, they quickly forget. Have you calmed down a little, Sabu? You're good now, let's go home."

Sabu said, "Okay." He sounded sure. "Thanks." In a near whisper, he added, "I'm sorry, Ei-chan."

Eiji said, "The next time, please, don't run off without a word. From now on, talk to me. I'll stand by you. Okay?"

Sabu slowly nodded.

They turned back. When they reached Ryōgoku Bridge, a twelve- or thirteen-year-old girl caught up with them from behind, held out an umbrella, and between gasps said, "Please, open this. I'm taking it to my big sister but went the wrong way. Please, open it."

Eiji looked at the girl. A hole pierced the umbrella he was opening. She wore a secondhand, lined, two-color-striped kimono dotted with patches. Her obi sash was frayed. Her worn-out geta sandals were for adults. The sandal's straps were stretched and had turned her mud-splattered toes into vipers.

"I don't need it," said Eiji. "We're going to Kobuna-chō and will be home soon."

"Then it's perfect, okay?" said the girl happily smiling. "I'm going to Horie-chō. To the shop called Sumiyoshi in Horie-chō. That's where my sister works. I'll go home with you."

"You're a pest," said Eiji. "I said we don't need an umbrella."

"But you two are soaked. Hey, open it."

"Sabu," said Eiji. "Run!"

The two ran out into the light rain.

"You jerks," shouted the girl. "Good. Get wet, losers!"

Eiji and Sabu were both fifteen back then and soon forgot about the girl.

1.2

On February 15, Eiji and Sabu turned twenty years old. For the first time in their lives, they went out together to drink sake. However, this was not their first time tasting sake. On celebratory days when sake was brought out at the shop, they drank two or three cups but never went out and paid to drink. They were half scared because the proprietor Hōbei forbade it. He loved to say, "Don't drink until you're twenty because your bones will be soft if sake is drunk before the body hardens."

Hōko-dō was a well-known, established premier shop of picture framers and scroll mounters. From the previous generation, they specialized in serving five or six well-known calligraphers and artists of the day. They worked only for long-established antique shops, samurai families, and large shops, and refused cheap jobs.

Obviously, the eight craftsmen underwent rigorous training that began at a young age. Of course, they learned to read and write but also learned flower arranging, the tea ceremony, and, from a young age, the appreciation of authentic items, such as the quality of calligraphy and paintings.

The shop currently employed eight craftsmen: Wasuke, the head craftsman, a 29-year-old; Taichi, 27; Shigeshichi, Gorō, Eiji, and Sabu, all 20; Denroku, 17; and Hanji, 15.

Thirteen craftsmen who used to work at the shop came and went. They had independent shops. When Hōko-dō overflowed with work or had special orders, they called on these suitable thirteen men for assistance.

This was the shop's tradition. The craftsmen's routines were regulated. Other than the first and fifteenth days of each month, they were forbidden to go out at night for amusement. One cup of sake with the evening meal was allowed with dinner from the age of twenty but not one drop more. Not everyone lived this life with strict obedience, but they were fine and not a cause for concern.

Work stopped at five regardless of the work backlog. They quit work at five, cleaned up, went to the public bathhouse, and after the evening meal were expected to go to bed at nine. During the time until bed, one could do as he wished: read a book, practice calligraphy, or play a game of go or shogi. However, no one should sneak out to drink sake or visit a woman.

The proprietor Hōbei knew these things happened but said nothing. If sneaking out became a frequent habit, naturally, the craftsman's work would be affected. At those times, first came a reprimand and then dismissal if he did not correct his behavior. This happened to about two craftsmen every five years. They could not be allowed to remain at Hōko-dō.

Eiji's and Sabu's hearts were pounding.

"I can't believe we're twenty. It feels so strange," Sabu said slowly. "I've been thinking it feels stranger than when I was sixteen and got my head shaved bald on top like a samurai."

"You're right," said Eiji.

They wore two-striped haori half-coats over handwoven cotton, striped lined kimonos tied closed with Kokura obi sashes, and zori sandals with hemp soles.

At dusk, they walked east on the streets of Kobuna-chō crowded with passersby. They had no destination in mind but seemed to be thinking about going to Hirokōji Bridge in Ryōgoku.

Sabu said, "Eiji, you're doing good work. You already set up folding screens and are an expert at painting the undercoat on *fusuma* sliding screens. But all I get to do is prepare paste."

"That's work, too," said Eiji.

"I think sometime I can't stand it when I'm kneading a sack underwater. I think about being twenty and still doing this."

"That's work, too, Sabu. The quality of the paste determines the results of the work of the mounters and framers. Do you understand?"

"I guess so."

"If you understand, then stop complaining. If you become Japan's best paste preparer, you'll be a fine craftsman. You must become Japan's best paste preparer."

"I guess so."

Sabu wanted to say "If I become a craftsman at Hōko-dō, I want to frame, mount, and make fusuma sliding screens for mansions," but couldn't.

"Wait a minute," said Eiji and stopped.

They were at the canal between Horie-chō and Shinzaimoku-machi. Five or six scattered buildings and a small restaurant appeared beside the canal. In front of the building at the end, a woman was hanging up a half-sized *noren* shop curtain with Sumiyoshi written in kana characters dyed white on dark blue cloth. She was small with a slender build. A *tasuki* sash held back her kimono sleeves as she worked. Slim, flexible-looking white shins peeked from under the tucked-up hem of her checkered yellow kimono.

"What is it, Ei-chan?"

"Sumiyoshi," whispered Eiji in his mouth. "I've heard that name before."

"It's a restaurant in Yanagibashi. Aren't you a regular customer there?"

"No, not the one in Yanagibashi. I've heard about another one somewhere else."

The woman finished hanging up the noren curtain and avoided the salt pile for good luck at her feet and went inside.

Eiji narrowed his eyes and thought for a short time like he was trying to recall a memory. No matter how hard he tried, he couldn't remember. He softly clicked his tongue in exasperation, said it'd be okay to go see then nudged Sabu in that direction.

When they entered the restaurant, a man in his forties was raising a large lit hanging paper lantern to the ceiling. In the room, about thirty feet by eighteen feet, two dining tables were placed on both sides. Built-in benches were provided for each table. Round straw mats woven from cattail were placed about two feet apart. The many customers were not crammed together but drank in comfort.

In the kitchen, a lattice woven from bamboo was on the right side. Another noren, a light yellow one with Sumiyoshi written in blue, hung at the other end.

"It's early," said Eiji when he entered the restaurant and asked the man hanging up the lantern, "Are you open?"

"Welcome," answered the man. "Please come in." He gestured for them to come inside and shouted, "We have customers."

Eiji nudged Sabu's shoulder and chose a table and sat at the far end.

Two young women came right out, touching their hands to their hair, greeted them, and took their orders. Neither was the woman who was hanging up the noren earlier. One was eighteen or nineteen. The other was twenty-two or -three. Both were plump, wore face powder, and smelled of strong perfumed oil. As he blushed, Eiji ordered a dish of pickled and braised foods and two bottles of sake.

"I know who you are," said the older one to Sabu. "You're from Hōko-dō in Kobuna-chō."

A confused Sabu looked at Eiji. The other woman passed on their order. The older one sat down.

"No, not me," said a flustered Sabu but corrected himself. "No, you're right. The boss and his wife let us come today. Ei-chan here and me, I'm Sabu, have the same birthday."

"Stop it," said Eiji. "You talk too much."

"What's wrong? It's all right," said the woman. "Sabu-chan and Ei-chan, I'm Okame, a turtle. That's not a nickname. It's my real name. Nice to meet you."

Sabu laughed. Eiji scowled.

"We'd like to drink alone," Eiji said to the woman.

"I'll pour your drinks then leave you two alone. All right?"

"For privacy, you should go inside," she said out of nowhere like she was annoyed. "Soon it'll be crowded in here and we won't be able to easily chat. It's cramped, but if I sit across from you, we can talk quietly."

"Yeah," said Eiji and put his hands inside his kimono. "We don't have much money."

She laughed and told him not to worry about that, made them stand, and escorted them further inside. They passed through the noren and saw a row of three small 4½-tatami-mat rooms.

The fence with the neighbor was on the right side. Planted bamboo hid the fence. Scattered leaves had withered to a brown color. Stones with moss, probably an arrangement, were placed at the base of the plants. The moss was also shriveled.

"Here's a good place," she said as she took them into the room at the end. "I'll get a lantern."

Although a small room, a futon covered half the floor. Two small two-panel folding screens were set up to hide the sliding door to the adjoining room. A square hibachi heater made of paulownia wood was lit.

Okame probably told the truth about her name. She soon returned with a lit standing lantern. Another woman followed carrying two *choashi* trays, each one with legs shaped like a butterfly with wings spread.

"Should we be doing this?" asked Sabu in a whisper, sounding helpless. "What about the bill?"

"Oh, shut up," said Eiji while trying to hide his pounding heart. "They know the name of our shop. We could get fired. Stop fidgeting."

Eventually, Okame brought the food and drinks they ordered and served them on the two trays. She told them to clap if they needed anything and left.

"I won't hesitate," said Eiji. "That would be a problem. We won't be sharing drinks of friendship. We'll pour our own drinks. Okay?"

While staring at his tray, Sabu said, "Okay, but ... aren't you a little scared?"

"Scared of what?" asked the third woman, who opened the sliding door, stuck out her face, and flashed a grin.

"I'm terribly sorry. I thought you were the riverbank boss. Pardon me."

It was the woman who hung out the noren in front. Her slender face was tense. Her lips parted when she smiled; a double tooth peeked out. Eiji coldly turned away.

1.3

"Don't sulk," she said. "No one's here."

"We're fine," said Eiji, still looking away. "You don't need to pour the sake."

"This looks like a wake," she said. "And that's bad advice no one should have to listen to."

Eiji turned and said, "You're a pest."

She smiled, but her face tensed when she looked at Eiji's eyes.

"Excuse me," she said softly and closed the sliding door. Her double tooth exposed when she smiled stayed in Eiji's eyes.

Eiji did not take the day off on March 1. He repapered a sliding screen in the tatami room for a large money-exchange business customer called Watabun in Honchō, Nihonbashi. To inspect the paper alignment, he went with the senior apprentice Taichi.

Watabun was an old special customer of Hōko-dō. Once a year, they repapered the sliding doors. Every year since he was thirteen, Eiji assisted Taichi and Shigeshichi and became familiar with the family and the servants.

The proprietor Tokubei had a large frame and was portly. His breath always smelled of sake. He rarely came out to the shop but toyed with antiques and loved classical literature.

His wife Miyo was slender and petite. Her face was small, too. More than the proprietress of a large shop, she seemed more like a proprietress on a backstreet.

They had no sons, and their two daughters, Kimi and Sono, were two years apart. Both were attractive. The older sister inherited her father's immense physique and carefree personality. The younger sister was thin, had a narrow face, spoke like an adult, and took swift actions.

Watabun was a corner shop with a storehouse with two entrances. An inner garden separated the two-story shop from the one-story residence that had a gate on the side and the entryway in the front.

Following the earthen wall for fire protection on the right led to a well with a bucket. It wasn't the kitchen but where the family, guests, various merchants and craftsmen came and went.

As a house with many visitors, one apprentice was also the doorman. At the landing, the size of six tatami mats, he was hitting a hemp sack filled with small grains of gold and *koban* gold coins against a wooden board.

This monotonous and stupid action opened the sack and knocked it onto the board. Small amounts of gold stuck to the sack. If the sack was burned up after some fixed time, the collected gold scraps could be picked out.

Since its discovery by a government official would be unfortunate, this shouldn't be done at the shop but is likely done at money-exchange shops anywhere. Eiji felt contempt when he heard that because this large shop was so miserly.

As Eiji and Taichi passed through the tatami room carrying a bundle of sample paper, Sue, a fifteen- or sixteen-year-old maid, brought in tea and pastry. Eiji had not come to this house last year or the year before last but came every year until three years ago and was friendly with the two daughters and known to Sue.

Sue greeted Taichi and then saw Eiji.

"It's been a long time, hasn't it, Ei-san? You've grown up. At first, I thought my eyes were tricking me."

"Stop it," said a smiling Taichi. "That's pitiful. He's already twenty."

"Excuse me," said a redder Sue. "I was trying to say he's become a fine young man but blurted out the wrong words."

Eiji also blushed and avoided looking at Sue.

"How old are you, Sue?"

"I'm sixteen," she said to Taichi. "I'm small so people often think I'm twelve or thirteen. It's embarrassing."

Somebody stood in the hall watching them. She was the older daughter of the house. Someone else was there. The younger sister was passing by and peeked out from behind her sister and said, "Oh, it's Ei-chan."

The older sister didn't move, but the younger, Sono, leaped into the tatami room, flopped down to sit in front of Eiji, and stared wide-eyed at him. Sue slightly bowed and slipped away. Eiji glimpsed her retreating figure from the corner of his eye.

"What a shock. You're Ei-chan?" said Sono, her face beaming. "You've grown big. I'm surprised."

Taichi smiled only with his lips and said, "Not long ago, someone else said that."

"Ei-chan," said Sono staring at Eiji's eyes, ignoring Taichi. "Do you know who I am?"

"You're Sono-san. It's not like we haven't seen each other in ages. It's only been two years since I was last here."

"I've grown, too. Haven't I?"

"Hello," said Eiji to Kimi in the hall. "It's been a long time."

Kimi gently nodded and leisurely said, "Welcome back."

1.4

The proprietor Tokubei appeared. Taichi spread out the paper samples. As usual, Tokubei's breath wreaked of alcohol.

"Come here for a moment, Ei-chan," said Sono. "I want to show you something."

"Sono-chan," snapped Kimi in the hall.

"Is that all right, Father?" asked Sono's nasally voice. "I want to show Ei-chan something. Can he come with me?"

Kimi scolded her, "Sono-chan!"

Tokubei waved his hand, unconcerned. "Stop bothering me. Do as you wish."

Eiji looked at Taichi for help. Taichi only smiled and jerked his chin to say, "Go."

Sono grabbed his hand.

"Come this way. Hurry."

She hasn't changed, thought Eiji. When the apprentices came to do a job here, the sisters always made them their playmates. Since the sliding doors were repapered every December, he played games with cards, shuttlecocks, beanbags, or marbles but felt humiliated when he played these girls' games.

However, this is an important customer, so as an apprentice, he could not refuse. Although he participated reluctantly, he was the best in any game. The strong-willed Sono became frustrated and often cried.

He was taken to the sisters' room. Everything, their dressers with two decorative shelves occupied by their dolls, the musical instruments of a koto and a shamisen, *chadansu* chests for tea utensils, and vermillion-lacquered clothes racks overflowed with gorgeous colors befitting the daughters and smelled of perfume.

"I'm sixteen," said Sono while kneeling in front of her dresser. "I had a long-sleeved silk kimono custom made from a Yuzen print. It's beautiful."

She opened a drawer and, with both hands and great care, passed it to Eiji.

"Spread it out and look at it," said Sono. "The pattern is called

The Flowers of the Four Seasons. The cloth was dyed at Tamaruya in Kyoto."

"My kimono has a susomoyo pattern on the hem," said Kimi from the side. "I'll show you mine, too."

"Show him later," barked Sono. "You're always copying me. Stop butting in."

Eiji spread out the kimono.

"This is pretty," he said.

For the daughters of a wealthy man, a Yuzen kimono dyed in Kyoto was to be expected. Deliberately bringing someone to see it revealed the open nature of these down-to-earth residents of downtown. These sisters were not showing off.

The older sister scolded by her little sister did not mope but quietly opened her dresser. She seemed about to take out her kimono, but Sono was faster. While announcing she would show him her obi sash next, she opened the lower drawer. She shrieked, jumped up, and hugged Eiji with both arms.

"Eek!" she shouted and held tight to him. "A mouse ... there's a mouse in there!"

The surprised Kimi moved backward. Eiji freed himself from Sono's arms. However, the power of her clutch was surprisingly strong. He couldn't immediately break free.

"You have to let go," said Eiji. "That mouse isn't chasing you."

"No, I'm scared," said Sono and tightened her grip. "I can't breathe."

"You chased away the mouse," said Eiji. Finally, he could move his body and push Sono away. "Kimi-san, please come back."

He looked in the drawer but didn't see any mouse. He stuck in his hand and opened each sash in the pile until he felt the bottom, but did not see one mouse or bug. He returned the sashes to the drawer, stood, and glared at Sono's face.

Kimi hugged his chest with both arms and looked up at Eiji with a frightened expression.

"It's true. I'm not lying," said Sono, avoiding staring into Eiji's eyes. "If I try to pick up a sash, the mouse in there tries to bite me."

Eiji was about to speak when he heard his name being called from the hall. He turned and saw Sue.

"Taichi-san wants you," said Sue without looking. "Please come to take the measurements."

Eiji nodded at her, pointing at the drawer packed with sashes, and said to Sono, "There's not enough room in there for a small mouse to squat."

Sono shrugged.

"But it's in there. It's squatting in there like this. I think it'll bite me. It bared its teeth like this."

Sono showed him, but Eiji said nothing and left.

1.5

When he finished his work, Eiji left through the kitchen door. Sue saw him as he passed through the lattice door carrying the package of sample papers and the notebook of measurements. She seemed to have been waiting for him by the well. Her grinning face never took her eyes off Eiji as she ran to him. An earnest brooding light filled her eyes. Her grin warped like she was about to cry.

"Please forgive what I did earlier."

"About what?" he asked.

"About you being bigger," said Sue, never looking away. "I wanted to say how nice you looked."

"Oh, forget about it," said Eiji as he shifted the package. "I'm not mad at you."

"Really?" whispered Sue as tears fell. "Thank you."

"All of this over nothing."

"Ei-san, I first met you when you were thirteen. I remember thinking you were full of anger and scary."

Not knowing what to say, Eiji blushed and said angrily, "I remembered you."

"Thank you," Sue softly said, spun around, and jogged away. Eiji did not watch her. As long as his face was flush, he took breaths so deep his chest seemed to roll like waves.

A voice called, "Eiji, come here."

Taichi was peeking from inside the lattice door. Eiji thought he was caught doing something wrong and nervously walked over.

"You can go home before me," said Taichi. "I have to have a drink with the customer. It's boring, but what can I do? Please, tell the boss."

On the landing, the shop boy was still hitting the board with the heavy-looking hemp sack. Eiji nodded to Taichi and left.

"So I've gotten big?" Eiji muttered while walking and smiled. "I'm bigger, but my build and face haven't changed since I was thirteen."

When a girl becomes thirteen, her face and body become those of a young woman. He found that thought strange and was still smiling.

He returned home to Kobuna-chō. The shop was closed because it was a day off. Eiji entered from the wooden side door. Sabu was preparing paste in the narrow empty lot out back.

He sat on a small bench in front of a ten-quart bucket. He had tucked up the hem of his kimono and pulled back its sleeves with a cord. Both of his hands were in the bucket. He was kneading a sack containing wheat flour with a generous amount of water.

Milky water flowed out. After deposits formed, he poured it into a jar. The half-full jar was set on the ground in the shade and covered to rest.

Only paste made this way can be used in mounting or lining the backing of a folding screen. The jar is left alone for two to three years.

"Sabu, what happened?" Eiji called out as he approached. "Didn't you have the day off? What are you doing? Worse than that, why are you here out back?"

Sabu did not answer and turned away. Eiji noticed wetness on the side of his face.

"What happened?" Eiji said softly. "What happened?"

"Nothing," said Sabu, shaking his head. "Nothing happened."

"Are you crying?"

"No, I'm not crying." Sabu rubbed his eyes with his arm. "Flour gets in my eyes when I'm making the paste."

Eiji stared at Sabu's profile, but Sabu didn't turn to face him.

"I thought we could go out somewhere so I hurried home," said Eiji. "It looks like we can't because you're in the middle of your work."

Once the kneading began, Sabu couldn't stop until the mixture was in the jar. If Eiji went out drinking with Sabu, he wanted to talk about Sue despite being unsure about what. He managed to wind down without talking.

"It's okay. You can go," said Sabu, his white hands never stopped kneading. "Don't worry about me."

"Don't be stupid. By myself? If you're working, so will I," said Eiji. "I have the measurements for the fusuma screens at Watabun. I can gather the paper. But not here, why don't you come around to the workshop?"

"I'm okay here." Sabu sounded like his throat was throttled. "Please, leave me alone."

He plunged his hands into the bucket, slouched, and began to cry quietly.

Eiji bent over and said, "Sabu, tell me what's wrong. Why won't you talk to me?"

"Please, leave me alone."

The sniffling Sabu turned his face away.

"I mean it. Nothing's wrong. I'm asking you to leave me alone."

"Okay, if that's what you want."

Sabu gave a sharp nod. His stout body slouched over and his nodding head radiated childlike honesty. Eiji's heart was touched, What a pitiful guy.

CHAPTER 2

2.1

Two months later on April 15, Eiji and Sabu entered Sumiyoshi in Horie-chō. When they left after dinner, the lamps were already lit in the shop and five or six customers were there. Okame, who they met before, seemed to have forgotten Eiji and Sabu. She welcomed them but didn't mingle with the customers.

Eiji was a little bewildered.

All the customers were middle-aged and appeared to be regulars at this shop. He felt out of place and had no idea where to sit. The noren near the end of the dirt-floor room parted and out came the young woman who peeked into the small tatami room the last time.

She saw Eiji and Sabu and stared at them with wide-open eyes. She clapped her hands as she scurried toward them.

"Welcome," she said. "I know you two. The tatami room would be nice again. Please, this way."

She turned around and left through the noren curtain. Eiji winked at Sabu and followed her. She entered the small tatami room, took out an ashtray, and set up a folding screen.

"Calm down," said Eiji as he stepped into the room. "There's no point in getting giddy."

"Oh, I say that to everyone," she said and shrugged. "Sake and side dishes. What side dishes would you like?"

"We came to have a meal. How about two or three dishes that won't leave us hungry?"

"That's like the last time," she said and looked at Eiji then Sabu. "I wouldn't have recognized either of you alone, but together, I knew you right away. No, that's not so. I knew after you went home the last time. Ah, it was those two."

"You're a pest," said Eiji and scowled. "Hurry up and bring our order."

She stuck her face in front of Eiji and said, "Calling me a pest again ... and you don't remember me."

"I know someone like you."

"Like me? But not me."

Eiji thought she resembled Sono and laughed when he recalled the time she feared a mouse was going to bite her.

"You're horrible ... and have no heart," said the woman as she left to get the order.

She returned with the sake.

"The side dishes will be here soon."

She placed a tray and the sake-warming bottle between the two. While pouring sake beside Sabu, she said, "You still don't remember me."

Holding the cup, Eiji told her she talked too much. She clapped her hands again.

"You're the pest," she said, a little agitated. "At Ryōgoku Bridge, you told me I was a pest."

"Aah," Sabu slowly said and nodded still holding the cup. "The umbrella."

"Yes, the umbrella."

"That was five years ago," said Sabu.

"Yes. It was raining, and you opened an umbrella with a hole."

"That's right."

"What are you talking about?" asked Eiji.

"Hey, five years ago, I ... uh," said Sabu but stopped. "Weren't we going from Azuma Ryōgoku to Yokoami? We were soaking wet from the rain."

Now, Eiji turned his eyes, which looked he just woke up from a nap, to the woman.

"Oh, now I remember. That time I opened the umbrella for that bratty kid. That was you?"

"My name is Nobu," she said smiling and showing her double tooth and bowed. "It's lovely to see you again."

"I'm Eiji, and this is Sabu. You were a shrimp back then, and I forgot all about you. Well, you've grown," said Eiji then feeling vengeful added, "I remember that tooth."

"Oh, you're awful. A meanie," said Nobu and stared at Eiji as her hand pressed her mouth. She poured Sabu another drink. "This tooth can be pulled out. I'm eighteen. When I turn twenty, I will have it pulled out."

"You're eighteen? A mere child."

Trying to help, Sabu broke in. "And pretty. She's a pretty girl."

"I'll go get the side dishes," Nobu said and left.

Sabu tried to pour Eiji a drink, but he refused, poured himself a drink, and took a sip.

"Something's still bothering me," said Eiji quietly while looking to the side. "What happened on the first of last month?"

Sabu was surprised, dropped his eyes like they were struck by a bright light, and hung his head down.

"Can't you tell me now?"

"I'm sorry about that," mumbled Sabu. "I'm sorry I made you worry. I think I did."

Eiji cut him off. "Stop it. You always say you think. Please get to the point."

"Okay." Sabu nodded. He sipped the sake and said, "Mitsu-chan visited that day."

2.2

Mitsu was the daughter at Hōko-dō. This year she turned nineteen. In the spring of last year, she married into the family of the comb merchant Sawamura in Himono-chō in Nihonbashi.

Hōbei and his wife had two children. Their younger child Yoshijiro, now fifteen, was a sickly boy and stayed with a farming family in Tamagawa. The farmer, Heisaemon, was married to Yu, their relative, and owned a fairly large amount of farmland. They had a family visit once a month.

Mitsu was no beauty but picky because of her family. She found fault with the workers and made up reasons to complain to her parents.

Hōbei and his wife were aware of her disposition and, for the most part, paid little attention to her complaints. This served to heighten Mitsu's stubbornness. After marrying, she became more dissatisfied and often returned to her parents' home and picked on everyone.

"She came home and saw me. She said I shouldn't be fooling around because it's a day off."

Sabu forced a smile.

"She said, 'If you're going to eat other people's food and have the least bit of gratitude, you should work. For example, if the shop gives you time off, shouldn't you work to show gratitude? A grain of rice is not free.'"

"I don't need to hear the rest," said Eiji. "You understand Mitsu-chan's personality, don't you? She gets into an argument at Himono-chō and comes here to take her anger out on someone. Forget about it."

"It's all right for you, but I was born slow and still can only make paste. She told me a grain of rice is not free."

"What a stupid thing to say. We don't eat for free," said an angry Eiji. "We work and aren't fooling around. Since I was small, I've hated my chapped hands and feet. I've worked so hard I dripped sweat. Hōko-dō stays in business because of us, the craftsmen. Don't let it get to you, Sabu."

Nobu stepped into the tatami room carrying the side dishes and asked to pour their drinks. She removed the tasuki sash to untuck her sleeves and sat between the two.

"I remember now," said Eiji and looked at Nobu. "That time, didn't you say you had an older sister?"

"Yes, I was bringing the umbrella to her."

"Does she still work here?"

"She died," said Nobu, shaking her head. "My sister was sickly. Her death was pitiful. Talking about it makes me cry. Now, here's your drink, Sabu."

"Do you live in Honchō?" he asked.

"Yes, in Koizumi-chō," she said as she poured Eiji's drink. "I don't want to talk about me. I don't want to make people listen to my story. It's miserable. A day doesn't go by when I don't think I'd rather leave home even if I had to become a beggar."

"Stop talking about that," said Eiji. "You said you didn't want us to hear it."

"You're right," she said and shrugged her narrow shoulders. "I'm sorry. Here's your drink."

"Your tooth is cute," said Sabu, sipping his sake. His bright eyes stared at Nobu's mouth. "I think it'd be better if you don't get it pulled."

"Not get it pulled? Of course, I am going to get it pulled out."

"Why?"

"Oh, I don't know," said a staring Nobu. "I was born with this extra tooth out of place. It has been pushed out of the way, but I'll get it removed one day."

Eiji hurriedly said, "If it's not taken out, it will drill a hole in your lip. Drink up, Sabu."

"Maybe I said something wrong," said Nobu, glancing at Eiji's face.

"It's okay. That's not it," said Sabu, giving her a big-hearted smile. "I think Ei-chan only worries about me, but I'm used to it. Don't worry about saying the wrong thing.

"If a hole opened up in your lip, then taking out the tooth would be a good idea."

"I don't understand you at all. I feel like you say hateful things."

"I'm sorry. Let's talk about something else," said Eiji and held out a cup to Nobu. "Can you have a drink?"

"I can hold my liquor."

"Great. Is there another cup?"

"I brought one." She turned over a cup and stood. "It's still early, so don't drink too much."

"My purse is not bottomless," said Eiji to Nobu's retreating figure. "That goes for the food you like, too."

Nobu stepped down to the dirt-floor room and turned around to stare at Eiji's face. "Thank you for the treat."

2.3

In May, Wasuke left Hōko-dō and opened a shop called Kōwa-dō in Higashi Naka-chō in Asakusa. He was loaned the apprentice Hanji who turned fifteen. Previously, there were two apprentices, Ukichi and Sado. Since Hōko-dō was closed until the fall, Hanji was sent.

On their days off, Eiji and Sabu went to Sumiyoshi. Sabu grew fond of Nobu and would make up any reason to buy a present and bring it. He lacked the courage to give it to her and asked Eiji.

It was October 15, and the air would soon get chilly. After dinner, the two went to Sumiyoshi for drinks. That night, Sabu bought an embroidered kimono collar and had Eiji hold onto it. When they entered the usual small tatami room, Eiji passed the package back to Sabu.

Deliberately sounding cold, he said, "Enough of this. You're not a seventeen- or eighteen-year-old apprentice. From now on, you do it."

"I know," said Sabu. His eyes seem to plead. "But I can't."

"Nobu knows," said Eiji. "I didn't tell her. She figured it out, said I wasn't that type of guy, and called you 'the poor fellow.'"

"When?"

"A few moments ago, when you went to the bathroom."

Sabu placed the package beside him and lowered his head in embarrassment. Nobu soon returned. After passing on the order, she came back only carrying the sake. Then, as always, the drinking started and interrupted Sabu. Unusually, the cups piled up, but no one was drunk. Not even a little of the good mood bounced back. A short time later, Eiji and Sabu left Sumiyoshi.

"Why didn't you give it to her?" asked Eiji when they walked along the dark canal to Kobuna-chō. "She saw the package."

Sabu quickly stopped at a corner of the canal.

"I got drunk," said the staggering Sabu and squatted. "Tonight, I want to talk to you, Ei-chan."

"What? Here, by this canal? We'll catch a cold."

"Wasuke has a shop," Sabu haltingly said. "Someday, you'll have a shop, too. But I never will."

"We'll talk about this when we get home."

"I think," said Sabu in a weak, miserable voice, "If I have no hope for the future, wouldn't it be better if I change my job?"

"Don't say stupid things. Nobody's better than you at making paste. The boss always says so. You've heard him and know it."

Sabu was quiet for a while then said, "Ei-chan, if I become the best paste maker in Japan, when will that happen? Then I'll be called a fine craftsman. Only then I'll feel better. They always say I can't have a shop only for making paste. Won't Hōko-dō keep me for my whole life like a useless pet?"

"So they say things like that?" asked Eiji like he was searching for an answer but none came. He nodded alone and quietly said, "People can't guess what's gonna happen tomorrow or next week let alone five or ten years in the future. Buddha doesn't know either. You say that and I feel that. If I ever have a shop, I think we will work together."

Sabu slowly looked up at Eiji who crouched next to him.

"I don't know what kind of shop I'll have, but we'll live together. I'll use your paste as a picture framer or scroll mounter and do fine work. We'll both find wives in time and have children. We'll be together in the future, too."

Eiji's emotions charged his quiet voice.

"At some time, we'll work together. We'll create the best shop in

Edo and won't be defeated by Hōko-dō. That's what I think, but what do you think? Is working with me a bad idea?"

After Sabu thought, he shook his head.

"No, it's no good. Thanks for thinking about me, but I'll only be a burden to you."

2.4

"Oh, that again. Sabu, that's your worst habit," said Eiji. "Both of us will run the shop, so why will you become a burden? You make paste that can't be beaten by anyone. I'll do my work using that paste. If we combine our strengths, don't you think saying anyone's a burden is ridiculous?"

Sabu stuttered, "I, I think so but ..."

"Cut it out."

"But that's what I think," Sabu stubbornly said. "Like with Nobu, I'm too cowardly and cause trouble for you."

"Did I say it was a problem?"

"You didn't and wouldn't say that, but more than that, I can't stand being a weakling."

Sabu seemed to search in the darkness for Eiji.

"Ei-chan, remember the winter when we were fifteen and I ran out of the shop, you followed me, got soaked in the rain, chased me to the riverbank at Yokoami, and took me back."

"You got soaked in the rain."

"I'll never forget that for as long as I live. On the way back, I thought about only one thing. I'm a burden to Ei-chan and will always cause problems for you."

"I'll speak honestly, too," said Eiji, took a deep breath and exhaled a gust of air.

"Sabu, do I think you're a burden to me? You're an important friend who has always supported me. Since I'm being honest, don't get mad, but everyone always says you're slow and a dummy. Despite that, you never give up and don't complain. Like moss on a stone, you keep working hard at your job. Each time I see you like that, I say to myself, He has the spirit of a true craftsman."

"Hey, enough of that," said a voice from behind them. "I don't know what you two are talking about, but we're tired of waiting, so why don't you two stand up?"

Eiji and Sabu turned. Three men stood there. It was dark and they couldn't see them well, but they looked like gangsters. Sabu tried to scramble to his feet, but Eiji stopped him.

Still crouching, Eiji quietly said, "Wait. We're in the middle of an important conversation. If you have business with us, please wait."

In a reasonable voice, the next man said, "We can't. We've waited long enough and are tired of waiting. Stand up, youngsters."

"Ei-chan," said Sabu.

"Don't worry," said Eiji. "Just do what I say."

One man moved forward and grabbed Sabu's kimono by the collar. As if he had been waiting for that, Eiji stood, turned around, and flew at one of the men behind them. He violently thrust his right knee into the man's stomach. The man yowled and doubled over. Without giving him a second look, Eiji hit the next man in the body and straddled him when he fell to the ground. With his left hand, he strangled his neck while two fingers of his right hand pressed on the man's eyelids.

"I'll poke your eyes out," Eiji screamed. "You two over there watch me poke out this squirming punk's eyes."

The man pinned down by Eiji did not move. The man kicked in the stomach was still doubled over and groaning. The man who grabbed Sabu stood upright in shock.

Astonished by Eiji's unexpected agility and familiarity with fighting moves, the man standing upright moved away from Sabu. His mouth dropped open, and he frantically waved around his right hand.

The man said, "Hey, stop. We were joking. We only wanted to talk."

"Don't move," said Eiji while putting a little strength in his fingers on the man's eyelids. "If you move, these fingers will poke your eyes."

"Please stop him. Katsu, help," cried the man under Eiji. "Don't crush my eyes!"

"What do you want?" said Eiji. "Say it straight. You better explain yourselves."

"It's about Nobu," said the standing man, still waving his hand. He groveled as he answered. "Nobu at Sumiyoshi. I think you understand now."

"What about Nobu?" asked Sabu as he stood.

"I'm her older brother," said the man. "Nobu promised to marry someone last year. Then you two showed up, and she suddenly started saying he was no good."

Meanwhile, Eiji noticed a stick nearby. The man continued. When Eiji released the pinned man and jumped up, he grabbed the stick with his right hand. It was an oak branch about three feet long and two inches thick that fell from a load of firewood.

"What are you gonna do?" the man asked, never taking his eyes off Eiji. He put his right hand in front and stuttered, "Please, no more violence. You listened to me. I told you the reason, right?"

"Keep talking," said Eiji. "If you try something funny, I'll beat you to death. Some hoodlums picked a fight with me, a respectable craftsman, but I don't want to commit the crime of killing one or two of them. You three, stand over there."

The stooped-over man and the pinned man got up, hesitated, and then stood beside Nobu's brother.

2.5

After they got home and went to bed, Sabu said his heart was still pounding. They slept in a ten-tatami room next to the workspace. Eiji and Sabu shared this bedroom with the seventeen-year-old Denroku, Ukichi, and Sado; the last two joined the other three apprentices in March. Taichi, Shigeshichi, and Gorō each had a 4½-tatami room.

The five roommates packed anything, clothes, daily articles, futons, and belongings inside an eighteen-foot closet that served as a partition. The walls were opposite the closet. On one wall was the wooden door that passed to the workshop. The eastern side had a window where Eiji and Sabu lined up their beds.

The three apprentices were already asleep. Snoring, Denroku's flaw, seemed to fill the ten-tatami room.

"Who were those three?" asked Sabu. "Is that man who said he's Nobu's brother really her brother?"

"I'm sure he was lying."

"He said she's been engaged since last year."

Eiji broke in, "It's a lie. We went there two times a month. You brought her some presents. From the beginning, she was open and said whatever she wanted. Nobu had no reason not to tell us she was engaged if she were."

After thinking for a short time, Sabu said, "So who were those men?"

"I don't know," said Eiji, shaking his head left and right on his pillow. "I think they're local punks circling Nobu, but I won't know unless I ask."

"It's sad," whispered Sabu. "What can Nobu do if those guys are following her around?"

Eiji didn't answer. Denroku's snores got louder. Sabu stopped talking.

After a short time, Eiji broke the silence.

"People don't know the future. We don't have money or power. We're not even full-fledged craftsmen.

"Sabu, I understand how you feel. The most important things to us now are ourselves. In the next few years, we'll decide what our lives will be like. This is tough to say, but please forget about Nobu. I not saying this to be hard on only you. I will forget about women, too."

Sabu only breathed, turned over, and looked at Eiji.

"Forget?" asked Sabu. "Eiji, is there someone you will forget?"

"I never told you?"

"If you did, I don't remember."

"It's from long ago," said Eiji, rubbing his chest under his bedclothes. "At the money exchange shop in Honchō, you know, the one at the customer called Watabun."

"Oh, I only went there once."

"A young lady named Sue is a maid there. She has black eyes and is petite. She said I had grown big."

"Sorry for butting in, Ei-chan, but is a young lady at Watabun who you want to marry?"

"Don't be stupid," said Eiji and quickly turned to Sabu. "Why'd you say that?"

"I heard Taichi say so." Sabu felt awkward and mumbled, "I know nothing, but Ei-chan wants to marry the young lady at Watabun."

"No," said Eiji, lifting his head from the pillow and shaking it no. "You talk too much. Plus, I'm still training to be a craftsman, and she's the daughter of a rich man. It's not funny. If I married a girl like her, she would be a burden my whole life."

In a lazy tone, Sabu asked like he was fishing for something, "In that case, you're through with Sue-chan?"

"No, not at all," said Eiji, trying to dodge Sabu's question. "I don't know about her, but I already know this. I've liked her for a long time and think I'd like to marry her if I could, but only tonight, I'm not thinking about that."

A short time later, Sabu mumbled, "Yeah, a lot is going on."

Eiji said nothing. Denroku's snores softened, and the apprentice Sado started talking in his sleep. When he thought everyone was asleep, Eiji's whispering voice could be heard saying, "If I'm alive …" he sighed and said, "While I'm alive …"

CHAPTER 3

3.1

H*e is twenty-three years old,* Sabu read the characters on the paper scrap and said, "'He is twenty-three years old' means our age because we're the same age."

Eiji adjusted the tasuki cord tucking up his sleeves as he spread the paste on a paste dish and rubbed his forehead with the palm of his left hand.

"Stop reading," he said without looking at Sabu. "If it's wrinkled, we won't be able to use it."

"I'll iron them properly."

"That's why I told you to stop reading. You're always fooling around like a kid." Then offhandedly Eiji said, "You can be a pain."

Sabu gently put the paper down.

The two were now twenty-three. For the first time, they went alone to repaper the sliding screen doors at the Watabun residence. Each tatami room had two eight-panel sliding screens.

This day was the fifth day when they painted the undercoat. Eiji tensed when he held a brush and faced a sturdy sliding screen the size of a tatami mat with a Yoshino cedar frame at the vermillionpainted edges. His entire body surged with excitement over the work to do.

The maid Sue came and peeked in to ask if they'd like tea. Sabu looked at Eiji. When Eiji was about to respond, Sono, the younger Watabun sister, came running, pushed Sue to the side, and sat beside Eiji.

"I was practicing," she said and placed her hand on Eiji's thigh. "Did you hear me, Ei-chan?"

"Yes," he said and turned to Sue. "Yes, we would like tea. Thank you."

"All right," said Sue.

While Sono shook Eiji's thigh with her hand and wondered whether he heard her, he did not answer. Sue averted her eyes and left. Eiji gently pushed aside Sono's hand.

"You said you were practicing. What?"

"You're horrible. An epic song."

Sono slapped Eiji's thigh. "You didn't come to the dress rehearsal before. Right, Sabu-chan?"

"Yes," said Sabu and placed his hand behind his head out of embarrassment. "You played Yanokura's *Izumirō*."

"Ei-chan didn't come to see me."

"I went," said Eiji while carefully wiping one finger of his left hand with a hand towel. "Dōjō-ji temple, the same as the year before last, I was surprised at how boring it was."

"You're so hateful. Who is not boring?"

"The master."

Sono's big eyes looked daggers at him. Eiji stood and said, "I'm going to wash my hands," and went out to the hall.

“He's teasing," stammered Sabu like he was trying to placate her, "The truth is he was impressed."

"Liar. Who's impressed? I'm fed up with myself," said a surprised-looking Sono. "Ei-chan spoke the truth."

Then she smiled and said, "The truth is, the proprietor isn't a patient man. Her chest tightened. She stooped down and laughed.

Sabu's round face reddened like he had blundered. He moved the paste dish to his side and layered the scrap paper.

"Aaah."

Sono stopped laughing and said, "I didn't mean to laugh."

Eiji returned right after Sue brought the tea and pastry. Sue poured the tea, removed the lid from the pastry bowl, and hurried out without looking at anyone's face.

"There's talk about her getting married," said Sono as she picked up a pastry. She waved a hand at Sabu, "A tea for me, too, please. That cup is fine."

Sabu offered the cup poured by Sue on the tray. Eiji looked nonchalant and again asked, "Who?"

"Sue. She's engaged," said Sono, enjoying her pastry and drinking her tea. "We're both nineteen. She should get married, but she hasn't said yes. What will she do if she's left behind?"

"What will you do? Sono-san, if you're the same age, then—"

Sono interrupted Eiji, "No, you're wrong. My sister and I have little chance of marrying by nature. She is twenty-one but has never had one proposal. Please hand me a pastry."

A nervous Sabu picked up a pastry. Eiji drank his tea and then said, "You've had little chance of getting married since birth. What carefree people."

"But it's true," said Sono, swaying her narrow shoulders from side to side and watching Eiji from the corner of her eye. "Ei-chan, maybe you can make me your bride?"

3.2

The day after he finished painting the undercoat was the fifteenth, a day off. Work should have continued in December. Nevertheless, after he ate breakfast and was about to go out, the proprietor Hōbei came and called him over.

"Gorō will be going to Watabun, not you."

"Why?" Eiji was confused. "I can't go?"

"Gorō will go with Sabu. You'll take a little break."

"A break?"

Hōbei sounded cold when he spoke. "Everything about work has a process. For now, there's nothing for you to do. There are no more days. There will be work next year. Taking time off for the end of the year is best."

"I don't understand why. Did I make some mistake?"

Hōbei looked away.

"Don't hear what I'm not saying. Sabu and Gorō will go."

Sabu silently nodded. Hōbei left. As Sabu prepared his work bundle, he searched Eiji's face for answers. Eiji was pale, and his tightened lips had no blood.

"What happened?" Sabu whispered. "Up to yesterday, nothing happened."

Looking preoccupied, Eiji said, "It's okay. Go to work."

He returned the tool bag he was carrying to the shelf and changed out of his work clothes.

Because his work assignment at Hōko-dō was decided, he had only free time after being discharged from this job. Although there was no free time for an apprentice, at twenty-three, Eiji was not fully skilled and worked under three senior apprentices. At this time, placing him was a problem.

He dismissed the apprentice Ukichi and went out. Hōbei said not to hear what he didn't say. He couldn't tell me why. There must be a reason for the change of craftsmen during a job. He thought there must be some reason for not stating the reason. Of course, he couldn't guess. As a road without a destination opens up, his head became chaotic. He became desperate, wondering, Should I drink more sake?

"Why won't he tell me?" Eiji asked himself as he headed toward Ōkawabata. "Although I've trained for the past ten years since I was young, why is he treating me like a stranger?"

He couldn't find a shop where he could drink all morning. Rough bars with companions of river laborers and samurais' manservants are in the area behind Hirokō-ji in Ryōgoku and between the roadside teahouses on the riverbank. These places would be incomprehensible to the uninitiated. Eiji passed by these establishments oblivious to them and crossed the bridge in a daze.

A woman hugging a bundle wrapped in a *furoshiki* cloth was

running over the bridge toward him from the east. She recognized Eiji, stared at him, stopped, and jogged over to him.

"Is that you, Eiji-san? What happened to you?"

Eiji saw her, staggered out of surprise, and moved his body to avoid her. When he realized it was Nobu from Sumiyoshi in Horie-chō, his joy, like meeting an old friend in a strange land, warmed his heart.

Unlike himself, he pleasantly said, "What about you? What are you doing out so early in the morning?"

"I'm on my way to the restaurant. I went back home for three days. Where are you going?"

"Nowhere special." As he started to walk with Nobu, he said, "Do you want to get a drink somewhere?"

"If you like, come to the restaurant. The proprietor and his wife can't say no to Ei-san. I'll treat you."

"As you can see, I'm not feeling good."

"What's making you feel bad? That's not so unusual."

On her own, Nobu decided on a rare instance of indulgence and quickened her pace.

They entered Sumiyoshi through the back. Eiji went to the same small tatami room. The room was lightly cleaned after last night's guests, but wastepaper and chopsticks littered the corners. Four or five sitting cushions were pushed against the walls. The air was heavy with the strong scent of sake.

The women might still be asleep. Inside the house behind closed storm shutters, Eiji heard Nobu's voice, sounding like a distant voice in the mountains, talking in a soft tone to the proprietor and his wife.

"It'd be better if she'd stop," muttered Eiji, shivering in the cold. "They're discussing whether it would be better for me to go to the Kōwa-dō shop or directly ask Watabun for an explanation."

"Yes, that's right," he said to himself. "What the hell did I do? I have to find that out first. Why am I drinking? It's not helping."

Nobu carried in leftover lit and unlit charcoal on a fire shovel.

3.3

Three sake-warming bottles were arranged with several small side dishes on a serving tray. Eiji's face was already red. The area around Nobu's eyes was flush.

"It's like a lie. There should be some reason," said Nobu, shaking her head and carrying sake cups. "When I saw you coming over the bridge, Ei-san, you looked like you were going to jump."

"That's stupid," said Eiji and blinked like it was too bright, "I wanted to have a drink."

"But you sure looked like you would."

Nobu sipped the sake then poured sake for Eiji.

Looking at his cup, he said, "You went home for a few days. Did something happen?"

"We're not talking about that." Noticing the look in his eyes, she asked, "What do you have to say?"

Eiji emptied the sake in his cup into the sake cup stand and immediately poured himself another drink.

"It's nothing. Garbage," he said, stared into his cup again, and drank.

Eiji said, "One time when we were going home from here, three hoodlums picked a fight."

"Something that happened three years ago," said Nobu after counting with her fingers. "I have regrets about that time. The one who said he was my brother is a pimp called Roku. He sold me for money."

"You never mentioned this before."

After the fight with the three punks, Eiji told the story, and Nobu made up a plausible tale and strayed from the subject. Eiji guessed from the way she spoke she couldn't tell the truth, but he kept asking questions.

"I didn't say, so I can't say."

"Can you talk about it now?"

"Ei-san, what happened today?" asked Nobu, seeming to search Eiji's face. "You never take any interest in me, so don't be so concerned about me today. It's not flattering."

"I'm sorry. That wasn't my intention."

"No, don't apologize. Lying is okay. Ei-san, please worry a little. Nothing would make me happier."

In the next moment, Nobu hid her face behind her sleeve and looked about to cry. Eiji was startled.

He gruffly said, "More sake. It's all gone."

Without a word, Nobu stood, turned her face away, and stepped down to the dirt-floor room. She soon returned carrying two sake-warming bottles. Her face looked freshly washed. A friendly grin rose on her mouth, and the double tooth poked out.

"Excuse me," she said, placing the bottles on the tray and moving the empty bottles to a bowl. While sitting, she said, "This time, I'm gonna get tipsy and cry into my drink. I'm at that age."

"That age. How old are you?"

"I'm an old lady. I'm twenty-one."

"So you're an old lady? You're good-natured," he said as he poured himself and then Nobu another drink. In a quieter tone, Eiji said, "I think I mentioned it once, you probably know this, but Sabu likes you."

"Yes, I know," she said seriously and nodded. Her laugh had no emotion. "This someone likes another one. You look like a bug."

"I'm not joking. Listen."

"If it's not a joke, stand in the corner. Because I said it's Ei-san, I don't like Sabu-chan in that way. He's a fun guest, but if it's about love or hate, it's no good. I'm sorry. Please forgive me."

"He's a good guy and has fallen hard for you."

She shut her eyes and softly said, "Well then, I have a terrible family and don't have the constitution to become someone's bride."

"Didn't you once say you wanted to leave home?"

"My parents are unreliable, have a lot of kids, and all my brothers are lazy bums. My older sister, me, and a younger sister under seventeen are the only girls and have hard lives. Our future lives will be hard, too."

"Your older sister is dead."

Nobu was quiet for a short time. Her eyes still closed, she said, "She killed herself for love."

"She what?"

"She killed herself with her lover. A man loved her, but she was going to be sold," said Nobu while shaking her head. "My sister was not strong-willed like me but docile and small-minded. Somehow, she was ready to die and hung herself in the graveyard of Shōmo-ji Temple in Kōme."

Eiji poured sake for her and said, "Drink." She sipped the sake like she was licking it.

3.4

When Eiji left Sumiyoshi, he went to Wasuke's shop in Asakusa. Wasuke had been the chief craftsman at Hōko-dō. Three years ago in May, he opened a shop called Kōwa-dō in Higashi Naka-chō, and did well as a scroll mounter.

As he walked, Eiji grumbled to himself, "The boss is awful. He heard a story, but are bosses like that?"

After her sister died, Nobu would be pestered to be sold next. Being poor is horrible, but daughters don't have to be sold. If everyone worked a little bit more, food for the day wouldn't be a problem. Unfortunately, parents don't want to work and want to take it easy and eat good food, so they grab for fast money.

Nobu won't give in even a little. There are five younger siblings, so any money she gets disappears in a flash. Who will look after the younger ones? Since she will protect their futures, Nobu insists on not being sold even if she had to die and tried to convince her parents. However, they're impatiently waiting for her younger sister, Shino, to turn seventeen.

They set their sights on Shino and started to coax her. Four or five days ago, Shino came to her in tears. Nobu stayed over and talked to her parents. For three days, she tried to persuade them. If something strange happened to Shino-chan, Nobu said she'd kill her father and mother.

In a person's life, it's not unusual for parents to be more frightening than strangers. To protect yourself, according to Nobu, you must be brave. Burdened by that family, not only Sabu, she couldn't marry anyone. In this life, Nobu said she works for her younger brothers and sister.

Eiji said to himself, like a reprimand, "There are situations in this world where a girl's body must be thought about like that. You're still too naive."

He turned the same thoughts in his head over and over until he reached Higashi Naka-chō. Several times he frowned and clicked his tongue.

The workshop with the wood floor occupied two-thirds of the storefront of Kōwa-dō. The building was three six-tatami-mat rooms deep. The apprentice Hanji who came with Wasuke from Kobuna-chō was eighteen. Two more apprentices worked there. Wasuke married last spring. This summer, twin daughters were born. The cramped house was a problem.

"Welcome," said Hanji in the shop and smiled brightly when he saw Eiji. "A message from Kobuna-chō came earlier."

"Is the boss in?" asked Eiji then looked out of the corner of his eyes. "What came from Kobuna-chō?"

"Sado brought a letter. The boss is eating breakfast now. He was up all last night working," said Hanji and frowned. "Eiji, you can't. You reek of booze."

Eiji brought his hand to his mouth. Wasuke never drank one drop of sake and hated it so much it sickened him. Now close to noon on the fifteenth at the end of the year, Eiji blushed when he realized Wasuke would be bothered by the smell of sake and lecture or scold him.

"Oh, I've already forgotten," he said and waved his hand. "I came to talk, but I stink of sake."

"Yes," said Hanji like a grown-up and already shaking his head. "You can't see him like that."

"I'll come again later. Please, don't say anything."

As he was about to go out, Wasuke picking his teeth with a toothpick slid open the shoji door opposite him and called to stop him. He turned back while still crossing the threshold, bowed, and said, "I'll come back later."

"Come here," said Wasuke. "It's a small house, so I couldn't help hearing you mention sake."

Eiji scratched his head.

"I won't scold you about sake today, but there's something I want to talk to you about. Please, come here."

Eiji went in, and Wasuke led him into the six-mat room on the right. He called into the adjoining room for tea. He sat facing Eiji. The other room was the sitting room. The voice of his wife and the sounds of a rice bowl and chopsticks, perhaps, someone still eating, could be heard coming from the room.

Still picking his teeth, Wasuke said, "Earlier, a message came from Kobuna-chō."

He made a loud sound when he sucked his teeth.

"You have helped here for some time. Later, your belongings will be delivered here—"

"What? Wait a minute. I don't know why, but what do you mean by help at this shop?"

"I asked Kobuna-chō."

Eiji shook his head. His face paled and his eyes gleamed.

"I don't believe it. That's not true. Wasuke, what are you hiding?"

His wife brought the tea and greeted Eiji, who returned a curt bow. He didn't take his eyes off Wasuke's expression. When his wife left, Wasuke took his large teacup and began asking questions while he sipped tea.

"What am I hiding?"

Eiji said, "It's about Watabun in Honchō. Something about them was written in the letter from Kobuna-chō. That's it."

Wasuke said nothing and sipped his tea.

3.5

Wasuke spoke with his head turned away.

"He didn't say."

Eiji said, "I'm twenty-three years old. This job at Watabun was my first outside job. Because I'm an apprentice, I accompanied senior apprentices and was known by everyone at the shop. All of them should know and trust me."

He wanted to say more but hesitated. The words welled up in his throat, but he stopped himself and checked his passion.

"Until yesterday, nothing was wrong. I think I did my job well," said Eiji in a quiet but powerful voice. "You know this. I repapered two sliding screens in two of the customer's tatami rooms. It wasn't that difficult and not too technical, but I took great care because it was my first outside job. All of a sudden, the boss tells me I don't have to go to work this morning and takes me off the job."

Wasuke said, "Please, drink your tea."

Eiji continued, "I felt blindsided. What's the reason? What was the failure? I paid attention to what the boss said, but he wouldn't give me an answer. He said I was off for the rest of the year and didn't listen to me. That's it."

"Drink a little tea and calm down," Wasuke quietly said. "You're already chilly. Have a sip."

Eiji had one sip. His throat got hot, and he became aware of his thirst. He drank the rest of the tea in one gulp.

Wasuke said, "You were popular at the Honchō shop. The two daughters liked you. When you were small, you became their play-mate in all sorts of games involving cards, shuttlecocks, beanbags, or marbles. Their parents seemed delighted, too. Therefore, you thought there was mutual friendship and trust."

"Wasn't there?"

"People's feelings aren't always the same. There are times when they smile even while being smacked. Sometimes when only being teased, they want to kill their companion. After all, at the Honchō shop, you were a craftsman on a job. The other side was a rich man. Whatever happens, a person, no matter how favored, should not act without reserve."

"If something happened," said Eiji and licked his lips, "What was it?"

"You don't know?"

"Well, what happened?"

Wasuke stared into Eiji's eyes. Eiji wanted to ask again, but Wasuke interrupted and said he'd tell him.

"You knew the layout of the shop in Honchō."

Eiji thought about it and said, "I'm not sure how well I knew it. I was with Kimi-san or Sono-san and didn't get lost."

"You knew about the master's sitting room?"

"It was one room away from the guest room."

"There's a small chest of drawers for storage in there. Antique gold broaches were in one drawer. The master went to get one to show a guest, but one plain gold broach with antique gold leaf was missing."

Wasuke watched Eiji's face, but his expression did not show the tiniest change. He only saw an unsure look in his eyes.

"They searched for this expensive item. Only the master and his wife searched without telling anyone else. In short, as a precaution, your tool bag and Sabu's in the guest room were searched. The broach was found in your bag."

Eiji laughed.

"You're joking. Stop teasing me, Wasuke."

"It came out of your bag," said Wasuke. "The master found it. The bag was yours. A man like Watabun-sama has no reason to concoct this lie."

Eiji was silent. His laughing mouth stiffened. His eyes searched Wasuke's face. He inhaled a long, deep breath and slowly exhaled in short puffs of air.

Eiji said, "So I stole that piece and put it in my bag?"

"Last evening, the boss came from Kobuna-chō to see me and told me that story. I know nothing else. He said to stop visits there."

Eiji started to say something, but Wasuke raised his hand to stop him and said, "There's more. After returning to Kobuna-chō, the boss thought about it and consulted his wife. They couldn't believe you'd do such a thing and thought it was a mistake but recalled something from seven or eight years ago."

"Something from seven or eight years ago?" asked Eiji.

"Think back," Wasuke said quietly. "I had forgotten all about that until I read the boss's letter and remembered."

Eiji looked puzzled for a short time. Eventually, his eyes opened wide as if he had been smacked. His mouth fell open.

"Ah!"

His right hand curled into a fist and pushed into his knee with all his strength. His fist seemed to draw blood from his joints and tremble.

"The reception desk ..." Eiji's tongue seemed to turn to lead. His words were lifeless. "The cashbox?"

Wasuke said nothing and only stared at Eiji. His gaze mixed the feeling of it's wrong to cheat with the question of what is the truth. Blood rose in Eiji's cheeks and disappeared as he watched. His cheeks twitched and his lips trembled.

He stuttered, "That thing then ..." He licked his lips. "That's being dug up again now."

Wasuke said nothing.

Eiji said, "I absolutely stole coins from the cashbox. The aroma of the broiled eel from a food cart beside Wakoku Bridge conquered me. After the missus discovered me, I never did it again. She promised she would never tell anyone."

Wasuke said, "It's what happened after she discovered that," and stared at Eiji again. "Do you remember what I was doing at the reception desk at that time?"

Eiji tried to remember but shook his head.

"I was in charge of reception. I was the first to discover you were swiping money from the cashbox. I thought I should immediately scold you, but I couldn't do that and secretly consulted with the boss. He chewed me out."

Eiji's eyes didn't move. Wasuke continued as if confessing.

"The boss said, 'If no one's looking and money is in a place hands can reach, anyone may unexpectedly reach out. That's what people do. More than the thief, the one who leaves an opening for the thief is worse. More than Eiji, you failed.' I said nothing. As the boss said, I was wrong to leave that opening. Because I believed that, I said nothing to you. Until today, no one other than the boss and his wife knew."

"So this means, no ..." said Eiji, shaking his head. Keeping his eyes fixed on one point, he asked, "So you're saying the gold broach this time is the same as the cashbox."

"You know the layout of that house and worked a room away from the guest room. If someone among the two daughters and the shop workers has a grudge against you, it would be different, but I don't think that person exists. Not only that. The master said there was proof. With that, wouldn't someone think of you?"

Eiji shook his head, which hung down like his neck was broken.

"I don't think you did it," said Wasuke, "But the circumstances match too well, and right now, there's nothing we can do about it. There's no proof you didn't do it."

"And the cashbox makes matters worse?"

"Don't sound so desperate," said Wasuke then spoke in a softer tone. "During one's life, without warning, you loan to or borrow from the world. Right now, you're expected to give a loan to the world. Without saying a word, for a short time, you are to help in the work here."

Eiji mumbled, "More than the world, the boss is terrifying."

Wasuke looked at Eiji with doubt.

Eiji raised his eyes. "Wasuke, you said my belongings will be delivered here."

"Yes, sometime today."

"I hate to ask, but could you please lend me a little money? I have twenty *ryo* saved at Kobuna-chō." Eiji didn't give Wasuke the chance to refuse. "Don't ask me why now. Please lend it. I beg you. Please."

He dropped both of his hands to the ground and lowered his head.

CHAPTER 4

4.1

He heard a woman's voice.

"Is this your first time?"

The warmth of her skin vividly lingered on his chest and thighs. No matter how much he wiped, he could not get rid of the feeling of the slimy tracks left by a crawling slug.

Eiji scowled and spat a few times.

"If you're a man, please act like one. What's wrong? Are you ill? Oh, I know. You came to be by my side because you're sick. You're too stuck up."

"Hmph, this guy is some young daimyo."

"Don't make me laugh. What flat broke guy comes to this sort of place to put on airs?'

"I don't put on airs. Shut up."

"You're a nice man. I've fallen in love. Hey, come here."

"Stop it, I wanna sleep."

"Oh, you're awful. This isn't an inn. Hey, don't be so cruel. All right? It's my living."

"Shut up. I'm going to sleep. Let go of me."

Hot lips like fire, truly like fire, sucked his ears and cheeks.

"Aah," Eiji moaned and violently shook his head back and forth.

He had no idea where he was on this dark street. The canal or the river was to his right. He occasionally heard the sounds of waves lapping the shore. The wind blew gently.

Eiji said to himself, "If this is Monzen Naka-chō, the lumber-yards may be nearby.... It's so dark. I can't see anything no matter which way I look. This doesn't look like a world where people live."

Stars twinkled between the clouds in the sky. In the intermittent light from the stars, he discovered lumber stacked on the left side of the road, went over, and carefully sat down. The lumber was a little unstable. Eiji had to use his legs for balance. He sat down and sighed.

"What's gonna happen now? I don't understand any of this."

He shook his head while his elbow poked into his knee, and his hand supported his chin.

"Dammit. What happened? I've never even seen a plain gold leaf broach, but that thing was in my tool bag. In my tool bag ..."

He broke down in tears. Still supporting his chin, he shook his head causing tears to spill from both eyes. Moans welled up in his throat. He heard a sobbing voice that wasn't coming from his throat. It sounded like the whimpering of a sopping-wet stray dog having trouble finding shelter from the rain.

"Was it Sabu?" he said to himself, still weeping. "No, I lived with Sabu like brothers. He had no reason to do something like that. He depended on me. If I disappeared, he'd be lost. Someone at that house must have done it."

Deep in his ears, he heard the woman's voice, "What are you crying about? In this world, you do things for lust and money. Suddenly, you're full of yourself. When you die, you're no different than a beggar or man in the lowest caste. Whether a daimyo or a dog or a cat, you become bones. Hey, in a flash, there's no more whining."

Another woman's voice said, "I'm madly in love. It's true. This is the first time I've felt this way. Hey, please make me your wife."

"Make you my wife, ha!" said Eiji, while his hand wiped around his wet eyes and cheeks, and he spat again. "Everyone says the same thing. 'Won't you make me your wife?'"

Eiji's body stiffened. His eyes stared, fixed at one point on the dark ground.

He heard the other woman's voice again.

"Don't be so rough. I'm new at this and don't know much. Be gentle. Please be tender and teach me. Oh, that's strange.... Why at such an important moment, you're so mean? Oh, suit yourself.

"To hell with parents, brothers, and sisters. It's not for the sake of others, doesn't everyone work, even if they don't like it, for their own good? They all say it's for their family, but that's a lie.

"Hey, come closer. I can't resist your skin's hot stickiness. It's like a mochi rice cake."

Vigorously shaking his head no, Eiji stood and walked out, stumbling a little.

"Make me your bride," he muttered as he walked. "Who said, 'Maybe you can make me your bride?'"

Eiji stopped and looked somewhere into space from beneath lowered brows. The wind fluttered the hem of his kimono and toyed with his messy hair.

"Sono," he mumbled. "My rival is the daughter at the large shop in Honchō. Even if she was joking, that sort of thing affects the reputation of the shop. We've been friends since I was thirteen or fourteen. That's it. She said she had little chance of marrying since birth then asked me to marry her.

"That would be dangerous for a parent. With me going in and out of their home, he might have thought there was the slightest chance."

Eiji thought, Is that it? Did her father plan this to stop me from going there? Eiji believed he was closer to the truth.

"I have to make sure," he said and tightened his fist. "I have no choice. I can't live knowing I was made to look like a thief. To live my life, I gotta find out for sure."

4.2

"Hey, let me see the proprietor," said Eiji, sitting at the Watabun storefront. "I'm Eiji from Hōko-dō. Please ask him to come here."

It was still morning. The shop opened moments earlier, and no customers had arrived. Three shop boys were dusting and sweeping. Eiji had been on a five-day drinking bender and quite drunk. A shop boy was not behind the lattice at the reception desk. Eiji believed he was a sales clerk or the head clerk.

One shop boy said, "I understand, Ei-san. How many times do I have to tell you, the proprietor is still asleep?"

"Hey shop boy, this is none of your business," said Eiji and yawned. His yawn reeked of sake and made him frown. "Hey you, keep smacking that sack of coins against the board all day long like a dope. I'm here to see the proprietor, the boss of Watabun. Tell Tokubei to come out."

Then Eiji toppled over sideways.

He told himself, Don't act like a fool. Calm down. I can't shout and shame him to be heard. I'll behave humbly. Since a rich man hates being unjustly suspected, he'll pretend not to know and throw his opponent off guard. The lie or truth is revealed in the eyes. Even if the mouth lies, the eyes don't. The eyes are the key.

He heard a woman's voice, "Oh, you've come again. This is no good. You're miserable and look like you'll hang yourself. You need to cheer up. Right now. All right.

"You look drunk. You can't come here drunk to complain. Go somewhere and sober up. What are you going to do? You're not the only customer. Hurry, get going. This fellow is disgusting."

Eiji groaned, "Aaah."

"Mother, I can't stand this pain, Mother."

He began sobbing. Again he heard a voice that sounded like the whine of a hungry, stray dog.

"LOOK OUT, A PUDDLE."

"Let go." Eiji tried to free his left arm. "Let go of my hand."

"It's a little further. You're gonna fall, Ei-chan."

"Oh, it's you, Sabu. What happened?"

"I'm going to Horie-chō. I have nothing else to do. Do you want to go to the Asakusa shop?"

"That's ridiculous. I gotta go to Watabun to negotiate."

"You can't. You're too drunk. Go after you sober up," said Sabu and hung Eiji's arm over his shoulder. "It's been four days. It'll be okay."

"How did you find out about me?"

"I went to the job at the Honchō shop. They said Ei-chan is dead drunk. They wanted to put you in the maids' room to sleep, but you were too loud. They had to take you outside."

"I don't get it," said Eiji, strongly shaking his head. "Dreams and reality are jumbled together. I can't remember where I was or what I did. What's today?"

"The twenty-first," said Sabu. "Didn't you leave the Asakusa shop on the fifteenth?"

"I need a drink of water."

"After we go around this corner, we'll be at Sumiyoshi. Hold on a little longer."

"No. I can't take one more step."

Eiji's knees gave out, and he sank to the ground. Sabu couldn't support him, stumbled, and nearly fell on top of him.

At the corner of Horie-chō, many people passed back and forth. Sabu was dismayed as if he saw himself. He told Eiji to wait there and ran over to Sumiyoshi.

Eiji heard a woman say, "I've given up. That is the luck I was born with. I carry hardship in this life. At least, when born this time, my only wish was to be born a child to a slightly better family. Although any place in Sado is called hell on Earth, all the time from the day I was born until now I've lived in hell."

Eiji said, "Ah, that's true. This world is hell. People should do whatever they want."

"Here's your water," said a woman. "Don't choke when you drink."

Eiji drank water from a teacup and immediately drank more. He turned his head and looked up.

"Nobu, right? Is this Sumiyoshi?"

"You should lie down for a while," said Nobu. She folded over a seat cushion to use as a pillow and made Eiji lie on his side. "I'll get a cover for you. If you're sleepy, please rest."

"Where's Sabu?"

"At work. He said he'll come back after work. He's at the Honchō shop."

"I have work to do at Honchō, too," said Eiji and tried to get up. Nobu held him down.

"No, don't touch me," said Eiji. "My body is not back to normal. I'm filthy with mud. I'm worthless."

4.3

When Nobu was sure Eiji would not try to get up again, she left the small tatami room and brought back a sleeved quilt to cover him.

"Nobu?" Eiji opened his eyes. "I'm sorry for causing so much trouble."

"I hate it when you're like this, Ei-san."

"I know. Even I hate me. Forgive me."

"What happened to you? You were drunk on the fifteenth. They said you came again then left. Then there was no news like dry leaves blown around by a cold wind. Finally, Sabu-chan came carrying you on his back. You seem to have lost control. Pull yourself together."

"Finish me off," said Eiji, closing his eyes. "Because no matter what you say, I don't think there's anything good to say about me."

"Please rest. Sleep now, I'll listen to you after you wake up."

"Can I sleep? If you come closer, Nobu, my body is caked with mud. I can't move to the side."

"What's covered in mud? There's only a little dirt on your kimono. Wipe it off."

"That's not mud."

He thought about saying, "I slept with women and don't

remember the faces of the women I didn't like," but his tongue didn't move.

"Please forget about that," said Nobu as if she heard his confession. "This is the first time I'm talking about this, but when I was eleven, I kissed a guy named Roku from the neighborhood. Back then, I felt my body had been spoiled. I cried about not being able to be clean for the rest of my life. I thought seriously about killing myself. After five to ten days passed, I slowly calmed down. My body was not dirty. I wondered if that tainted me."

"You were an eleven-year-old child."

"I talked about that guy Roku before. At fifteen or sixteen, he ended up a pimp who sold women into prostitution."

Eiji remembered that time the punk said he was Nobu's older brother.

"Was he one of those yakuza?"

"I don't know where he is or what sort of disgraceful things his gang is up to. It looks like they left Edo. If they casually come back, they'll be shunned," said Nobu and smiled to soothe him. "Now, do you feel a little better?"

"I'll try to sleep," said Eiji.

Nobu left to get water, and Eiji shut his eyes. Although he thought he wouldn't be able to sleep, he dozed off. He hazily remembered Nobu returning and placing the water near his pillow. He opened his eyes when he heard people talking. The room was growing dark. He stripped off the sleeved kimono and tried to sleep but noticed a chill in his arm from his right shoulder.

Nobu said, "Sleep a little longer. You haven't slept properly in days."

He heard Sabu's voice.

"I'm going to the shop. I'll apologize to the senior apprentices."

"I want to wait but can I stay here?" asked the thin voice of a woman.

"It's okay. Customers will be coming soon. I can't stay. You'll be a great help if you look after Ei-san for me," said Nobu. "What about the shop?"

"They're fine. That's why I came."

It's Sue, thought Eiji. That's her voice. Why has she come?

He sat up and didn't pour water from the pitcher provided at his bedside but drank from the pitcher. Water as cold as ice slid pleasantly down his throat. Three or four sneezes came out when the water trickled to his nose.

Nobu opened the shoji door and peeked in to ask if he was awake. Eiji sat up again, shivering as he pulled the sleeved quilt up to his shoulders.

"Did you catch a cold? You're sneezing."

"Did somebody come?"

"Yes," said Nobu and looked back. "She said she was from the Honchō shop. Please come in."

Nobu stepped out of the room. Sue appeared and bowed. Her pale face, as if made of porcelain, looked cold and expressionless. Nobu said she was going to get a lantern and left.

"Please go home," said Eiji. "You shouldn't be in this sort of place."

Sue began crying.

4.4

Standing in the cramped dirt-floor room, Sue hid her face behind her sleeve, stifled her voice, and cried.

"I'm already good for nothing," said Eiji recklessly. "I'm ashamed to show you my face, so please go home."

"I'm not going home," said Sue between sobs. "I took time off from the Honchō shop and came here."

No matter what Sue said, Eiji acted like he did not understand.

"Time off? For what?"

"You're alone, Ei-san," she stuttered and again said, "Ei-san, you mustn't be alone."

"Sue-chan, you don't understand."

"I do."

Nobu returned with a lit lantern.

"You don't have to stand out there, come in. I'll bring a fire," said Nobu, urging Sue. "Please, come in. You'll get cold standing out there."

Sue peeked at Eiji's expression as she stepped into the small tatami room and sat in a corner. Nobu went to get the lit fire and asked if they would like sake. Eiji shook his head no.

"Sue-chan, do you know about the gold broach?"

Sue gently nodded.

"I didn't tell you that," said Eiji, pulling up the sleeved quilt. "Somebody put the gold broach in my tool bag by mistake. If it wasn't a mistake, someone had a reason to get me in trouble. I have no idea which it is."

Sue nodded again.

"I haven't become a good-for-nothing. That's not true at all. I'm not bad."

Sue's moist eyes wiped free of tears gently looked at Eiji. Nobu came with the fire on the fire shovel, went over to the brazier, and put in charcoal. Eiji lowered his head and said nothing. A few minutes ago, customers began showing up at the restaurant. They could hear the sounds of maids coming and going in the dirt-floor room and the kitchen. The place livened up.

"Call if you need anything," said Nobu. "Take your time, other customers won't come in here."

Eiji thanked her, and Nobu left. He sneezed again and fumbled around in his pocket with one hand. Sue sieged the opportunity and took some papers from her sleeve and handed them to him. He took the several sheets of paper folded in half and, after wiping his eyes, blew his nose.

"Don't laugh," he said while laughing at himself. "It looks like I caught a cold."

Sue said, "You must rest. Come to my house. It's a brush maker's shop in Shitaya, Kanasugi. It's small, but there's room for you to sleep."

"That's nice of you, but I'm already useless."

Sue pressed him.

"What's wrong? You're still Ei-san. You're not another person. To me, you're the same old Ei-san."

"That's not true."

Eiji quickly turned away. In his heart, he felt I'll never get back to my old self. My heart and body were pure. However, after the gold broach incident, people don't trust me anymore. I polluted my body by sleeping with women I don't know. People are fragile. My heart and my body were changed by a tiny piece of metal. I'm no longer that guy.

"Sue-chan, you've tried hard to console me. A bum like me can't go back to the old me," he said and turned away. "Your concern cheers me up, but please forget about me."

"You bully yourself! That's the most dangerous thing to do at this time, and you're doing it. Listen to me," said Sue. Not yielding, she continued, "I may be a little brash, but when I saw you laying there in the maids' room at Watabun, I made up my mind. I knew you were in danger, and someone had to stand by your side. If not, something horrible would happen. I knew this and had to take time off from the shop."

"That's no good," said Eiji and turned his head. "I'm not worth it. Apologize and go back to Watabun."

"I'm not leaving you, Ei-san," said Sue and drew closer on her knees. "As a girl, I'm embarrassed to say this, but I've been thinking for a long time. I'm ready for whatever hardships for Ei-san's sake. I was happy when Sabu-san told me what you thought about me."

Sue still covering her face behind her sleeve was sobbing.

Eiji grumbled, "Sabu. Oh, Sabu."

In a broken, shaky voice, Sue said, "Now, let's go to my house. You'll be one more worker. The name Hōko-dō will die away, and you'll become a skilled craftsman. Please, listen to me."

Sue pressed her hands together in prayer. Eiji was upset, waved her away, and asked her to leave him alone. He heard soft coughs from the dirt-floor room then Sabu's voice say, "Excuse me."

Sue sat up properly and wiped her eyes. Eiji folded his arms.

"Can I come in?"

"Don't worry. Come in," said Eiji.

Sabu slid open the shoji door and stepped in without looking at the two.

"How are you feeling?" asked Sabu as he sat next to the brazier. "Sorry, I thought I'd get here earlier but didn't finish until late."

Eiji stared at Sabu's face.

"You shouldn't have come."

"I had to," mumbled Sabu, blinking at the brightness. He stuttered, "I wanted to drink sake, but we can't, right?"

"I asked before," said Eiji, not taking his eyes off the expression on Sabu's face. "Did the boss say anything to you?"

"I'd like a drink," Sabu said, then quickly added, "It's freezing outside. I'm cold to the center of my body."

"Can't you tell me without getting drunk?"

"Excuse me," said Sabu and stood. "I've had nothing to eat."

He stepped down to the dirt-floor room, went to place an order, returned, and retook his seat, still fidgeting.

Sue looked at Eiji and asked, "Should I stay?"

Before Eiji answered, Sabu said, "I'd like you to stay."

"There's something I want to ask you, Sue-chan," said Sabu. "Of course, everything's become so hard."

Eiji sneezed and blew his nose. Sabu wanted to ask a question and glanced at Sue. She nodded in response to his gaze. Eiji noticed but turned away without saying a word. They were worried about him and had some secret plan. This thought crushed Eiji's spirit and made him feel worse.

He felt another sneeze brewing, brought a piece of paper to his nose, and massaged his nose with two fingers. He felt exasperated at times like this when a choice had to be made. Isn't sneezing at an important moment farcical?

Two young women Hatsu and Take, not Nobu, brought the trays of food and drinks. The restaurant was crowded with customers who came to talk, laugh, and get drunk. Voices complaining over drinks created a racket along with the sounds of containers and utensils.

"I'll have the big one," said Sabu and took the lid off the soup bowl. "Ei-chan, do you want one?"

Eiji turned his head. Sabu anxiously asked, "A little drink is okay?"

Sue poured for him, and he drank three in a row.

"Stop it. You're not a strong drinker," said Eiji. "If you keep drinking like that, you'll get dead drunk."

"Even if I get drunk, if it's sake, I'll sober up eventually," said Sabu and put a fourth drink to his mouth. "If a person's reputation is harmed, can't it be cleaned up a little, Ei-chan?"

Eiji was silent until Sabu drank his fourth cup then asked, "Was that one mine?"

"I think so," said Sabu, wiping his mouth with his palm. "Ei-chan is a skilled craftsman. Without help from the boss and the shop, he can proudly stand on his own. He doesn't have to hold back for anyone. Right? Ei-chan."

Eiji watched Sabu's eyes and asked, "Okay, but what about the cash box from the shop?"

"Don't talk about that. I was thinking—"

Eiji interrupted him. "You don't think. I remember what I did. I raged at a long-time customer from the previous generation of Hōko-dō. I was drunk and raged at the storefront of a superior, established shop in Honchō. When he heard, could the proprietor turn a blind eye? He would have to apologize to Watabun for the disturbance I caused. Sabu, tell me what happened. I'll probably be driven from the shop."

4.5

Wisely, Sabu tried to gloss over the bad parts. However, he could never make false accusations or insinuate anything. The boss Hōbei immediately went to apologize to Watabun and promised to fire Eiji from the shop. Then he called on Wasuke in Asakusa and ordered him not to hire Eiji in the Higashi Naka-chō shop.

Eiji said, "Yeah, I thought he was going to do that."

"Wasuke has smoothed things over several times," said Sabu like he made a mistake then hesitated. "He said he can't give you work this time and needs to think a little more for your sake."

"Enough," said Eiji shaking his head and taking the lid off the bowl on his tray. "If he's made his decision, I have nothing to say. I'm drinking, too."

"Ei-chan," Sabu said as Sue poured their drinks she had been waiting to pour.

"The boss is an honest man," said Eiji as he stared at the sake in his cup. "So that others couldn't criticize him behind his back, he'd never allow bad behavior, even by an apprentice trained from an early age, to shake the foundation of Hōko-dō. That's fair and makes sense."

Eiji took a gulp of sake.

"I say this, but please don't think I'm desperate. After the connection to Hōko-dō is broken, whatever I do shouldn't cause problems for the boss. He or anyone in the shop no longer has the right to say anything about me. Right, Sabu?"

"I think you're right," said an unsure Sabu. "Even if that's not decided, you might as well keep listening to the senior apprentices in the shop."

"I won't," said Eiji like he punched something. "I don't know how fine a shop Hōko-dō is or how important is the shop's reputation. I'm disgusted by how this was handled. If they asked me to go back, I would never step foot in that shop again. No way."

Sue's face paled but she said nothing and poured a drink for Eiji and then Sabu. Eiji drank the second drink in one gulp and had her pour a third. Sabu didn't touch his drink and timidly stared at Eiji.

"Sabu, I have a favor to ask you."

"Okay, I'll do anything."

"Go to Higashi Naka-chō and get my baggage. I think the money I left at Kobuna-chō was also delivered there. If it's not there, go get it at Kobuna-chō and bring it here."

"That'll be easy to do," said Sabu and looked at Sue, "Better than bringing it here, should I take it to the new address?"

She quickly said, "Yes, my house is better. Ei-san is going to need money soon. At my house, money is not wasted, and it's where he'll start working."

Eiji shook his head decisively and said, "Because she's helping me clean up."

Sue was about to speak, but Eiji raised his hand to stop her.

He said, "First, I will erase the dishonor of stealing. My body is unclean. Sabu also knows this, but I never fooled around with women until I was twenty-three. I drank sake but didn't go near the red-light district because of you. Sue-chan, at one time, I thought I wanted to marry you and keep my body pure until then."

Sue's head dropped a little, still holding a sake-warming bottle in her left hand, the fingers of her right hand pressed on the bridge of her nose.

Eiji continued, "I haven't heard a good reason for the false accusation. I can't forget that and being driven from the shop where I worked for ten years.

"For the first time since the day I was born, I no longer believe in the world or people. While being eaten up by desperation, I casually slept with random women."

He thought, Maybe I slept with several women somewhere and can't remember their faces. Sleeping with women I can't remember, even a little, makes me feel more disgusting. Until I get rid of this dirty feeling, I don't want to get close to Sue.

Eiji said to Sue, "If you took a break from Watabun, please go to your home in Kanasugi. If I figure out how to survive, I'll bring a new story. I'll be straight with you. I don't know when this will be and have no idea whether I'll feel this way six months or two years from now. Sue-chan, I can't tell you to wait for me."

Sue's eyes opened wide and stared at Eiji.

"Let's consider this settled," said Eiji and gulped down the sake. "Now, if it's all right, Sabu, go to Asakusa, and Sue-chan, go home to Kanasugi. I'm sorry for being selfish. Now, please leave me alone."

Sabu sipped the now cool sake in the bowl lid he was holding. Sue set down the sake-warming bottle and said, "My home is the shop called Yarokudana in 3-chome, Kanasugi. My father's name is Heizō."

"I'll say it again, but it'll be better if you don't wait for me, Sue-chan," Eiji said and turned away, "When you live in this world, you don't know what's gonna happen or when?"

CHAPTER 5

5.1

Ice, possibly formed from the light rain that began falling moments ago, spread over the paving stones to the entryway. Eiji closed the umbrella and leaned it against the shutter box. When he slid open the lattice and went in, the usual shop boy on the six-tatami landing was holding a hemp sack and slamming it against the board. His frostbitten hands were swollen and purple. Blood oozed in places on his fingers.

When Eiji asked to be announced, the shop boy stood and left. Soon the sales clerk Shokichi appeared.

Eiji greeted him.

"I'm sorry for the commotion I caused the other day. Today, there will be no rowdy behavior. I'd like to see the proprietor. Please tell him I won't be long."

Eiji thought he should kneel in the dirt-floor room. The sales clerk left. The shop boy resumed smacking the hemp sack. Eiji thought this big shop had no shame about having the shop boy steal tiny amounts of gold dust from the government-issued gold currency on this landing with no fire.

It doesn't matter how hard it is to learn about business. Isn't this kid breaking the law? That's a merchant's shame.

He spat from his core. The sales clerk returned and told Eiji to come in. They passed through into an eight-tatami room. Then the head clerk appeared instead of the sales clerk. Still standing, he asked Eiji, "What is your business here?"

Eiji said, "I'd like to see the proprietor."

"I'm the head clerk of this shop," said Gihei, while picking his teeth with a toothpick. "Anything related to this shop is entrusted to me. If you have an issue, you can tell me."

Eiji placed both hands on the ground, pointing toward the head clerk.

"It's about the gold broach. If possible, I'd like to see the proprietor."

"Hasn't that been settled?"

"It hasn't been to me."

"The matter is settled," said Gihei, loudly sucking his teeth, "You've been coming here for a long time and have a future, so the proprietor didn't go to court. If you're a master paperer, you should have a rough idea. That broach was valued at 100 ryo. Why do you think the proprietor asked to settle out of court?"

"Gihei-san, even you think I did it?"

"The proprietor found it in your tool bag. What else could I think?"

"That's why I want to see the proprietor," said Eiji with great patience. "Why was that broach in my tool bag? I have no memory of that at all. A child would understand. If I did it, I have no reason to carelessly drop it in my tool bag. Wouldn't I hide it where no one would find it?"

"We are merchants, not investigators. Every thief does something different with a stolen object. There is no confusion over the fact that the broach was in your tool bag."

"Something happened, but I swear to god I did not do it. I had no reason to do it. Why can't I see the proprietor? If people say I'm a thief, I will no longer show my face in public for the rest of my life."

"All right," said Gihei, still standing and looking down at Eiji. He broke the toothpick in his right hand in half.

"I thought we might come to an understanding, but you're quite stubborn. Wait here," said the head clerk and left.

The rumor was Eiji became too friendly with the two daughters and one of them wanted to marry him. Sabu heard this from the apprentice Taichi. No one knows where the rumor started, but it was probably known to people associated with Watabun. Eiji believed someone planned this to get rid of him. Maybe, it was Tokubei, the father; the mother; or anyone else connected to the shop.

He made a disgraceful mistake as an apprentice. The proprietress discovered his theft at Hōko-dō and pardoned him. He thought only she knew, but the senior apprentice Wasuke and the proprietor knew. Even though they forgave him at that time, no one believed him now. Instead, that previous incident led them to conclude he stole the broach this time.

"It can't end like this," Eiji said to himself, "Somehow, the truth must be known."

A short time later, he heard approaching footsteps. The sliding door opened and three men stepped in. They weren't the head clerk or anyone connected to the shop. All three men wore work aprons over workmen's *happi* coats with the insignia *Squad One* and navy blue work trousers. Two were twenty-five or -six years old. The other was in his forties. The undyed word *Chief* was on his coat lapel. Eiji thought, He's the neighborhood boss.

He said, "Hey, are you trying to pick a fight with this shop?"

Surprised, Eiji stuttered, "What do you mean by trying to pick a fight? This is serious. I want to talk to the proprietor. That's it."

"Get up, kid," said the boss and jerked his chin, "This isn't the place for quarrels. If you have something to say, step outside, then we'll listen."

The head clerk had summoned these men, almost certainly, under the proprietor's orders. Eiji thought this was cowardly. His body shook from anger he couldn't suppress.

"No! I'm not budging until I see the proprietor. My whole life depends on it, but you guys wouldn't understand."

"Get him up," said the boss to the younger men, "You're causing trouble at this shop. Drag him out."

Eiji sat with his legs crossed and arms folded. The two younger men quietly approached from the left and right, determined but wondering whether he would move. While telling him to cooperate, they grabbed Eiji's arms and hauled him away. He tried to free himself but was no match for their strength. They dragged him to the entryway. The startled shop boy slamming down the hemp sack jumped out of the way. Eiji was enraged.

"This is how you treat people here," shouted Eiji, "You dishonor an innocent man by calling him a thief then treat him like a swindler?"

"You punk," said one of the young men and punched the side of Eiji's face, "Can't you shut up?"

The other man hit him, too. When they pulled Eiji down into the dirt-floor room, they tripped and fell. Although barefoot, they dragged him, like a sack of rice, from the lattice to the stone pavement, and outside the gate. In a few moments, the light rain turned into snow, and then the frozen wet road turned white.

The two young men tossed Eiji onto the road and took turns straddling him and punching him indiscriminately.

At first, Eiji was punched in the ears and lost hearing in his right ear. Blood flowed from his split lip and mixed with the blood from his nose. His face was covered by red mud.

"Dammit. You bastards," shouted Eiji with all his might, "Kill me."

He thought he was going to die. Instead of him dying, he would kill one of his attackers and flailed his arms and legs with full power. They seemed to be young firemen and used to this. They skillfully handled Eiji, pushing him down to the ground prostrate and rubbing his face against the road.

"Take him to the guardhouse," said the boss, "Don't draw a crowd. This is embarrassing."

"Stop struggling, you dope," said one young man and thrust his clenched fist into Eiji's side, "If you don't behave, you'll end up a cripple."

The poke stopped Eiji's breathing. He rounded his body, crouched, and did what they said.

The guardhouse was located on the corner of Honchō facing the outer canal. The three brought Eiji inside to face the contract private policeman and his assistant. They seemed to know each other. After a quick explanation of the situation, they handed over Eiji and went home. He later found out the private policeman was Ōtaya Sukejiro, and his assistant was Shimazo.

Eiji fell over into the wood-floor room. His whole body ached, particularly, the pain in his side. He lay groaning on the floor. Needless to say, more than the physical pain, the pain in his heart was unbearable. He cursed the people of Watabun and the boss and his men. He could only think of anger and spat up several times out of frustration.

"Hey, kid," said the elderly watchman, shaking Eiji's shoulder, "Wake up. Get up and wipe your face."

The old man wrung warm water from a hand towel and made Eiji take it.

"Your head and clothes are wet and covered in mud. Get up and go over to the fire. You'll dry faster if you're right next to the open fire."

"I'll set it on fire," muttered Eiji, still gripping the hand towel but making no attempt to get up. "I'll burn down Watabun's mansion and kill those three firemen."

"You don't talk nice," said the policeman in the dirt-floor room with the fire stood and walked toward him. "Hey kid, you can't talk nonsense and think you can get away with it."

"What if I get away with it?" asked Eiji, sitting up halfway, "Anyway, is there anything to eat?"

He spat at the face of his adversary.

5.2

Eiji's hands were tied behind his back. He lay in a corner of the guardhouse's dirt-floor room. He did not know his companions, but the private policeman he spat at was angry and badly beat him with a hooked *jitte* truncheon. Then his assistant tied up Eiji, kicked, doused him with a bucket of water, and knocked him over.

Eiji was half-conscious, caused by extreme mental anguish more than by physical pain. Blood and mud covering half of his face had dried like plaster and gave his face a horrifying, bloodless look. His half-open eyes stared blankly at something. With each shallow, quick breath, strands of his disheveled hair freed by the broken paper hair tie swayed at constant intervals.

Eiji vaguely heard a man's voice say, "You're Sukejiro from Yumichō. Why do you always overdo it? Tell me what happened."

He must be a samurai, thought Eiji hazily. He sounded like a samurai. Maybe, he's some type of police officer. Eiji listened to him for the details, then Sukejiro began a tedious explanation. Eiji could barely hear his low, hoarse voice talking quickly but didn't care.

Not fully conscious, he repeatedly mumbled, "Do whatever, who cares?"

"Anyway, loosen the rope. Get him closer to the fire," said the samurai, "If he stays there, he'll die."

The two sat Eiji up, untied the rope, and carried him to the fire. In no time he felt the fire's warmth. He later found out that the three men, Aoki Kōnoshin, a patrol officer; Yasui Tomoemon, a policeman; and a junior official, Okamura Jihei, stopped by the guardhouse on their patrols and reprimanded the contract policeman.

The official Okamura dipped a hand towel into warm water, wiped Eiji's face, arms, and legs, and put ointment on his split lip and the bruises that appeared all over. Eiji grimaced in pain only when the bruises were touched. Otherwise, his face was blank like he was senile. He didn't see the others' faces and seemed to hear but did not answer.

Eiji had no idea whether the contract policeman, Sukejiro,

heard some story from the Honchō fire chief or what Aoki Kōnoshin said. Judging from Aoki's questions, Eiji appeared to have committed blackmail at Watabun in Honchō although he hadn't given his address, name, or job.

"Looking at you, I don't believe you're the sort," said Aoki, "I'm Patrol Officer Aoki Kōnoshin. I think there may be some reason for this but can't say what."

Eiji didn't answer. Aoki waited.

"I'll burn down that shop," said Eiji to himself in his throat, "and kill those three firemen then those two detectives."

His muttering between his swollen lips was unintelligible, but Aoki heard and looked with narrowed eyes at Eiji.

Aoki Kōnoshin was a tall, slender twenty-seven or -eight-year-old. His eyes and nose were prominent on his tan, narrow face. His expression reflected self-control and a strong will.

"If you have a home address and a guarantor, you can go home."

With great patience, Aoki asked, "Where do you live?"

Eiji did not respond.

"I don't understand your silence. If you don't answer, I'll have to take you to the magistrate's office."

Eiji said nothing.

"It looks like the contract police officer was rough with you. You're mad," said Aoki, then quietly added, "Listen carefully, in my role of investigating suspicious people, I have no reason to welcome anyone as a guest. The slightest misstep will lead to rougher methods. The longer you insist on being stubborn, you'll be suspected of other crimes and, eventually, you'll be tortured. Think carefully, will you tell me what happened, leaving nothing out?"

Steam began to rise from Eiji's kimono. As he warmed, the muscles and joints in his entire body began to ache like they were heated up.

Damn those jerks at Watabun, those firemen, and those cops. I'll kill them all. Even if I'm thirty-five or fifty, I'll kill them all. Eiji pledged this in his mind as pain surged throughout his body.

"Well, you give me no choice," said Aoki and sighed deeply. "I will take you to the magistrate's office for a thorough investigation."

He ordered the elderly watchman to call for a palanquin.

Eiji rode the palanquin to the Kita-chō magistrate's office and was jailed. The magistrate had to give permission to jail him. However, Aoki spoke with a man called Matazaemon, a government police official, and put Eiji in an empty cell.

Matazaemon's family name was also Aoki. He was forty-five years old, a relative of Kōnoshin, and a senior police officer in the Kita-chō magistrate's office. Eiji was indifferent to these facts. Of course, he knew nothing about jails or the Kita-chō magistrate's office. He shut down inside himself and let nothing from the outside in. He must never forget the entire world was his enemy.

The rich man through the power of money and the government official through his authority can turn an innocent man into a criminal. Someone like him with neither money nor authority cannot oppose them. This is the truth, he thought, and fury rose in him again.

Eiji looked around. The cell had wooden plank walls on three sides and faced the hallway. The rage pushing up made him dizzy. The solid latticework appeared to repeatedly pulse forward and then recede.

"Dammit," Eiji screamed like he would burst and jumped to his feet, "Let me out of here!"

He rammed his body against the lattice. Although sharp pains stabbed his muscles and bones, he slammed his body two more times and used both hands to shake the lattice with all his might.

"Let me out," he continued shouting, "I'm gonna kill every last one of you bastards."

5.3

On his seventh day in jail, Eiji was sent to the labor detention camp in Ishikawajima. Matazaemon conducted a careful investigation and extended various kindnesses to Eiji. Yasui Tomoemon, a policeman, and Okamura Jihei, a junior public official went to the Honchō guardhouse with Aoki Kōnoshin, a patrol officer and member of Matazaemon's family. These three men sympathized with Eiji, informally discussed and quietly wondered over and over what was the source of his misfortune.

Eiji maintained his silence even with Matazaemon. During a fight in jail, the toenail on the big toe of his right foot ripped off, and he wrapped it in cotton cloth. His fingers hurt. Other parts of his body, bones of his shoulders and hips radiated dull pain. He grimaced each time he moved his body. Staring at a point in front, his face hardened like it had become stone, and he remained silent.

During this time, Kōnoshin conducted his investigation of Watabun. But there, they only said, "He stormed in and was violent." They said nothing about Eiji's family or upbringing. That situation occurred often in Matazaemon's investigation. Eiji smiled coldly in his heart but didn't show it on his face any more than the tip of his toenail.

Instead of Matazaemon, a police investigator called Ishikawa So-and-so investigated for three days. The investigation was scrupulous and merciless, but he didn't throw his hands up and scream. On the seventh day, Matazaemon took over again.

"What should I believe are the details?" asked Matazaemon in a businesslike way, "Government officials are extremely busy and have no time. No other crimes have been uncovered in the investigation, so this matter can be retired. You have not told us an address, guarantor, or whether you have a job. You should understand you can't escape the penalty for vagrancy and will be sent to the labor detention camp in Ishikawajima."

Nevertheless, Eiji said nothing.

Eiji and five others dressed in their everyday clothes and wearing zori sandals were sent to Ishikawajima. Eiji and another youth were tied together by a rope around their waists. Only those two looked like they may be violent. Three policemen and three junior officials guarded them. Eiji and the youth he was tied to were jumpy and snorted, sniffed, and twisted their heads left and right.

"Hey, I'm Kinta," whispered the youth to Eiji as they came out in single file to the street, "I was ratted on by a stingy gambler and sent to the island."

"Quiet," shouted one of the officials, "No talking."

As the youth twisted his head, he stuck out his tongue, an extremely long and pale one. Eiji did not engage. He had no sense of what the other four men were like and could not see where the street led.

People among passersby knew criminals were on the move. These men and women stopped. Their curious eyes watched them with disgust. Most noticed but hurried to avert their eyes.

Eiji thought, So they're afraid of us with ropes tied around our waists. Maybe, they see me as a villain, a man who robbed or killed. That's fine. Now, watch me become the man you think I am.

He hated and challenged everything he saw. If he saw a row of houses, he hated seeing others enjoying their tranquil lives. If he saw a happy couple satisfied among the people coming and going, he ridiculed them in his heart and cursed them.

However, when they reached the Echizen Canal, Eiji's heart was enchanted only once. Along the storehouses of the merchants facing the canal, two seven- or eight-year-old girls spread out a rush mat at a sunny spot on the ground, sat on the mat, and played bean bag games.

He could hear one girl singing, "Ride on my hand. Ride on my hand. Fall down. Now play again."

Eiji stopped and watched them. They seemed to be about the same age and tied their hair up in the *otabakobon* style of young girls. They both wore aprons over their colorful kimonos.

"Grab one. Grab one. Grab one. Let them fall. Now, play again," chanted one girl as she skillfully tossed up and grabbed the bean bags.

Exactly like that time, Watabun's daughters, Kimi and Sono, invited him to play bean bag games with them. For no reason, those thoughts brought on warm emotions like a hot spring to his chest. Tears dampened Eiji's eyes.

"Wake up," said an official, pushing Eiji, "Pick up the pace."

Eiji resumed walking.

Behind him, he heard a girl's voice say, "Long sleeve. Long sleeve. Long sleeve. Pull down the long sleeve. Play again!"

Eiji slowly turned his head to the left and right.

5.4

"This labor camp is not a jail," said a camp guard, "You've heard the declaration once, but delinquents and vagrants are sent to Sado Island. With mercy particular to the emperor, you are ordered to serve as temporary workers."

This labor camp was different from other jails in that the detainees did not look like criminals. According to regulations, their clothes were made from reddish-brown cloth with undyed water droplets. Their hairstyles were unchanged. Married women were allowed to blacken their teeth.

Skilled craftsmen were encouraged to work. The unskilled could learn the trade of their choosing. They were paid wages for their work. This money became the capital to build an honest trade when eventually released back into society.

Eiji did not hear a word the camp guard said. Deep in his ears, he could still hear the voices of the two small girls he saw playing with bean bags in Echizen.

On the left. On the left. The dolly on the left.

Eiji bit his lip and closed his eyes. In the inner sitting room when he was an apprentice, he could see himself playing with his friends, the little girls Kimi and Sono.

"Hey," said the youth Kinta sitting beside Eiji and poking him, "Stand up."

The guard's speech ended, and the five men sitting on the rough mats put on their zori sandals. The four junior police on their left and right said to follow them, led them to an expansive courtyard, and introduced other junior policemen waiting there. They were the men in charge of handcrafts, oysters, the farm, oil pressing, the millstone, the guardhouse, as well as, the camp warden, the doctor, and the teacher. They would be introduced later.

After the introductions, a man about fifty stepped forward. He was built like an ox. Flesh rose on his shoulders like swellings. His reddish-brown face looked natural and not caused by salty winds or the sun. His eyes and mouth were ridiculously big. His voice sounded like the teeth of a saw passing through wood.

"I am Matsuda Gonzo, the camp warden," said the man like he was screaming, "The laborers here call me The Red Demon behind my back. I don't give a damn about that. You can call me that if you want. I won't get mad. Remember this, that fellow over there who talked to you, Okayasu Kihei, a police officer in the government office and an administrator, take him at his word. If you think this place is paradise, you're making a big mistake. They say the gold mine on Sado Island is Hell on Earth. The name is different, but never forget this place, Ishikawajima, will be no less hell than Sado depending on how you behave."

Then he looked annoyed at the five men, spat on the ground, and took long strides to leave. Next, a forty-four- or -five-year-old man came forward. He didn't look his age. The closed collar of his kimono seemed to strangle him. In a sugary-sweet voice, he told a soothing tale.

He said, "I am Kojima Ryōjirō, the watchman," and smiled. "The watchman is here to serve all of you. As Okayasu-dono said earlier, this camp is not a place to bring you pain. Those with a trade will be encouraged to work. Those without will—"

"Is that a womanly Buddha?" Kinta whispered to Eiji, "That one's The Phony. He's worse than The Red Demon."

Kojima continued, "For that reason, the man who works a trade is given that work. The man who thinks he has no trade and wishes to learn one will be offered the desired work. Depending on the circumstance, the rest will be assigned to work on the riverbank, on the farm, in construction, or in the rice granary. Those skilled in a trade and those who wish to learn a trade may apply."

Of the five, the three middle-aged men were a carpenter, a plasterer, and a tabi sock maker. Kinta had no trade and said he didn't want to learn one. Eiji did not answer.

In a sluggish tone like saliva was building up in his mouth, the watchman, Kojima, asked a variety of long-winded questions. From the first to the last, Eiji did not say one word.

"You won't even give your name," said Kojima, frowning as he looked at the register he was holding, "If you come here and are not obedient, it will be painful."

Then he said, "Kinta and you will be in The Dirt Basket Room."

That is where the people only able to work on the riverbank or in construction are gathered.

Eiji thought, Who cares? Whatever. The world is my enemy.

5.5

Twenty-three laborers worked in The Dirt Basket Room. Kinta and Eiji brought the total to twenty-five. The leaders were Denshichi, Sōta, and Saiji. Denshichi was around fifty-five or -six; Sōta, forty-seven or -eight; and Saiji, twenty-eight or -nine. The three were professional construction workers and proud of having been jailed in the Tenma-chō prison.

The crew bosses called Eiji, Bushū, a reference to his birthplace in the Musashi Province. He should not have put himself in the power of the town magistrate by not giving his name. Perhaps, the two policemen named Aoki thought about giving him special treatment. They notified the officials at this labor camp, whispered to the leaders in The Dirt Basket Room, said bad things and made insinuations, but there would be no violence or unreasonable work forced on him although Eiji was stubborn, defiant, and befriended no one.

For the first fifty days, he worked on the river dike south of the labor camp. Ishikawajima was a nearly triangular island with the mansion of Ishikawa Osumi no Kami separated by a canal to the east and Tsukudajima to the west. The mouth of the big river was north, and the ocean spread out to the south.

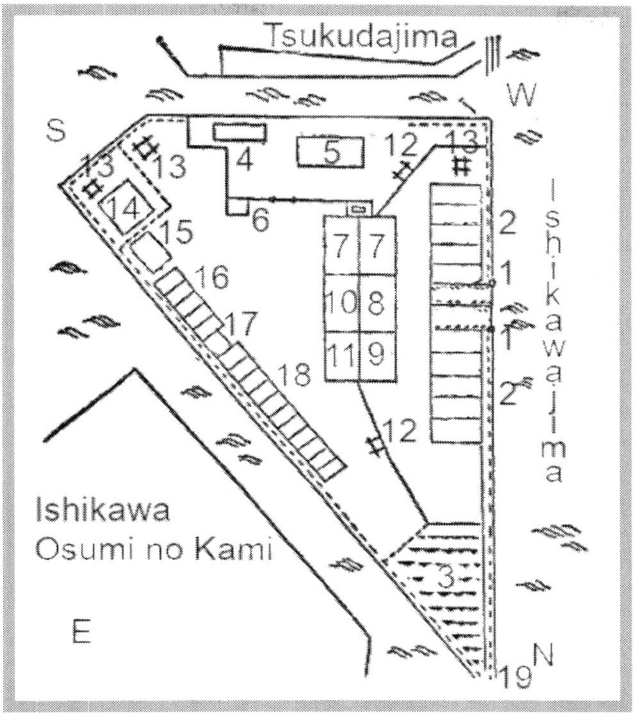

Special Labor Camp Map on Ishikawajima

1 Guard, 2 Workshops, 3 Farm fields, 4 Charcoal, 5 Whitewashed building, 6 Watchtower, 7 Sitting room, 8 Entry, 9 Office, 10 Middle room, 11 Kitchen, 12 Gate, 13 Well, 14 Women's camp, 15 Infirmary, 16 Doctor's office, men's dorm, workshops, 17 Bathhouse, 18 Workshops and offices, 19 Bamboo stick fence (---)

At the mouth of the river, merchants' houses in Funamatsu-chō, Jikken-chō, and Akashi-chō were lined up on the flat land by the wide river. A boat landing and a gate faced north. Longhouses for the inmates were built on the left and right sides of the gate. Another longhouse was on the east side where a bathhouse was located.

The office and the houses where the officials lived faced the gate entryway. Inside the nearly triangular inner court, a solitary guard watchtower was built in the center of the grounds. This position was excellent for watching the laborers' movements.

The south side where the river dike was being constructed was much narrower than the island. One end to the other was no more than three hundred feet. The ocean was at a shoal. At low tide, the sea floor usually appeared for more than one thousand feet. At the beginning of the month and around the time of the full moon, the water ebbed as far as five thousand feet.

Stone walls were constructed on the other three sides of the island. The southern tip was covered by ocean waves. About once every three years, it was destroyed by storms. To keep that from happening this time, more than ten feet were being dug from the coastline. The work advanced by deeply driving in stumps of cedar logs and leveling the ground to strengthen it.

Four or five days after joining The Dirt Basket Room, Eiji caught the attention of one of his fellow laborers. This eighteen- or nineteen-year-old's shaved face had angular cheeks. He forced an insincere smile and spoke to curry favor. He did not look directly at peoples' faces because his sunken eyes never rested but constantly scanned the surroundings.

Eiji mumbled to himself that he had seen that face somewhere. He was sure he would remember that face.

He soon discovered the man was called Jirōkichi but could not recall where he met him. Eventually, a man named Yohei approached. Eiji forgot about Jirōkichi.

"I'm Yohei. It's been about half a month since you came here. You must have some reason, but you've been quiet and that's bad for your health."

It was a break period at the work site. Eiji leaned against a pile of stones and stared at the placid ocean of early spring. Yohei came over to him to talk, but Eiji did not respond or turn around to look.

"I'm talking about this for the first time. I botched killing my wife," he said like he was talking to himself, "Eight years ago, I worked at a small kimono shop in Shiba no Kanasugi. Although small, it was fairly prosperous. I rose from a shop boy to an apprentice. I married the daughter of the proprietor."

Eiji listened in silence but was fascinated by his talk of botching the killing of his wife. It wasn't unusual for the wife with a strong spirit from the proprietor's family to marry a timid husband who rose from a shop boy. He was married for more than a decade. Despite having three children, he was never treated as the head of the household, harangued from morning to night, and pushed around. Even the children called him Dim Daddy. During meals, he was made to eat in the wood-floor room of the kitchen like he was still an apprentice.

"My wife wasn't the only one who was bad. We should never have married and made a mistake. Thinking about it now, my wife probably thought it intolerable, right?" said Yohei and sighed, "But I didn't think so. People often say, a man's thoughts center on himself. For three years, I've endured the pain of others but couldn't bear my pain. One day, my patience finally gave out."

The break ended and interrupted Yohei's speech.

It rained the next day, and work was suspended. Half of the laborers in The Dirt Basket Room were sent out to repair the bamboo fence. They replaced old sections in the nine-foot-tall bamboo fence built along the shore of the island. As he watched the laborers, Matsuda Gonzo, the warden, barked orders in his loud, hoarse voice. His nickname, The Red Demon, was fitting. Eiji thought, He's oddly good-natured. He lay face up while looking ahead, weaved his fingers behind his head, and freed a long yawn.

"Hey, you kid over there," said Matsuda, pointing his pudgy finger at Eiji. His face reddened, and his eyes opened wide, nearly bulging out. When he was sure he found Eiji, his finger quickly pointed to the other laborers, and he yelled louder, "Hey, stray dogs, can't you work faster? Kid, go slap those whining lazy bums for me."

Eiji snorted a laugh through his nose.

He mobilized thirteen laborers. The young Saiji was a sub-foreman, and Yohei was added to them. It rained for three days. The fence was repaired in three days.

On the second day, Eiji went out, but Yohei was removed from the laborers. On the third day, they were together but had no time to talk.

Yohei was a thin, small man around forty. His face, hands, and feet were full of wrinkles and dried up like an old man close to sixty. He was soft-spoken and talked slowly and cautiously. When he laughed, his laugh was a breath behind others. He always behaved to escape being noticed.

When the rain stopped, they worked on the river dike. Again during the afternoon break, Yohei started to talk.

"Am I bothering a young guy like you with my boring talk?"

Eiji shook his head slightly. This time, too, he didn't look at Yohei but at the ocean with muddy, choppy waves caused by the rain.

"Eight years ago on September 3 of the first year of Koshin. Right?" said Yohei, "The silver coin was changed in June of that year. Its value fluctuated too much. This damaged my business a lot, and the bad effects piled up. More than thirty yards of the fabric I stocked were damaged goods. The uneven dying was less than a foot short in ten yards of cheap woven silk from Isesaki for women's clothes was unevenly dyed.

As usual, my wife began abusing me.

"'You're a plague, a curse that will destroy this shop,' she said and knocked me down in front of the children."

He was on the landing of the shop, rolled down into the dirt-floor room into a corner, and hit his head on the sill. The gash in his temple was about two inches long.

"I touched my hand to the blood and looked. I was blinded by frustration and wanted to hit my wife. For the first time in my life, I couldn't help it. I wiped the cut using a kimono scrap and treated the wound myself."

His entire body shook from frustration. He couldn't stop the tears from welling up.

That evening, he recalled his time as an apprentice to the ten years since getting married and wondered if he had been living. He decided to kill his wife and die, too.

He quietly got up and took the traveling sword from the storage room. Of course, it was his late father-in-law's and hadn't been taken out in a long time. The blade was rusty.

He held the naked sword, returned to the bedroom, and shook his wife awake. She opened her eyes. When she realized he was holding a blade, she screamed, jumped up, knocked down the paper sliding door, and fled out back through the kitchen door.

"It was so quick," said Yohei, quietly laughing in his throat, "I was an insane cat whose tail was on fire. Yes, I chased after her. As my wife screamed, 'Murderer! Murderer!' she shoved open the wicket gate, ran down the street, and begged for help. Her voice sounded like her throat would rupture as she screamed, 'Murderer!'"

Neighbors came out and chaos arose when they saw Yohei had a sword. People came out carrying long six-foot wooden poles and laundry-hanging poles. Others ran to the guardhouse. As they protected his wife, she shouted, 'He's a murderer!'"

He continued, "Since I was carrying a sword, I was dragged to the guardhouse. My wife recited false complaints about me. She said if they let me go, I would kill her and the children, and she wanted a divorce. Blood rushed to my head. I saw no point in divorce and threatened to kill her again. That's why I was sent to this labor camp. Right?"

There are some awful women, thought Eiji in his heart. He remembered being dragged to the guardhouse. Anger welled up in him and contorted his face.

"After coming here, I began to understand things differently," said Yohei and sighed, "My wife truly thought I was a plague. I was a complete dimwit to my children. Depending on their nature, people see and think differently about things. I only pitied myself and never thought about my wife's or children's feelings. Until now, I think I've been bad. Right?"

Eiji was becoming irritated and wanted to scream, "And that's why your wife looked down on you."

He wanted to scream, but at that moment, the sub-foreman said, "Back to work."

In contrast to what he was thinking, Eiji turned to Yohei and quietly said, "I'm Eiji."

"Nice to meet you, Eiji."

CHAPTER 6

6.1

One evening in the last weeks of February, Jirōkichi went berserk in The Dirt Basket Room. He said money disappeared from his bundle. The room had a storage partition for each laborer's belongings. Money earned while on the island was stored in the office. It was registered in an account book and totaled each month. The money held from the beginning and the money and goods sent by friends could be kept at hand. This is one example of how the camp differed from prison.

The rewards for good behavior were permission to wear everyday clothes, to leave the camp, and to meet with visitors. Therefore, most of the laborers had some money.

"Search carefully for it," said one man, "I've never heard about one case of stealing money on this island."

"But it's gone," said Jirōkichi, claiming he thoroughly searched the bundle, "I know I put it in my wallet that I put in this kimono."

While listening to this exchange, Eiji thought, Ah! I've seen Jirōkichi's face somewhere and heard his voice before. He couldn't stop thinking he was certain he heard that voice with its crafty talk to curry favor.

The same laborer said, "Hey, hey, your partition is next to mine. Are you trying to falsely accuse me?"

"Don't be stupid," said Jirōkichi, furiously shaking his head, "I'm not accusing you. Not at all. I simply had money in the wallet."

"Yo, Jirō," said another laborer sprawled on his bed, "Looks like something's falling out of your breast pocket."

"Huh?" said Jirōkichi. He looked down and saw the wallet about to fall out. His mouth dropped open in surprise.

"Oh, excuse me," he said, scratching his head, "Sorry. This idiot made a big mistake. I forgot I put the wallet in my breast pocket when I opened the bundle. I'm so ashamed. I guess I'll be the laughingstock for a while."

"Stop joking. What do you mean a laughingstock?" shouted the first man, "You skip over making suspects of others. A laughingstock. Hmph. You don't get off so easy pretending it's a joke."

"Wait a minute," said Jirōkichi, sticking out one hand and stepping back. In a servile voice, he said, "I suspected you of nothing. That's ridiculous. It's my stupidity that is laughable."

Eiji, who had been listening, stood. As he walked toward Jirōkichi, he called, "Katsu."

Jirōkichi turned, and the other laborers surrounding him looked at both of them like something was happening.

"I called Katsu knowing that was you," said Eiji, "We've got things to talk about. Let's go outside."

"What? Why?" asked a frowning Jirōkichi, then stuttered, "Uh, I ... my name is Jirōkichi. I don't know any Katsu."

"If you come outside, you'll find out."

"You've mistaken me for someone else."

"I said go outside!"

Eiji raised a fist and punched Jirōkichi in the face.

"Maybe you forgot. Do you remember this? If the pimp Roku doesn't go outside, why don't I tell everyone here about what you did?"

"I ... I ..."

Jirōkichi was tongue-tied. No words followed. He looked around at the others seeking help.

"Help me, fellows, this man is ..."

Jirōkichi started to speak but only saw scorn and hatred on their faces. He jumped down into the dirt-floor room, opened the sliding door, and ran outside. Eiji followed close behind. Most of the laborers in the room ran out after them.

A crazy cat with its tail on fire.

While chasing after Jirōkichi, Eiji thought about the words spoken by Yohei. His rival's cowardice and prissiness more than his strangeness enraged Eiji.

The inner courtyard was dark. The shoji sliding door of the guardhouse across the way was dimly lit by a fire. Jirōkichi intended to run there, but Matsuda Gonzo grabbed him along the way.

"Please, help me," pleaded Jirōkichi's crying voice, "They're all trying to cast me out. Please protect me."

Eiji ran closer to them. When he got there, he realized The Red Demon was holding onto Jirōkichi. Eiji raised both hands and stopped.

"You're driving out this man," said Matsuda's gravelly voice, "There seems to be a crowd. Can't you handle this man without the mob?"

"Please, hand him over," said Eiji, "I alone am his rival. The others came to watch."

"You're Bushū," said Matsuda, "What's your grudge against this guy?"

"It's nothing you'd know about," said Eiji in a low, clear voice, "Please, give him to me."

Then he sprang at Jirōkichi.

6.2

Jirōkichi ducked behind Matsuda Gonzo who held him with one hand and pushed him toward Eiji.

"No violence!" said Matsuda, "You can't attack him. Fights and acts of violence are forbidden. Patience is essential in a man. A man without patience will harm others. Bushū, control yourself."

Eiji punched Jirōkichi's head on the left and right sides. Both fists punched from the left and right with full force. Jirōkichi's body staggered to the left and right. Naturally, a strange cry rose. Jirōkichi grabbed hold of Eiji but was knocked over with a leg lock, straddled and pushed down, and hit on his face from the left and right again.

Jirōkichi whined, "Help. He's gonna kill me."

Matsuda walked closer and hit Eiji's shoulder.

"Enough. You don't want to alert the office. Now behave."

Eiji stopped the beating. Breathing heavily, he still held down Jirōkichi. Eventually, he stood and left for the dark inner courtyard to escape the crowd.

He passed the front of the longhouse in the south, the infirmary, and the front of the women's camp to the river dike works at the water's edge. He sat on withered grass and shut his eyes until his breathing calmed. As he listened to the whispers of the waves nearing the shore five or six feet in front of him, he smelled the scent of seawater in the occasional soft breezes.

As he opened his eyes, "It's good I stopped," he whispered and deeply sighed. "Why did I do that? Spitting at that cowardly worm would have been enough."

He saw the lights of boats night fishing reflected in the water on the dark sea. Maybe, three or four are out there, he thought and stared for a short time. He noticed many lights standing still or moving nearby and far away.

"Nobu, instead of you, Roku is hurt," muttered Eiji while staring at the boats' lights, "To die because of that coward, he toyed with your sister."

Nobu was not defeated. Roku was not defeated either and threatened her parents.

Nobu said, "For poor folks like us, sometimes parents are scarier than strangers."

That may be true, you may not understand your parents, but I respected Hōbei as a parent for ten years and trusted him. I became familiar with the people at Watabun. How did they treat me? Nobu's parents and good-for-nothing brothers hounded her older sister until she killed herself. Sabu has family in Kasai, his grandfather, grandmother, and siblings, but Sabu has no place to live there. Why? What's going on? Eiji had questions for no one in particular.

"What's wrong?" asked a gravelly voice approaching from behind, "Are you feeling regrets?"

That's The Red Demon, thought Eiji and didn't answer.

"Why did you beat up that asshole?" asked Matsuda, standing to Eiji's right, "Is it some grudge from the outside?"

"It's got nothing to do with you."

"I've heard that line before," Matsuda yelled back and breathed out a long blast of air, "Your roommates said you called the asshole a pimp named Roku. What's that about?"

Eiji was silent. Matsuda stomped forward and cursed using unfamiliar words.

"I let you smack around that ass. That sniveling brown-noser is scum. I look at his face and want to puke, so I let you punch him.

"And I've taken a liking to you and support you. I'm not afraid to do that. Because I like you, I've overlooked your selfish behavior. If I wanted to, I could punish you for tonight's incident, Bushū," said Matsuda and squatted.

"I'll listen to what you have to say about that asshole. It looks like he's committed other crimes in society. If you tell me what you know, his true colors will be exposed. Well, Bushū? Will you tell me?"

Eiji was quiet but eventually stood and walked back to the longhouse. Matsuda immediately got up, followed, and grabbed Eiji's shoulder from behind.

6.3

"Wait, dammit," shouted Matsuda and spun Eiji around by the shoulder to face him and slapped his cheek. "Don't get smart with me."

Eiji's strength drained, both hands hung limp, and he stared at Matsuda's face. Matsuda raised his hand to slap him again, but considered Eiji's situation, slowly dropped his hand, and squeezed Eiji's shoulder.

"You are one irritating brat," said Matsuda through clenched teeth.

"I've put up with a lot of crap." He stomped and shouted, "Now, get the hell out of here."

Eiji went back to the longhouse.

All the laborers in The Dirt Basket Room watched Eiji. Roku, aka Jirōkichi, looked fearfully at Eiji. Of course in the room, but also at the work site, he avoided Eiji as much as possible and always shrunk his body.

Only one laborer, the young Saiji, did not behave that way. He openly antagonized Eiji. Even when assigning jobs or during work, he singled out Eiji for harsh treatment. The expression in his eyes and his manner exposed the meaning of "How about it? Will you give up?"

Eiji didn't show any reaction to this change in the environment. He never looked twice at the pimp Roku, talked to no one, and closed down.

No matter how spiteful Saiji acted, Eiji never rebelled. Anyone could see it was not out of submission but simply ignoring everything. This further annoyed Saiji and drove his anger. One day close to the completion of the dike work, he lost all patience and challenged Eiji.

Eiji was carrying a stone for the stone wall. It was Mikage stone weighing about forty pounds with a broken corner. He carried it on his shoulder covered by a piece of quilted cloth and held it with both hands.

Saiji's hands came from behind, pushed him in the back, and sent Eiji flying. He fell forward. Still holding the stone as it dropped off his shoulder, he slammed into the ground.

"Damn you! What happened?" yelled Saiji, "Can't your lazy ass carry a small stone."

Eiji turned to look at Saiji and slowly stood. His movements were sluggish like a sleepy person waking up, but he got up.

The instant he brushed off the dirt stuck to his hands, he pulled back his right elbow, then with full force, rammed his clenched fist into Saiji's face. The blow was swift and accurately hit the bridge of Saiji's nose. He stumbled.

Eiji crouched and viciously headbutted his opponent's chest. Saiji rolled over to face up. One hand pressed his nose. While screaming, he doubled over and tried to stand. Eiji stepped on his face and kicked a place best to avoid. He didn't hesitate in the least or show any mercy in this action.

His feet wearing straw sandals trampled his rival's face and chest, and then he kicked and stomped him.

"Enough. Stop it, Eiji," said Kinta from behind as he put him in a full nelson and pulled him off. "Stop it or you'll kill him."

His face smeared with blood and mud, Saiji lay face up on the ground. On the verge of losing consciousness, his mouth hung open and he gasped for air.

"Let go!" said Eiji to Kinta, "I'm sorry. Please, let go."

The watchman Kojima Ryōjirō came running, carrying a six-foot pole. Once the laborers spotted him, they quickly scattered. Eiji picked up the quilted cloth that fell to the ground, put it over his shoulder, and lifted the stone back onto his shoulder.

"What's going on here?" shouted the running Kojima. In a sugary voice, he said, "Who committed this violence? Who did this? Who was it?"

The laborers were engrossed in their work and no one answered. Kojima located the other two sub-foremen, Denshichi and Sōta, at the edge of the work site and went to ask what they knew. Both knew nothing and returned with Kojima. The three carried off Saiji.

"You're a strong guy," said a thirtyish-looking laborer to Eiji. "If you're gonna do something, you gotta be determined like you are. I haven't felt this good in a long time."

Without looking at the man, Eiji carried the stone in silence like he heard nothing. The laborers' expressions were a mixture of admiration and awe. They snuck peeks at Eiji. Only one man, Yohei, looked sad. From time to time, he looked at Eiji and shook his head. In his sadness, he felt it would have been better if this had not happened.

6.4

Saiji was in the infirmary for more than ten days. Meanwhile, March arrived. As a fill-in for Saiji, a middle-aged man named Kyūshichi worked as the sub-foreman. Eiji was not blamed at all.

From the beginning, the laborers and Saiji hid the truth. Laborers nearby at the time might have seen who started it. In that case, they were quiet because they would put themselves in a bad light.

However, the officials seemed to know. Tatematsu Hakuo, the professor of religious ethics, touched on the incident in his lecture.

In this labor camp, an ethics lecture was held once every ten days. The meeting place was the hall in the government office. The women residents also attended.

The lecture was not complex and resembled teaching that quoted historical events and anecdotes. Nonetheless, all of the laborers hated them. No one would have attended if they weren't ordered to go.

Some went to listen if only to see the women for a short time. At those times, they weren't listening to the lecture but fixating on the women. Consequently, the teacher tried to keep women from attending.

For the evening lecture held on March 5, Okayasu Kihei, a government administrator, nominated Eiji.

Every other day was bath day, and the lecture fell on his bath day. He was bothered by a listless feeling after a bath and never before attended a lecture but was specifically nominated this time. With no way out, he went.

The hall's width was thirty tatami mats. The government office was on the south side and rose from the outside corridor facing the inner courtyard.

Fourteen or fifteen men in addition to Eiji and about the same number of women were present. The sexes sat apart on either the left or the right side. The teacher was seated in the center.

Tatematsu Hakuo was a fat, old man around sixty years old. His large bald head and plump, round face radiated a light-brown greasy light. The redness of his large, thick lips gave him a freakish look.

Eiji imagined an ethics teacher to be a slim man of refined elegance and was amused by the vast difference. He would have taken this man to be a monk or priest.

The watchman Kojima Ryōjirō and two police officers from the government office sat in a corner of the hall. Okayasu Kihei's face could be seen in the group.

The teacher Tatematsu's speech was boring. He alone was excited and moved by his words.

"Yes. That's it. This is the path of human righteousness. Yes."

He nodded vigorously and smacked his lap with a fan with great power.

What is in the *Book of Filial Piety*? How is this expressed in ethics? What is done in foreign countries? Hakuo randomly presented stories or strange poems that were read or heard before but not understood. He repeatedly said this was certainly the path to live one's life.

Eiji fought the urge to yawn. Hakuo suddenly raised his voice and caught Eiji by surprise with the tale of a military commander, Kimura So-and-so of the Toyotomi clan, who demonstrated patience despite being whacked in the head by a tea master.

"A full-fledged military commander was hit in the head by a tea master," said Hakuo, almost like a threat. He opened his eyes wide and looked at the seats on the left and right.

"However, Kimura Shigenari said nothing and did nothing. Even his face registered no pain. This is the difference among men. The problem here is not whether the tea master ends as a tea master. Shigenari became a samurai general and captain and fought in the Siege of Osaka. The Tokugawa forces were there, and he died in battle and became a great man whose name went down to posterity."

Hakuo continued, "I cannot say everyone here is a person like Shigeru, but among us are people who were nearly killed by a rival over an insignificant prank."

Eiji quickly looked over at the policemen's seats. No one was looking at him. Okayasu Kihei's face pointed up, and his eyes were shut.

Still glancing to the left and right, Hakuo said, "I want to listen to that man. If someone played a trick, what happened after the laughing stopped? If the trick is played two or three times or if I hold back my laughter, my rival's rhythm is thrown off, and he will surely apologize. That man, however, nearly kills his rival, it seems he couldn't stop himself. What happens later?

"Without the heavenly taboo on revenge after a first act of revenge, for instance, a child whose parent was killed in an act of revenge hates the killer, seeks revenge, and avenges his parent's death, an endless cycle of revenge would emerge in this world.

"However, grudges cannot be suppressed by taboos."

Then with more zeal, Hakuo said, "The nearly murdered man never regrets the trick he played and may hate his rival enough to retaliate."

The teacher's voice filled with his true feelings.

"If a fire breaks out, the house set alight is destroyed, and the fire burns out. That is to say, through the sacrifice of one house, a conflagration is prevented."

Eiji listened to this point and then stood.

He felt everyone's eyes on his back and, without saying a word, walked out of the hall and went back to The Dirt Basket Room.

The teacher's lecture was obviously aimed at him, which explains Okayasu Kihei's choosing him. Eiji thought the lecture was long-winded, tedious, and stupid.

If what I did was bad, I prefer to be punished up front. Don't tell me about a patient tea master or military general. I'm not a scholar about China, a tea master, or a military general. I'm Eiji, a nobody scroll mounter. I've been shamed with the label of thief, beaten up in public, sent to a labor camp on an island, and my life turned upside down.

"He should have asked, 'Was that your fate?'"

Eiji leaned on his side using his arm as a pillow and softly mumbled in his mouth, "When I stood up, I thought about slugging that bald fool of a priest. If Baldy got mad, I'd tell him to be patient. Yohei talked nonsense. I can endure for three years if it's someone else's pain. A lecture by a charlatan about pain he knows nothing about."

While mumbling, Eiji's eyes became hot, and he felt tears on the verge of spilling out.

Anybody would keep a distance from me. I've decided the world and all its people are my enemies. I'm closed inside a hard shell and quick to pity myself.

The other laborers were already in bed. Some were snoring. Their snores brought on stifling loneliness in him like he was the sole person in this wide world. As Eiji wisely held back his sobbing, he slipped, still dressed, into his bed.

Saiji returned from the infirmary wrapped in gauze from above his mouth. From the hole opened only at his eyes, he stared continuously at Eiji. Despite the smallness of the gap, the expression in his eyes seemed to assume an attitude for his entire body and leap out.

Saiji said to another laborer, "A man can be killed by a single needle.

"A pressure point is located at the hollow at the nape of the neck. You can stick a needle right there. It's all over in an instant. No wound is left behind, so no one knows.

"I've hurt five people in the outside world. If you're interested, I fought three of them at once."

Eiji heard the awful things he said but didn't look at him or act like he heard.

Yohei whispered, "Ei-san, you better be careful. That Saiji quit as a sub-foreman. He may hold a grudge, so you better keep your distance."

He slipped when he said Eiji's name and anxiously tried to apologize.

The dike work ended, and the clean-up lasted seven days. On the evening of the fifteenth, when he returned to the room and was washing his arms and legs, Kojima Ryōjirō appeared and called to him. Still wiping his hands, Eiji followed him.

They walked around the office building to the guardhouse beside the gate facing the mouth of the big river. Kojima walked up to the front and stopped and motioned to the guardhouse.

He said, "Someone's here who wants to see you. It's outside of the scheduled visiting hours, but special permission was given for this meeting."

He tended to talk like he was eating glue. Eiji entered the guardhouse still carrying the hand towel. The dirt-floor room was a hook-shaped space leading to a wood-floor room with an area of six-tatami mats. Another room faced the shoji door.

Sabu sat beside a package wrapped in a furoshiki cloth at one end of the wood-floor room while the elderly guard lit paper lanterns. Not knowing what to expect in the dim interior of the dirt-floor room, Eiji didn't immediately know who was there.

Sabu's quiet voice called, "Ei-chan. Oh good. I've been looking a long time for you."

Eiji was startled and stared with wide-open eyes. Sabu looked like he was pleading as he stared at Eiji, but his words got stuck in his throat. When Sabu quickly wiped his round cheeks, swallowed, and called again, Eiji turned his body around and took long strides back outside.

Sabu's tearful voice followed.

"Ei-chan, what's wrong? It's me Sabu, Ei-chan."

"I don't know that guy," shouted Eiji, never breaking his stride. "Anyone I know in this world means nothing. My name's not Ei-chan. Go home."

"Ei-chan."

Behind him, Eiji heard Sabu's heartbroken voice. His lips drew into a line. His face hardened and his eyes stared ahead, he walked back to the longhouse.

6.5

Kojima Ryōjirō was right behind Eiji when he stepped into The Dirt Basket Room. Kojima carried the package.

"That man left this for you."

Eiji glared at the package. Still pigheaded, he said, "I don't know him. I've got no reason to take that."

"Really?" Kojima nodded but sized up Eiji. "That fellow, Sabu, seemed concerned and asked whether you were over your cold."

Eiji's expression stayed frozen. His eyebrows, eyes, and mouth were as motionless as a mask. He turned away.

"But you don't know him?"

"Nope. Never seen him before." Eiji's voice sounded husky.

"In that case, I should leave this package in the office?"

"That's fine with me."

Several times while asleep that night, Eiji muttered, "That idiot."

The bedding rule was bedding for five for every three people. More beds than people allowed two more men other than the sub-foremen, Eiji, and the pimp Roku, to sleep alone.

"Am I over my cold?" Eiji pulled his cover to his head. He grumbled, "He never changes. It's been almost one hundred days since I had that cold, and he's wondering if I've recovered.

"He says such stupid things."

Eiji grabbed his cover to muffle the sobs welling up. This is a strange time to catch a cold, sneeze, and have a runny nose. For the first time in his life, he didn't know what to do about feelings of unjust treatment, sadness, and anger. He sneezed and snot shot out.

Eiji almost smiled when he thought about Nikki Danjō in a play in which he sneezes when wounded by a sword, but a vision of the Watabun sitting room came to him.

He saw himself sneezing in that unheated sitting room; the boss and his younger underlings entering the room; being dragged out by the younger two into the street piled with snow, and being punched, stomped, and kicked; and finally his time in the guardhouse. These vivid recollections rose in his mind. He felt like every blood vessel in his body bulged.

"Dammit."

With both hands clinging to the cover, Eiji said through clenched teeth, "What's he gonna do now?"

For the next several days, seventeen of the laborers in The Dirt Basket Room went to jobs off the island. The laborers with outside earnings were well-behaved and only those guaranteed to not run away.

Eiji was not selected and stayed behind to do other jobs. This allowed him to observe and gain experience in various jobs and crafts at the labor camp. He didn't enjoy baking oyster shell lime, but a more grueling job was pressing oil. Even men with superior physical strength did not last long.

The trades included engraving, making bamboo baskets, building palanquins, papermaking, making paper cords, making zori sandals, ropemaking, rice pounding, carpentry, plastering, farming, and making charcoal.

The laborers remaining in The Dirt Basket Room assisted in these jobs by unloading materials from the boats, loading finished goods, and working at jobs that lacked the needed workers.

Eiji was ordered to work and did not indicate any preference. Five men in the room where cheap thick paper was made always had a backlog of orders. That was the only job Eiji never did. He had been ordered to by the sub-foreman and the watchman, but he shook his head and never went because that job enraged him.

One time, Kinta said, "Have you heard? Saiji was transferred to Tenma-chō?"

The two men were covered in ashes from their heads from loading the oyster shell lime packed in straw sacks from the ash-burning pit to the boat.

"When?"

"Three days ago. I guess you didn't know."

"Why'd they move him?"

Kinta reluctantly said, "It seems whatever he did on the outside was exposed. I'm not sure, but they're saying he did something big. He went underground at the labor camp for some minor wrong to get away with a bigger crime."

"That's not good to hear," said Eiji.

"But that jerk Saiji held a grudge against you. He looked like he'd bite your windpipe if he had the chance."

Eiji lifted a sack and said, "I wondered what was with him and was waiting for him."

Kinta's mouth dropped open.

CHAPTER 7

7.1

Too bad, thought Eiji. I was gonna beat up Saiji again. He made the first move the last time, but I'll be on guard the next time. Victory or defeat could be decided on an equal footing. There is deception in protecting, taking good care of, comforting, or encouraging someone. Once you have a bad experience, kindness to someone else with an ulterior motive to benefit yourself goes up in smoke. The kind, smiling face of Ebisu until yesterday suddenly transforms into a demon's face.

Someone saying the gold broach was in my tool bag was enough to rupture a heart-to-heart connection lasting ten years, like a kite string snapping. In contrast, there is no lie or deception in Saiji's feelings of hating me on sight, wanting to get me, and being serious about looking for the chance. It's good that people brood over things that are good, bad, and real. I could clash with him again, but, fortunately, his hidden crime was exposed.

Eiji wondered, Did something like that happen? Like what happened to me, did he fall into a trap set by others in the world? If so, was what he did terrible?

After that, he paid more attention to the people and events around him. Spurred by Saiji, he realized everyone in the labor camp was an outcast from society. The people here are people like me. The people in the world are the enemy. Like me, the people in this labor camp were hurt, tricked, and swindled by the world. Yohei was driven away to the labor camp by his wife and children. Each of the others experienced a horrifying, dark event.

He grumbled, "That pimp Roku is different. He's human trash with no decency toward his companions. Nobu said he escaped Edo, but he changed his name to conceal himself, like human trash."

Since then Jirōkichi, aka Roku, has been quiet.

He didn't have a job off the island, but he never approached Eiji. Like the two ends of a pole that never meet, they were always far apart. That time he beat up Saiji, he could be said to have been reinvigorated as a man.

Later, whenever an opportunity arose, one man often talked to him without regard to Eiji's lack of interest in associating with him. His name was Mankichi.

He was a twenty-seven-year-old fireman in Squad Two. He enjoyed fighting and spent his free time walking around his base in the area of Hirokōji in Ryōgoku to pick a fight. The boss shut down brutal fights. However, in September two years ago, Mankichi lost all patience and held a bold fight. When he injured three opponents, the boss got mad at Mankichi, disowned him, and sent him to the labor camp. Mankichi had the habit of giving monetary value to everything.

Mankichi said, "When you beat up Saiji, the speed of your uppercut, Big Guy, was worth about one koban gold coin."

"Today's weather was worth 13 *mon*."

"Jirōkichi is one measly worthless coin."

Eiji smiled without realizing it as he listened to him talk about "paying the bill together."

Eiji once said, "Please stop calling me Big Guy. You're older."

"It's not about who's the older or younger brother. The standard-bearer of Squad Two was a big man but was three years younger than me but an important fellow. At a fire, he carried the standard and stood at the spot where they'd start putting out the fire. Without inflating the price, he was worth 1,000 ryo."

Mankichi had a sudden realization.

"Big Guy, you're the first person to listen to me."

After that, Eiji talked to the others little by little. At first, he said few words but as before, not a word to people he didn't like. However, the people he greeted grew from one or two. No one was happier about this than Yohei. He chose a work team and went off the island every day. Sometimes, he bought pastries that he shared with two or three compatible men as they chatted over tea.

7.2

One night, Yohei poured tea, opened a bag of cheap cakes, and called over Eiji and two other men for a talk.

The camp laborers were given monthly wages of 400 to 1,000 mon. They could freely use half of their wages for necessary expenses. The remaining half was deposited in the office and given to them when they left the island. Thus, they could enjoy moments like Yohei's tea and cakes.

The two men invited to the chat over tea were middle-aged men named Goichi and Isuke. Both were thirty-four or -five. Goichi lived in The Farming Room and Isuke in The Engraving Room.

Goichi said, "It's been more than five years since I got here. I don't think I'll see the outside again. I'm gonna become bones in this place."

Yohei said, "That's not something you decide. I was burned, so I'm afraid of fire. I'm sorry there'll be no fire while I'm alive."

"Well, that's how it is with fire," said Goichi and nodded. "No matter how stupid a man is, he can learn how to use fire. But if he's no match for the machinery in the world or crafty people, he is made to work hard like a cow or horse, in the end, hard enough to snap a hipbone, but his house and fields are taken."

Like he was talking to himself, Isuke quietly said, "There's nothing unusual about that. If I told you each one, the stories wouldn't end. Those plans are concocted in this world and are common."

Yohei said, "But that's not how it is for him. A man who has never been burned doesn't understand the pain of a burn. The pain is different for each man. Seeing the rising sun scares some folks out of their wits."

Eiji felt like his spirit wilted. What horrible experiences had Goichi and Isuke faced? Both could be said to be in the prime of manhood but have already given up on their futures in this world. Does a mechanism that beats them up so badly act *in the world*? A famous magistrate said, "Condemn the crime, not the criminal."

When Yohei tried to kill his wife, which one committed the crime? Yohei who tried to kill his wife or his wife who brought on those feelings in Yohei?

People say this labor camp is not a prison. The laborers here are treated differently than criminals in a prison. In either case, there were reasons for their separation from the world. I was falsely accused of stealing a gold broach. Who did that? I was beaten up and sent to this place. In my case, where is the crime?

If they discovered I approached a craftsman in small ornaments to crush them into small gold grains for use as raw material, the crime would be destroying gold metal.

Watabun uses a shop boy who often shaves koban gold coins with official sanction. This is done in the money-exchange business. Why isn't this a crime? The craftsman who melts down gold grains is poor and can't buy ore. Watabun's shaving gold coins is greedy and unnecessary. Which one was accused of a crime against truth? Eiji cross-examined no one in particular in his heart.

Goichi said, "My old man died young. I was eleven and started doing farm work. I had to work to support my mother, two younger twin brothers, and a little baby sister. On less than two acres of dry land full of bamboo grass, I irrigated the land to make a field. The agreement with the landowner said if I created a field, it would cover ten years of rent for tenant farming.

"But seven years ago, the landowner came to collect a loan for the rent for the new field and a loan made to my dead father. The rent for the field covered all the years from the start of cultivating the new field, and the loan contract for 25 ryo was from seventeen years ago.

Goichi said, "My dead father couldn't read or write. It was called a contract but was signed with his fingerprint. I couldn't tell whether that was my old man's thumbprint. The free rent for the new field for ten years was not written down, so I didn't have proof. I talked with other people, but money works with civil servants. I knew there was nothing I could do."

A field, a little over an acre, originally owned by Goichi's family, and the new field, almost two acres, eventually produced high-quality rice, the result of his late father's and Goichi's hard work. The landowner, however, coveted the land.

"Since the old man didn't say anything before he died, I don't know whether the loan for 25 ryo was the truth or a lie, but I know the truth about the field."

With no emotion in his words, Goichi said, "For eighteen years from the age of eleven, I cultivated that new field. I did bone-breaking work for my mother and the twins for twelve years. I didn't even get married.

"Then one day, the landowner's agent came with a town official to seize the field, the house, and the loan collateral. My whole family was evicted on the spot. We were forced out and driven away. You guys know what I was thinking at that time."

Eiji dropped his head. He ground his teeth unknown to the other three, made fists with both hands, and pressed them into his lap like he was screwing them in. He listened until Goichi told how he set the landowner's mansion on fire and was arrested, then stood without saying a word and went outside.

"For eighteen years," he whispered as he walked south. "Eighteen whole years. That's crazy."

Eiji had no idea how backbreaking the job of cultivating wild land full of bamboo grass was. By cultivating wild land and providing water, land yielding superior rice was produced. After he worked for eighteen years without receiving a bride, the field he owned, the new field, and even his house were stolen. All because an old contract of questionable authenticity and a deed was written without mentioning no rent for ten years. Do things like that happen? Are injustices like that watched in silence by everyone around? People at that time knew about Goichi's hard work for eighteen years. But no one helped him? Eiji moaned.

Stars twinkled in the sky, but the area was dark. Only the shoji sliding door of the guardhouse glowed with light.

When he passed in front of the longhouse, he found himself at the women's camp. A rough bamboo fence surrounded the building. Men were forbidden to enter. As Eiji walked by, a black human shadow slipped out and appeared to jog to the southern coast.

"Oh, that's ..." Eiji muttered and stopped, "That's Toyo."

7.3

Sabu visited every five days. He came after work. Despite the strict closing time on the island, Sabu's visits were permitted. One time, The Red Demon said, "You have a supporter who favors you."

Eiji suspected he was receiving special treatment for this and other things. However, he didn't meet with Sabu. The watchman Kojima did not mention him but only brought the packages left for the prisoner and said nothing. The packages contained cakes, eel broiled in soy sauce, or sushi packed in a small wooden box; undergarments or loincloths. Eiji generously shared his bounty with the men around him.

When he first saw the pieces of broiled eel, Eiji frowned, grumbled, "What a dope," and certainly recalled often eating eel at the stall beside the Wakoku Bridge long ago.

Sabu probably didn't realize that reminded him of the cash box at the reception desk. Of course, Eiji didn't touch the broiled eel.

One night before bed in the last weeks of April, Mankichi went over to Eiji and quietly asked him to come outside. Eiji nodded, stood, and went out with him.

Eiji asked, "What is it?"

"Have you heard about Shozō and Toyo?"

"Not much, but I heard what I heard. What'd they do?"

"Someone's been spying on them. It's disgusting to talk about."

In no time, the woman Toyo in the women's camp got involved with the man Shozō, who makes paper cords. The woman had become the talk among the men. Shozō was well-behaved and a messenger who could freely go throughout the city. If he had a guarantor, they'd release him from the island.

In the labor camp, intimacy between men and women was forbidden. Despite the prohibition, people secretly fall in love. Those around them acted oblivious and had the custom of protecting them from the eyes of the officials. Eiji also heard whispers about Shozō and Toyo but also saw her slip out of the women's camp.

Mankichi said, "The couple became close. At night, they met on the coast in the south. I heard that from Shozō. Some of the guys were jealous, and a few went out snooping."

"What did they see?"

"Where do they meet?" asked Mankichi and spat. "Do you know about a punk called Bump, an oil presser?"

Eiji did not know him.

Mankichi continued, "The men working the oil presses have bodies like sumo wrestlers and are as strong as oxen. Bump is the nickname of one of them. That jerk has a bump here on his neck. He's a powerful beast and has never been beaten, even in a fight against four or five of his workmates."

Shozō was thirty-one and Toyo, thirty. They escaped the others to meet at night and couldn't go three days without seeing each other. If they could, they'd meet every night. But Bump noticed them and went to watch, so Shozō complained about this to Mankichi.

"He spied on people's lovemaking. That's disgusting. Right?" Mankichi breathed heavily through his nose. "I thought about giving him a beatdown. Too bad I can't do that by myself. He'd turn me upside down."

Eiji asked, "Is that what they said tonight?"

"I don't know. I don't know, but I think I want to go."

Eiji quietly walked away. Mankichi caught up and, in a whisper, asked if they should have a pole or something. Eiji shook his head no and said, "I'll go alone. You wait here."

Of course, Mankichi didn't agree. He shrugged, knowing this was happening because of what he said.

At the seashore where they worked on the dike, there were only ten farming fields and weed-covered vacant lots. When Eiji went to look at the sea one night during construction, there was no bamboo fence, but now the area was surrounded by a nine-foot-tall fence along the sea. The two men slipped between the fields. When they came to a vacant lot, Mankichi tugged on Eiji's sleeve.

"Shh!"

7.4

Eiji stopped. Mankichi crouched down and looked around. It looked like rain. He couldn't see one star in the dark sky, but orange lights from fishing boats flickered above the sea in the distance.

Eiji whispered, "What? Is he there?" Mankichi shushed him again and walked out as quietly as possible. He took five or six steps and stopped then gently pointed ahead. In the vacant lot of budding weeds, he could see a darkened human form sitting in the gloom.

"There's the bastard," said Mankichi then whispered into Eiji's ear, "It's Bump."

The dark figure moved. Had he heard their whispers? He called, "Toyo?"

Eiji said nothing and walked toward him. Mankichi tried to pull him back but missed and watched him walk away.

"Toyo?" asked the man again.

"No, it's not," answered Eiji, "I'm from The Dirt Basket Room."

Staying seated, the man only turned his head and looked up at Eiji who stood with arms folded to the right of the man and looked at the sea.

"The tide's coming in," muttered Eiji.

"You said you're from The Dirt Basket Room. What's your name?"

"Don't worry about that."

"I'm asking for your name."

"I said don't worry about it. I'm here to look at the ocean."

The man said nothing and looked up at Eiji. During the pause, the sounds of waves hitting the stone wall made him feel the volume of water coming in with the tide. From the faraway sea, they heard the sounds of oars.

The man said, "I'm here to meet someone.... You're in the way, standing there."

Like he was talking to himself, Eiji said, "It's a quiet night."

The man moved his body. Eiji thought, If he's Bump, he's gonna beat me up. But he only moved a little and didn't try to stand.

Eiji lost heart. According to Mankichi, Bump was an out-of-control thug who was jealous of Shozō and Toyo and spied on their meetings. If that were true, he'd chase him away. But he didn't move and wasn't talking tough, he only seemed confused.

Eiji found this odd and was about to speak to the man when jogging footsteps approached. A woman's voice asked, "Sei-san, where are you?"

The man turned and said, "Over here."

Through the darkness, he looked up at Eiji.

The woman rushed over and stopped when she saw Eiji. Gasping, she asked, "Who's he?"

"He's from The Dirt Basket Room. He came to look at the sea."

As he unfolded his arms, Eiji said to the man, "I have a strange question for you. If it's wrong, please forgive me. Are you the man who presses oil and has the nickname Bump?"

"What if I am?"

Eiji gestured toward the woman.

"And she is Toyo?"

The man stood. Eiji couldn't tell while he was sitting, but when he stood, the man was much bigger than Mankichi described. He was taller than six feet. His shoulders were thick like a bull's, and he had plenty of muscles.

"Who the hell are you?" the man asked, "You said you came to look at the ocean, but that's not true."

"I'm sorry. I was wrong," said Eiji and stepped back, "You misheard. I didn't mean to intrude and will go home now. Excuse me."

Eiji slowly walked away.

When he returned through the fields, Mankichi, who had been hiding somewhere, came out and caught up to him.

"Did you hear?" asked Eiji.

"Yeah, I heard. I don't get it," said Mankichi, cocking his head.

"You tricked me."

"I didn't mean to. Shozō's not that type of guy."

"What did I just see?"

"I don't get it?" Mankichi tilted his head. "I didn't only hear what I said before from Shozō. I also heard it from Toyo. We can't do a thing and shouldn't go near Bump."

Eiji turned to look at Mankichi.

"What about the woman?"

"I've talked to her a couple of times."

While he kept thinking about his confusing conversation with the massive Bump, Eiji said to Mankichi, "You're a good man."

7.5

The situation was soon uncovered.

"It's like you said, Big Guy," said Mankichi scratching his head. "I was tricked."

Mankichi had been cautiously asking around.

Simply stated, Toyo was a loose woman. She would give herself to any man who approached her. Bump, aka Sei-san, was her man before Shozō. Toyo and Bump's meetings were spied on by Shozō who began meddling. Toyo became passionate about Shozō, too.

Bump was a criminal who would immediately become violent but turned to jelly when Toyo became his. His only merit was giving her money and gifts. He didn't have the energy to be angry at or jealous of other men.

Mankichi said, "Toyo is a flirt, thinking she's a nun is nuts. But that's no mystery, she has warm feelings for someone and hasn't decided to be unfaithful.

"Bump is an oil presser and the biggest earner in the camp. It looks like he can work hard at giving money or things. But that's not what's going on. She hasn't changed how she treats even the most worthless man."

At that time, Shozō was most infatuated with her. In time, he'll be released back into the world and gave serious thought about wanting Toyo to become his wife. She cajoled Mankichi to create a split with Bump.

"What is it with women?"

"That's a mystery," said Mankichi, unable to understand. "Shozō and I talked many times with that nun, but she's not crazy in love with Sho-chan. It looks like that's the truth.

"If the men in a relationship with Toyo were asked, it's the same for any man. Many of the men she dumped say she gets too serious during the relationship and then dumps them."

Eiji said, "Enough. This conversation's going in circles. Stop, this is no longer amusing."

"Sorry for dragging you into this stupidity," said Mankichi and bowed his head. "But while I was asking around, I heard they've found out everything about your background, your name, and age."

Eiji's narrowed eyes looked at Mankichi.

Mankichi continued, "It looks like Jirōkichi spilled everything. When you knocked out that guy, the pimp Roku, he blabbed to the police in the office. That worthless punk didn't even hold out for one *sen* and spilled everything he knew about your past crimes."

"Sabu," muttered Eiji.

"Did you say something?" asked Mankichi.

"No, nothing," said Eiji. He was about to say more but shook his head. He seemed to have changed his mind.

He thought, the pimp Roku talked about Sumiyoshi in Horie. Even if he only talked about his fight with me and Sabu, he surely mentioned how often we stopped by Sumiyoshi to drink. If they looked into that, they'd find Nobu and immediately know about Hōko-dō. But what's the point of investigating my background?

They found out about me from Sabu's visits. Even so, nobody has said anything to me or treated me differently. What was the point?

He quietly said, "It's Aoki. The patrolman or the one at the magistrate's office. Officer Aoki did this."

Why? Did he do that to calm me? Did he think I'd get angry? This is not a joke. My ripped-off toenail has grown back, but I'm still wiping away the blood from the wound of my shredded spirit. This wound isn't fixed by using Sabu to make me cry. Eiji laughed with a heart filled with contempt.

Rain began falling at the end of April and lasted until the middle of May. Seventeen men from The Dirt Basket Room assigned to off-island jobs had been working on land reclamation of the coastline at Fukugawa. As long as the rain continued, the reclamation work was suspended. The men cooped up in the room lounged.

Sabu never failed to come every five days. After May came, however, he was no longer seen. He had no reason to come if he couldn't see Eiji, and only the package for the prisoner was accepted. The end of the packages was worrying. The men who always received portions of the pastries and sushi were concerned.

Several asked, "Hey, what happened to your visitor?"

Of course, Eiji only answered he had no idea and was mad at himself for being worried about Sabu.

The rain stopped, and the days turned into scorchers. In addition to going to the bathhouse every other day, the laborers were allowed to use the bathtub every day. Their outside jobs resumed. As usual, the men left behind in The Dirt Basket Room pursued various odd jobs in the labor camp.

One day at the start of June, the oil presser Bump went on a rampage causing an uproar. Eiji and five other workers were unloading straw bundles to be made into rope and woven mats. They heard shouts at the burning pit, saw officials running around, and, without thinking, ran there.

The Red Demon Matsuda Gonzo came toward them, swinging his arms.

"Stop! Don't come," Matsuda shouted, "Go back! Go back! You'll get hurt."

Kinta coming behind Eiji called out, "Warden, what's going on?"

"Bump, Seishichi, is on a rampage," Matsuda shouted back. "He's already flattened three men. That bastard has a wooden hammer. We can't do a thing. We can only wait for him to get tired."

Eiji kept walking as he listened.

"Stop!" yelled Matsuda.

Eiji ignored him, raised his hand to stop Kinta, and shouted, "That damn Bump is crazy. He doesn't care who you are. Stay away from him."

Eiji walked slowly. The oil-pressing hut was near the ash-burning pit. It was surrounded by a wide vacant area. The laborers and the officials formed a sparse wall of people.

Bump was in front of the oil-pressing hut. He was stripped to his waist and held a wooden hammer in his right hand. His bloodshot eyes glared. His naked shoulders were fleshy like a bull's. The bump at the base on the left side of his neck was only visible in the stimulation of healthy flesh. Black bristles densely grew from his arms to his chest. His fingertips were larger than other men's.

"Watch out!" shouted someone from the human wall, "Stop, Bushū!"

Eiji dodged the human fence and went out in front. Several men called, "Stop. Go back."

Not walking too fast or too slow, Eiji approached Bump.

"Now, it's you?" said Bump, getting a proper grip on the wooden hammer. "Do you wanna be a cripple, too?"

In a relaxed voice, Eiji said, "Wait, please. It's me. The guy from The Dirt Basket Room. We met on the southern coast one night."

Bump looked at Eiji from the corners of his eyes.

"I don't know what's going on," said Eiji with arms spread wide, "If you do this, you'll feel better. Everyone is terrified. Isn't that enough?"

"The guy from The Dirt Basket Room." Bump seemed to be thinking then dropped his chin. "So you came to butt in?"

"Because it reminds me of something," said Eiji.

Bump looked at him askance again.

"Oh, yeah. You beat up Saiji."

"I'm glad I did it. But it was for nothing. Later, all I got was trouble."

"That's no good. Go over there. I'm getting off this island."

"You'll get the death penalty if you escape the island," Eiji said and smiled. "How are you gonna get away in broad daylight?"

"I'll kill anyone who gets in my way."

"Everyone here?" Eiji drew a circle with one hand. "Those guys over there will be a problem. Calm down. Why don't we talk this out? Why's this happening?"

"He stole Toyo," said Bump and slammed the hammer on the ground. "Toyo said she wasn't going to leave when that shit Shozō left. I asked the administrator and many times bowed my head. But it didn't matter. That pig Shozō stole Toyo and left. The warden, nobody tried to stop her from leaving."

Bump's face was twisted. Eiji could see tears pouring from his eyes and quietly approached. He took the hammer.

"I'm getting off this island and gonna beat that shit Shozō to death."

He didn't realize the hammer was gone. Through his tears, he said, "Toyo promised to marry me. Without her, life isn't worth living. Is getting caught and executed so sad? I'm getting off this island and killing that shit."

"I get it. I do," said Eiji, placing his hand on Bump's shoulder. "There's no getting off the island from here. Sei-san, you know that. You can beat the crap out of Shozō before you kill him."

"Life sucks."

"Leave Toyo to Shozō."

Bump lowered his head.

"Sei-san, if you die here, Shozō will live a life free of worry."

Eiji rubbed Bump's shoulder with all his heart.

"I'm on your side, Sei-san. If I'm good enough, we can talk any time. That's a promise. For now, please, get a hold of yourself."

Seishichi slowly turned his head and looked at the three prone figures.

"Those officers had my back," said Eiji. "I had friendly chats with those three. Hey, Sei-san, if you're punished, I'll be punished with you. That's a promise, man to man. Okay?"

Still looking down, Seishichi nodded. Eiji turned around and gestured to signal everything was under control to the officials.

CHAPTER 8

8.1

"This year I'll be thirty-one," said Seishichi with gravity, "I've known Toyo for two years. I don't understand women at all. You'll laugh at me, but I've been scared of women, even little girls since I was a kid. When I look at one in the face, I feel like her mouth rips open from ear to ear. Enough of this talk."

Eiji said absentmindedly, "I've heard. You told me about the time you went to a hot spring with your mother."

Seishichi was from somewhere in Joshu Province. He was the third son born to a poor farmer. When he was five or six years old, his mother took him to a hot spring deep inside Tanigawa not far from a town. This open-air hot spring was several holes in the rocks along the course of a river. The hot spring water gushed up from the bottom. When his mother held Seishichi and got in, an unknown woman came in behind them. He was looking up from below and saw her get into the spring on one leg. Without thinking, he clung tight to his mother's neck and screamed, "It's a monster."

It must have left a deep impression. Long after he grew up, whenever he stared into a woman's face, he thought her mouth immediately ripped from ear to ear and her red tongue shot out.

Several times, Eiji had heard Seishichi talk about a dream in which his mother's mouth splits from ear to ear.

Seishichi continued. "It's funny but I've never been afraid of Toyo, not even a little. Maybe because I first heard her speak at night. It was on the southern coastline lit by the moon. The dike work had not started, and waves hit where the stone wall crumbled. There were always depressions in the sand. If you got into a depression, no one could see you."

Eiji rattled his shackles as he shooed away the mosquitoes. In an empty room of the longhouse facing the big river, the two men had been jailed together for over ten days.

After the melee, Eiji met with the administrative officer Okayasu Kihei and gave a detailed account of the incident and petitioned for a lenient verdict for Seishichi whose violence broke bones in the hands and legs of two officials and cracked the skull of the oil-pressing laborer who tried to stop him. According to the doctor's diagnosis, the broken leg of one official might leave him lame, but the other two were not seriously injured.

Seishichi was usually called an out-of-control violent thug. Therefore, the government took a tough position and sent him to jail. Eiji was defiant and asked to be sent to jail with Seishichi. He promised he would take the same punishment. His honor as a man was at stake. Seishichi trusted him and threw away the wooden hammer. He argued he couldn't betray the trust one man had for another.

The laborers were also questioned.

Matsuda Gonzo was investigated for his handling of Toyo, the cause of the chaos.

Of course, Seishichi made his request about Toyo to the warden. However, the warden knew Shozō would return to the outside world and had a home while Seishichi would be on the island for some time.

Naturally, if it was Toyo's wish, he had to give permission. In the end, Eiji's claim was validated. Thus, Seishichi's punishment was confinement for thirty days in shackles. Eiji received the same punishment. The tiring back and forth of questions and answers with the government office convinced the camp magistrate to visit the town magistrate. The situation was exceptional, but Eiji's stubborn claim triumphed.

Over more than ten days, they lived together as one. Eiji learned the uncontrollably violent thug Seishichi was a gentle, timid man and ridiculously good.

He was fifteen when he ran away from home to work as a laborer and came to Edo at twenty-two. Even here, he worked as a laborer. Not particularly wise or able, people always made a fool of him, worked him hard, and abandoned him when the job was done.

Four years ago, he got into a fight with three men and injured all of them. A pack of laborers ganged together, beat him up, and handed him over to the authorities.

He had no guarantor and refused to disclose his hometown, so he was treated as a vagabond and sent to the camp for five years. He said this place allowed him to live like a human being for the first time in his life.

Oil pressing was hard labor, but the endurance gained from being born a farmer and his enormous physique made him unbeatable. Now, no one made a fool of him or was scared of him. He told Eiji, "I want to spend my life here."

Seishichi continued. "Women are great. In this world, there's nothing better than women. When I first touched Toyo's body, it was so soft and warm, I thought she was gonna melt away."

He repeated this story often, but Seishichi never tired of it no matter how many times he told it. The story never lost its freshness.

"The worst part is I won't hear her voice again. Every time I heard her voice, I got dizzy."

Outside, footsteps approached, and the storm door opened. The evening light and the wind blew in. The fresh scent of the tide penetrated the stuffy air in the room. The usual official did not enter. The government administrative officer Okayasu Kihei stepped in.

"Bushū, someone wants to see you. Come out and I'll take off your shackles."

8.2

Eiji guessed the administrative officer came himself so he wouldn't refuse and said nothing. Okayasu Kihei looked over his shoulder, and a junior official entered and unlocked Eiji's shackles.

Okayasu said to the official, "The mosquitoes are terrible in here. Light a fire to repel them."

The official gave him a questioning look. This had never been done for anyone confined as punishment.

Again Okayasu said, "Light a fire," nodded to Eiji, and went outside. Eiji followed as he alternately rubbed his wrists. He was sweaty where the shackles had been clamped. Laborers finished with work were in the open space of the inner courtyard and looked at Eiji with sympathy. Some greeted him with their eyes.

He thought he was going to the gate guardhouse but was escorted to the small sitting room in the office building. They stepped in from the outside corridor into the center one on the left. Seated inside on the right side was Sue.

She wore an unlined kimono dyed with small tree flowers and tied with a plain brown sash. Her unoiled hair was tied in the back. In a short time, she was tanned enough by the sun to alter her appearance, but Eiji immediately recognized her.

Okayasu said, "Don't be stubborn today. This woman came to the camp to see you. Think hard about that. All right?"

"Have a relaxed talk until I call for you," said Okayasu and left.

The small sitting room had a window on the east and walls on the left and right. The shoji door facing the center corridor and the window were open, but little wind blew through the sweltering room. Handheld fans were left out, but Sue did not use one. She sat properly with a package wrapped in a furoshiki cloth beside her.

"It's been a while," said Sue still looking down and then slowly raising her head. "Are you in good health?"

"You shouldn't come to a place like this," said Eiji quietly, "I'm not someone you know. Don't come again."

Not listening to him, Sue said, "I received a letter from Sabu-chan and finally found out about this place. At the beginning of

May, Sabu-chan was stricken with beriberi and returned to his home in Kasai to recover. He thought he'd quickly get well but then came down with a stomach illness and couldn't go out for some time."

He wrote because he couldn't visit Eiji and wanted Sue to collect the items and deliver them. While talking, she opened the package and laid undergarments, loincloths, and fruit candies. For the first time, she raised her head. While staring at Eiji, she said in a loud whisper, "That's too much, Ei-san."

Then she shouted, "Why didn't you tell me you were here?"

"My body was tied up by the government's filthy ropes."

"Ei-san, you didn't do anything wrong, right?"

Eiji tightened his face. "What are you saying?"

"Sabu-chan shared the details in his letter."

Sue was excited and licked her dry lips. As usual, she became impatient with her tongue she couldn't move and coughed when she spoke.

"After you disappeared, Sabu-chan took time off from his job to look for you. As I told you, he went home to Kanasugi. He took care of your belongings and money and brought them to his home in Kanasugi."

Sabu didn't want to worry Sue and kept Eiji's disappearance from her. On his days off and after work, he asked around and never gave up. Watabun took careful steps. As if he became smoke and disappeared, news about Eiji couldn't be found anywhere.

Sue continued. "You came to my home, but you didn't tell me anything. Although I came to see how you are, you haven't shown the tiniest bit of thanks. Ei-san, the official said to relax. He seemed to mean it and said it to make me feel comfortable."

January and February passed. On March 2, Sabu was invited by Watabun to a seasonal festival held one evening. Together with the proprietor Hōbei, Sabu went to the shop in Honchō.

In the attendant's waiting room, Sabu enjoyed sweet white sake and sushi. There, he found out from the slip of the tongue of a shop boy that Eiji came to the shop one snowy day at the end of the year, was stomped and kicked by the town boss, and forced into the guardhouse.

Sabu went to ask the watchman, but his words were muddled and not truthful. Sabu had to go to Hatchōbori and asked for help from the town officials.

Sue said, "An Officer Aoki knew about Ei-san and said he tried to uncover your identity. He told me about your being here, your stubbornness and not speaking to anyone. He believed releasing you from the island might turn into a mistake."

The officer had no idea how the events unfolded. Then Sabu visited the Kawadō shop in Asakusa. From the beginning, Wasuke was not a willing partner but might have been defeated by Sabu's enthusiasm. He recounted in detail the story about the gold broach.

"Ei-san, it makes no sense for you to do something like that. For example, even if fire ignited ice, Ei-san had no reason to do that. Sabu-chan took great care in writing the letter."

A smirking Eiji said, "The broach was in my tool bag. How could I not see it? A proprietor like Watabun wouldn't lie about something like that. Sabu can get as mad as he wants but who'd believe him?"

Sue insisted, "That doesn't matter. Sabu-chan believes you. I also believe you, Ei-san. Isn't it better for people who want to believe to come to that conclusion on their own?"

"You don't understand."

Sue's blinking eyes opened wide and stared at his face. While holding it deep in her heart, she said nothing to anyone about the incident. She knew talking was useless and would not fix anything. However, the moment Sue's large staring eyes fixed on him, Eiji felt an irrepressible urge to speak.

"You know nothing and have no idea what it feels like to be falsely accused of stealing. I was at Hōko-dō for ten years from the age of thirteen. I slept and woke up in the same house and ate food simmered in the same pots.

"I thought it was all obvious from the bottom of my heart, but the boss wouldn't listen to my explanation, removed me from my job with no discussion, and quietly sent me away to the Asakusa shop.

"I went to Asakusa and heard the whole story from Wasuke. Then I got drunk, went to Honchō, and showed up drunk at Watabun's shop.

"When I visited the next time, the boss and two younger men from Squad One were called, dragged me outside, beat me up in the snow, and shoved me into the guardhouse. Half dead, I saw the private policeman there again."

"Please stop, Ei-san," said Sue and paled. She tried to control her shaking as she spoke. "That's horrible. I don't want to hear anymore. Please stop."

Eiji looked up from his lowered brow at the ceiling and bit his lower lip. His hands on his knees formed fists with such force blood was squeezed from his knuckles, turning them white.

He continued, "Why was I accused of stealing? Who planned it? I have only one guess.

"There was no proof. I was friendly with the people at Watabun. The two daughters were my childhood friends. The rumor was one daughter said she would one day be my wife. I thought it was a joke and never felt that way. She had already decided she would become my wife."

Sue lowered her eyes. Her pale face stiffened. She couldn't stop her body from shaking.

"But Watabun didn't know my true feelings and was upset by the spread of that queer rumor. It's no mystery someone felt something had to be done to keep me away from the shop.

"Of course, I'm guessing. I don't have a shred of proof. What else could it be? Are there other facts or a person who put the old gold broach in my tool bag and had to falsely accuse me? I've thought a lot about that since then.

"There's no one else. I can't imagine or guess what the situation could have been.

"I visited Watabun the second time because I thought I could figure out the circumstances."

Sue stumbled over her words. "Even now ... Ei-san, even now you want to find out."

Eiji slowly turned his head. "It's no good. If they poked around clumsily, the next time I will steal. My rival is the proprietor Watabun. I'm a lowly worker who was forced to take a break by the boss. That's why even when the magistrate's office kindly asked for my version, I said nothing. Even now they have no plans to find the facts.

"I'm only a creditor out to collect the debts."

Sue seemed frightened as she looked at Eiji.

"When I get out of here," Eiji whispered, "For the rest of my life, I will never forget what Watabun, the boss and his young men from Squad One, the private policemen Ōtaya and his assistant Shimazo did to me. I'll get them even if I lose my life."

Sue pressed both hands against her face. Through her sobs and breaking voice, she asked, "What can I do, Ei-san?"

8.3

"You can forget about me," said Eiji, still looking down, "I liked you from the first time I saw you. If I was gonna get married, in my heart, I wanted it to be you."

"I heard that from Sabu-chan," said Sue quietly to herself.

"That's why he took care of my money and belongings. At that time, I still wanted to be with you and wanted to run a small paper mounting and framing shop," said Eiji like he felt a wave of nausea. His eyebrows and mouth warped sharply. "But I can't do it and have to give up on that plan. If I leave this island, what will I do? Like I said, I'm not that Eiji anymore and have no connection to you or Sabu."

"Ei-san, you can't do that," said Sue, sobbing and shaking her head, "You can't decide that."

"Can you make a dead bird sing?"

"Ei-san, you're not a bird and you're not dead. What thoughts pain and frustrate you? My memory's bad so I may not understand, but after you disappeared, what did Sabu-chan feel when he searched for you? What did I feel when I read Sabu-chan's letter? You don't know.

"Don't friends or a husband and a wife have a mutual understanding?"

"I have a safe place to live," said Eiji and stood, "I already told you my feelings. Please don't come again. Tell Sabu not to come anymore. All right?"

"I don't know about Sabu-chan," said Sue, wiping away tears, "but I'll do what I want."

Eiji paid no attention to the items spread out on the floor, silently went out to the corridor, and left.

It was July when the thirty-day confinement ended. To celebrate Eiji's release, everyone in The Dirt Basket Room chipped in to buy sake. The guards were asked to turn a blind eye to the celebration, but after The Red Demon, Matsuda Gonzo, spoke his customary upbraiding, he donated to the collection.

"I'm indebted to you," Matsuda called Eiji aside, "If you hadn't stopped Bump that time, who knows what mayhem that crazy bastard would have caused? Because of Toyo, that fool sought revenge on me. Thankfully, you were able to calm him down. Although late, I wish to thank you."

"Forget about it," said Eiji with a smile, "because I didn't do it for you."

"I guess not," said Matsuda, a little disgruntled. Suddenly, his face looked redder and puffier. "I will pretend not to know about tonight's sake out of heartfelt gratitude. For the first time on this island, the prohibition of drinking by the camp laborers will be broken. If the administrator knew, I'd be exiled to Hachijo Island. I think of myself as a worthless slug."

"Don't worry. Don't drink so much you'll get drunk," Eiji said without smiling, "To be on the safe side, wouldn't it be better if you didn't come?"

Matsuda's bloated face loosened and relaxed further.

"Wouldn't it be ridiculous for the warden to behave like that even for a short time?" he asked and left, looking embarrassed.

The oldest sub-foreman, Denshichi, was the coordinator. The off-island workers bought fowl and fish. Along with the vegetables and rice scrounged from the camp's kitchen, trays for twenty-five men were whipped up.

One was for Bump, aka Seishichi. He was called when the tray was ready. The sight of chicken and vegetable stew, grilled fish, boiled greens, and white rice in miso soup served on one tray filled everyone with excitement.

Meals at the camp included large amounts of barley. The exceptions were New Year's soup and salted salmon for three days in January, red rice served during the Five Festivals or for the local Shinto deity or harvest god, loach soup during the dog days of summer, and fine white noodles for the Star Festival. The food was usually bland. The men wanted to cheer the slightest treat.

When everyone was seated, the meticulous coordinator Denshichi brought out the sake. First, Eiji and Seishichi held out their cups.

"Thank you," Seishichi quietly said to Eiji, "Thanks for everything. I apologize for being a pain in the ass for thirty days. Thanks for putting up with me."

"Same here," answered Eiji, "We'll get along fine in the future, too."

Their cups were the only two sake cups. The rest of the men drank from teacups. The non-drinkers Yohei and two others poured for everyone else while adjusting the amounts.

"This is strange," said Mankichi and sipped his sake. He cocked his head and said, "When I take a sip to enjoy, I feel like my stomach lining is being tickled."

The man next to him asked, "About how much is this worth in coins?"

Mankichi was about to answer but had a sudden realization. "Hey, stop it." Everyone laughed.

"If we could do this once a month," said one man in an emotional voice, "I think it'd be all right to spend my life in this camp."

Another man said, "That's right. This island is much more comfortable than the cold, cruel world outside where living is like pulling out the tongue of a live horse."

"Yup, that's true," another man quickly added, "Compared to life on the outside world that is like pulling the tongue out of a live horse, life on the island is a breeze."

Everyone shared another laugh.

8.4

The congenial moments continued for some time. Five men came over to drink with Eiji. Although he didn't drink and declined, the five weren't offended but relished drinking their sake. They talked about how they would help each other in the future.

Nihei looked thirty-four or -five. Take was around thirty. Sanpei, Yoshizo, and Tomisaburō seemed to be around Eiji's age.

"You're a popular guy now." Yohei came over to whisper at bedtime. "This'll be my eighth year here, and this is the first time I've seen everyone get along. One gulp of sake is no good for me, but seeing everyone drink and being so friendly makes me happy. I hate to say it, but I want to get drunk."

Eiji said nothing for a short time, then like he found his companion's true feelings, said, "Yohei-san, do you still want to live on this island forever?"

"Yes, I do. I'm one of those guys who has a tough time living on the outside.

"Like somebody said before, the cold, cruel world is like pulling an eye out of a live horse. It's not like that on this island. Nobody tries to trip you up, outsmart you, or swindle you here because there's no gain. Right?

"Of course, this place has its bad points. Some guys are warped or mean and nasty, and you have to do jobs you don't want to do. The thing is I can't put up with people, earn a living, and get ahead in life. By doing the job I'm told to do, I don't have to worry about being stabbed in the back like in the outside world.

"I say that but I'm the same as an incompetent old man and half dead."

"What do you mean 'old man?' Aren't you at the height of your working life?"

"I'm forty-one," said Yohei accompanied by a weak laugh. "When I talked about that night, the night I wanted to kill my wife, I felt like I aged twenty or thirty years. But it wasn't just a feeling. My body felt like an old man's. You probably don't believe me."

Yohei went back to his bed.

After lying down, Eiji had these thoughts.

Many people in this camp say they don't want to go back to society and want to spend their lives here. Because they have a weak spirit, lack an outstanding ability, or are too good, their lives in the wide world are hard. But those aren't the only reasons.

In addition to a hard life, society has pushed them around and served up assorted cruelties. The pimp Roku feared retaliation from his associates and chose this island to hide and be protected from them. These are pitiful people.

He said to himself, "This world is brutal. But I'm different. I will get my revenge and enjoy striking a blow twice as hard in return."

He didn't notice when the wind picked up, loudly rattled the storm doors, and blew a lukewarm breeze through the wooden walls. As he listened, Eiji fell asleep feeling tipsy for the first time in a long time.

Sue said, "I'll do what I want."

Her face was as pale as a corpse. The paper cord tying her hair had broken. She wanted to tie up her unraveling hair. Her eyes staring at Eiji looked like burning blue flames. Eiji asked, "What are you going to do?"

Sue's mouth dropped open, and both ends ripped open to her ears. Inside the bright red of her split-open mouth, he glimpsed a long tongue like a snake. Eiji held his breath out of fear and was about to flee. While squirming, he kept saying, "This isn't right. This is Bump's dream. I'm seeing his dream not mine."

Someone shouted, "Hey, Big Guy, wake up. The storm's gotten bad."

Eiji opened his eyes to a pitch-black room. The men already awake were in an uproar. A terrifying howl of wind attacked his ears.

A shout from the darkness. "It's gonna collapse soon. It'll fail without support."

Jostled by strong winds, the entire building screamed. The sounds of the wooden walls warping could be heard.

As he changed his clothes and tied his obi sash, Eiji shouted, "Everybody, calm down."

Unfortunately, his voice vanished in the blasts of wind hitting the wood roof. Wind blew in through a hole ripped in the roof and filled the room with a vortex.

"It's the sake," someone shouted. "The Red Demon ignored it, but god didn't and this storm is punishment for drinking."

Eiji shouted, "Go outside. The roof is peeling off and won't hold. Everybody, get out now!"

8.5

The man who was first outside screamed, "Water!"

The wind sliced up his voice so much that no one heard him. Everyone following him out shouted, "Water! Water!"

Their screams made several others hesitate to go outside. As they hung back at the doorway, the longhouse swayed to successive sounds of wood splintering and abruptly collapsed from the weak end.

Eiji intended to be the last man out. The group lingering by the door heard wood splintering.

"Get out! She's coming down!" Eiji shouted while pushing several of them out and then dashing outside. He barely escaped getting his back scraped by the eaves of the crumbling building.

The water came to their ankles. Each burst of wind sheared white splashes of water from the surface vividly seen in the darkness.

Men from the other rooms in the longhouse got out. Their shouts back and forth were drowned by and went unheard in the groaning wind.

The office and the watchtower were invisible in the dark. The water steadily rose to halfway up their shins.

Someone shouted, "Give me a hand over here. A man was inside when it fell."

Eiji turned.

"Really? Who is it?"

"I don't know, but the guy behind me was too slow and didn't get out."

"He can talk."

The wind came from the south. The longhouse faced southwest and fell forward. It felt like the pushing force lessened for a moment, and the section collapsed to the northeast pitched forward. When they got closer to listen, they could hear shouts coming from beneath the collapsed roof.

Eiji shouted, "I need help over here. Somebody's trapped. Hurry!"

Several men came running.

Eiji shouted under the collapsed roof.

"Hey, we're gonna get you out. Don't give up."

He guessed from the voice he heard that he should toss away the panels and pillar he was touching. Eiji instructed several men to remove debris but saw boards only nailed to the pillars, like in a crude hut, when the building was built. When he tried to straighten them, the weight of the pillar and the boards surprised him.

He heard The Red Demon shouting. "Hey, get over here. We're moving the infirmary patients to the office."

Eiji clung to a thick corner pillar. It looked like a part of the doorway. Mankichi came carrying a log he said to use as a lever. Because there was nothing below to leverage the log, Mankichi shoved one end under the corner pillar and placed his shoulder at the other end. When some part of the building looked about to collapse again, the sounds of splintering wood, muted earth tremors, and screams were heard.

Mankichi said, "It's not working. This pillar ain't budging."

"It's hopeless if we can't get this loose," said Eiji. "Let's give it another try."

The corner pillar was surprisingly heavy, and broken panels and beams had fallen on top. It didn't look like they would be able to move it. Only two men ran over to help Mankichi shoulder the round pillar.

They heard Matsuda Gonzo call out.

"Everyone get over here. Here! In front of the office."

The gale carried water sprays that hit hard enough to hurt their faces and hands.

Someone yelled, "This ain't rain. It's seawater. Look, it's salty."

The three men seemed about to tumble over when they used the round pillar as a lever to move the corner pillar. Eiji pushed the corner pillar as he avoided being scratched by the wood panel pieces below.

He called, "Are you okay? Where are you?"

"I'm here. Please hurry."

Eiji heard the response come from under the pile of wood.

"Please hurry. I'm gonna drown."

Eiji was worried. The water already reached his knees.

"Faster," Mankichi shouted. Almost trancelike, the four men tossed off the pieces of wood and roofing. The Red Demon Matsuda splashed his way over and shouted, "What the hell are you doing? Didn't you hear me call everyone over?"

All that shouting made his voice so hoarse he sounded like a *deroren saimon* street performer who caught a cold.

"A man is being crushed," said Eiji again. "Help us."

Matsuda cynically said, "What damn fool is getting crushed at a time like this? Who is it?"

While scoffing, he came to help whoever he was. Kinta was on all fours under the junction of two pillars. He turned his face, half submerged in the water, to the side to avoid the water.

"You're in danger," said Mankichi, trying to help, "Can you take another breath? You'll feel like you found ten ryo somewhere."

"I'm sorry. Tell everyone thanks," said Kinta while his hand pushed back his submerged hair and dropped his head several times. "I think this is it for me."

"Hurry up," said Matsuda waving his hands, "Stop wasting time and get in front of the office."

As he walked out with him, Eiji was overcome with terror for the first time. This is awful, he thought. This island started as a sandbar formed from the accumulation of sand spewed from the big river. The water rose to his knees. If the wind continues to blow over it, the entire island may be submerged. During these thoughts, someone asked, "When does the tide come in?"

Eiji heard the response.

"Around four in the morning."

He called back, "What time is it now?"

One man answered, "About three." Eiji couldn't hear the other voices.

The water was shallow in front of the office. The men were crowded together and jostling each other in an area where the water only reached their ankles. Officials and camp officers were also visible on the veranda. The box paper lanterns with oiled paper were surrounded by the wind. They could see the figures of the officials although no light flowed into the courtyard.

"Is everyone here?" asked Okayasu Kihei from the veranda, "Where are the women?"

"They're here," came the answer that could be heard at the edge of the group.

"The men are here, too," said Matsuda Gonzo, "How many?"

"We're ready," said Okayasu, "The magistrate will speak now. Quiet down and listen."

The camp magistrate was a tall, thin man about fifty-two or -three years old. His rank was junior to an Edo town magistrate but with audience privileges with the shogun.

"I am Narushima Jiemon." The magistrate's voice carried well. "In addition to the storm, high tide will be with us in moments. Life and death are uncertain here.

"Therefore, at the discretion of the magistrate, you all are temporarily freed. However, because you will be freed without the permission of the town magistrate, you must return within seven days. If even one person flees and doesn't return, I will take responsibility and commit seppuku. Do you understand?"

He ended with, "Three lighters are moored at the river. First, rescue the patients and then the women."

Shouts devoid of surprise or terror arose from the laborers. They were standing on the balls of their feet and toppled over.

"Quiet down. Keep your places."

A voice restrained them, but they didn't seem to hear and in a free for all, they pushed and shoved toward the gate.

Eiji was pushed and poked around a corner of the building and along the fence facing the river to the front of the landing. The wave of people stopped there. At the gate guardhouse across from them, someone was screaming constantly. Eiji roughly pushed his way through the crowd to get there where Bump was stripped to the waist and screaming. His ever-present wooden hammer was raised above his head.

Bump said, "Get back. You guys go to the back. The patients and the women come through. Healthy people stay behind. We came to live on this island and owe a great debt to it. We will live here in the future. I'll kill any jerk who escapes this island we owe so much to. If you think you can pass, try to."

From the crowd, Eiji shouted to his voice's breaking point.

"He's right. Stay here. Even if you get out of here and escape the island, you don't know what your fate will be."

His words *escape the island* echoed sharply in the laborers' ears. Eiji kept shouting.

"Escaping the island looks like a jailbreak."

Those words were passed from one laborer to the next.

One called out, "Who's escaping the island? Didn't the magistrate himself tell us we've been released?"

Eiji pointed at the man and yelled, "Can you believe that? The town magistrate hasn't approved of the release. It's only by the discretion of this magistrate. There's no history of this ad hoc release.

"A large number of guards will come out to the opposite shore in this great storm. Only the dot pattern on your uniforms coming in droves will be visible. Won't they think the camp laborers are trying to escape the island?"

Another man said, "Then what should we do? If we stay here, won't we drown? We're gonna die anyway."

Bump shouted back, "We don't have to die. The magistrate and the officials will stay. The foundation around the office is high. Everyone must have seen that. If we work together, we can save this island."

Eiji said, "If you want to escape, go! But don't cut the line. The patients and the women go first."

8.6

Facing the menace of Seishichi wielding the wooden hammer and the glib words of Eiji, the commotion brought on by the selfishness of every man for himself subsided.

After the patients and the women, the evacuees boarded the three lighters and rowed to the river without incident. Over seventy laborers stayed behind.

The stronger winds and greater volume of water made the breaking wave crests in the broad courtyard appear white. Seishichi came out carrying only a hemp rope, straw mat, and straw rope and called the carpenters and plasterers to the oil-pressing hut.

As Seishichi walked through water up to his chest, he said, "This hut is strong. The wind won't knock it down, but the jars of pressed oil will float away."

Eiji clung to the office building. All the police and officials were there. They lashed storm doors together to make a makeshift bridge, held back the hallway pillars with cords, used cedar logs as support pillars, and dug a ditch to divert the water around the building. Helping to dig the ditch, Eiji said, "Let me do it," to a man with a hoe.

"Okay," said the man and passed him the hoe. "Hey, you're Bushū? You did this."

It was The Red Demon, Matsuda Gonzo.

"That was clever to say escaping the island was a jailbreak. If it wasn't for you and that Bump, people would have left and died. You should get a reward."

While continuing to work the hoe, Eiji replied, "I wasn't trying to scare anyone. I said what I thought was true."

"You thought that was true."

Eiji said, "This huge storm has put the people on the opposite shore on edge. Without warning, droves of men in dotted uniforms on boats suddenly appear and come ashore. Matsuda-san, what do you think all those people would think?"

Matsuda was silent for a short time but went somewhere and returned carrying a hoe. He started digging the ditch beside Eiji.

Matsuda said, "You've gone through some hard times."

"Not just me. Everybody in this camp has had an awful time in this world."

Matsuda stopped working. "You're a fast-talking bastard," and stared at Eiji. "You're always humiliating people. Do you hate me that much?"

Eiji was surprised and looked at Matsuda.

"You're saying I humiliated you. I'm not kidding. I liked you from the start."

"Umph." Matsuda put all his strength into swinging the hoe. "Stop with the flattery. It won't work."

Water approached from the lapping waves and crossed the open ditch and washed out the front yard of the office building, now squeaking eerily. Roof tiles could be heard flying off. The eaves and awnings howled in the wind.

The sky was pitch black. Violent winds strangely pushed the clouds northward at high speed. Occasionally, twinkling stars were seen in strips of clouds.

They heard Okayasu Kihei say, "Stop digging. You've done enough. Everyone climb up."

Matsuda said to Eiji, "The water isn't going any higher. High tide has passed. Climb up."

"I'm gonna see how Bump is doing."

"What happened to Bump?"

"He went to the oil-pressing room to keep the oil jars from floating away."

"Stop, don't go. Waves have covered that place. You said you were there. What will you do? That fool is all right."

Eiji shouted, "I'm going to make sure."

Matsuda yelled, "Stop, Bushū."

Eiji poked the ground with the hoe and probed his way as he walked through the water. More than water, it should be called raging waves. The water reached his chest when he walked a little. He was continuously slammed by choppy waves. Spray from breaking waves pelted his face like sand. The water approached relentlessly, and he looked like he'd lose his balance. Eiji used the hoe like a cane to move forward as he fought the water's power.

The oil-pressing hut was less than 120 feet from the office building. He estimated it would take half an hour to get there. Once there, he saw the building solidly standing in the water. Through the sounds of the wind, he could hear the voices of a large group singing inside. The door was closed, and the entire hut was wrapped by ropes and cords.

"Hey, are you okay?" shouted Eiji while hitting the sliding door with all his might. "Is everyone safe?"

The singing voices inside stopped. Someone called from above Eiji's head. He looked up to see a small window. A man's head was sticking out.

"It's me, Bushū from The Dirt Basket Room. Is Sei-san all right?"

The head from the small window disappeared, and Seishichi's head popped out. Of course, Eiji couldn't see his face, but he recognized Seishichi's voice.

"I'm okay," said Seishichi. "What the hell are you doing here?"

"To see how you're doing."

"I can't hear you. I'll throw down a rope. Grab it."

The wind thrashed around the thrown rope. It took three tries for Eiji to grab it. A couple of men combined their strengths to lift him. When Eiji came through the small window, shouts of joy arose in the darkness on a mezzanine floor resembling a ledge.

Seishichi said, "Watch your head. Sacks of seeds are stacked in here. The width is five feet. The ceiling is right above your head. Come sit over here."

"It's good you came, Bushū. How's it going outside?"

Eiji heard unfamiliar voices on his left and right. Everyone sounded cheerful.

Eiji asked, "How are the jars of oil?"

Seishichi answered, "We tied them together with rope. This hut is sturdy."

"Is anyone from The Dirt Basket Room here?"

"I'm here, Eiji."

Eiji heard Kinta's voice answer his question.

"Sub-foreman Kyūshichi and Yohei-san are here, too."

Eiji shouted, "Good, you didn't give up. You fellows kept going."

"Whaah." A cheer rose again. A blast of wind swept in and shook the hut. The pillars and beams creaked. This prompted someone to start singing. The voices of four or five men who knew the song rose loudly in unison. Eiji did not know this song and didn't hear the verse very well, but strangely, the backs of his eyes burned and tears welled.

When the verse "... when you saw ..." pauses, he heard "... the hand that cuts the hay ... and don't come to the barn ... only shadows"

Eiji gently wiped his eyes. Again gusts of wind shook the hut. They heard the loud snap of a panel.

CHAPTER 9

9.1

Under the clear sky, the sea was murky brown, and the faraway mountains in Bōshū, blue.

While adjusting the package she brought wrapped in a furoshiki cloth, Sue said, "I've been thinking. Ei-san, from now on, I'll visit you every five days. You don't have to see me. Like Sabu-chan, I'll prepare and bring articles I think are needed.

"I thought about a few things after I returned home. I think I understand your feelings about why you don't want to see anyone or for anyone to worry about you."

If a man is tormented by injustice from the left and right over a trinket and his whole life is ruined, naturally, he will hate people and society. Since his heart is filled with hate, the sight of others living tranquil lives arouses only hatred in him. Until Ei-san quashes these feelings, it may be better not to approach him.

In a feeble voice, Sue said, "That's what I think. But sometimes I can't hold myself back, and leave my house in a trance. When I think about Ei-san being a laborer in this camp, my heart breaks. I can't help myself and fly out in a panic and often end up on the riverbank in Teppōzu across the waters from here."

But when she reaches the riverside and looks at Ishikawajima, she panics and can't move her legs. If she goes, she'll stir up anger in Ei-san who hates society and people. She must not go and will endure a little more. She'll remember this to soothe herself and then go home.

Sue said, "I thought about this long before the big storm." She paused. "After midnight, the winds gradually strengthened. My father said he was worried about the rising tide. He said if the winds didn't stop by high tide, the Fukugawa seaside would be underwater.

"If water submerged Fukugawa, the situation would be worse here. If it weren't for the town security doors, I would have flown here."

Roku boarded an evacuation boat. When he disembarked, an elderly craftsman fell into the sea, and Roku jumped in to rescue him. They both drowned.

Eiji wondered, Why did the pimp Roku do that?

Every last one of the evacuated laborers returned by the fifth day. Six or seven of them witnessed that incident. Roku's body was discovered before they came back.

The boat landed on a sandbar, but Roku's body floated away during low tide and got snagged by a pile on the shore at Tsukudajima.

The old man's body was carried further away although no one knew where he was discovered. The story of Roku's attempt to rescue the old man evoked great surprise and praise throughout the camp.

In the gales and raging waves, even a strong swimmer would find it impossible to rescue a drowning man.

Perhaps Roku jumped in not knowing how to swim. A man who commits the vile act of selling women seems to drink the blood of many women. What was he feeling when he did that? Eiji could not understand.

Sue asked, "Is it true nothing happened? Buildings were destroyed and washed away, but you weren't hurt?"

"Huh, oh me?" said Eiji lazily staring at the sea, "I'm fine as you see. Are you disappointed.?"

Sue said, "Ei-san."

As if speaking to himself, Eiji said, "People are a strange bunch. Very strange. I don't get it."

"What did you say?"

"I'm not talking to you." Eiji looked at Sue with emotionless eyes. "Why don't you go home? I'm in the middle of cleaning up and pretty busy."

Sue took several letters from her sleeve, put them on the package, and passed them to Eiji.

Looking away, Sue said, "These letters are from Sabu-chan. Although I came as close as the opposite riverbank, I always returned home with them, so there are four. I'm sorry."

Sue left like she was trying to get away from Eiji.

9.2

Sabu wrote no dates on the four letters. His handwriting was awful. He practiced writing with a brush since their apprentice days at Hōko-dō. Even after he became a full-fledged adult at twenty years old, he would practice whenever he had a break as if it were a shop rule.

Even a bungler who reached twenty with suitable ability could write fairly legible characters. Only Sabu never improved and still wrote like a child. He seemed to be aware of this and apologized for his writing at the beginning of all four letters.

Eiji snapped his tongue. "What a dummy. Rather than apologizing for his sloppy writing, why doesn't he write the dates so I don't have to guess which comes first?"

The letters were more or less the same. He worried about Eiji and described the latest events in his life. In no particular order, he wrote about his peaceful life in Kasai. He was gradually recovering from his illness, going out to the vegetable fields with his brothers, and weeding the rice fields. So many fireflies filled the rice fields and areas near the river when he went out at night, he had trouble figuring out where to step.

His mother and sister-in-law were kind to him and allowed him to regain his health with no worries. He was laid flat by problems with his bowels and thought he'd be healthy again around September.

His sister-in-law gave birth to her seventh child. The house was more cramped so he slept in the storeroom.

Eiji grumbled, "He still gets pushed too hard. He says he's taking it easy to get well, but he works in the gardens and fields and sleeps in a storeroom at night. He'll always be a hopeless fellow."

Maybe, he wrote those things so Eiji wouldn't worry but didn't have the skill to write convincingly. The more he tried to sound carefree, the more he exposed the harshness of his life.

Eiji finished reading the four letters and was about to roll them up.

"Ah!" he said and closely examined the handwriting. He realized the writing he thought resembled a child's although clumsy was somehow filled with simplicity and purity.

"What's going on here?" Eiji unrolled the other three letters. "This is strange. I've seen this handwriting somewhere."

It looked a lot like the writing on the rectangular hanging scrolls mounted by the boss Hōbei or one of the apprentices. He was certain they were written by an apprentice. He remembered wondering why the scrolls had these crappy-looking characters. Thinking about it later, the writing wasn't bad. If it was one of them, he knew the writing was stylized. That apprentice's writing shared the flavor of Sabu's writing he was looking at now.

"This makes no sense," Eiji said as he put away the letters. "Anyway, this has no connection to who I am now."

July was autumn on the calendar of course. The heat was worse than during the height of summer.

The big storm and high waves left only the office building and the oil-pressing hut standing. The three longhouses for the laborers, the women's camp, the infirmary, other small buildings, and the fence were destroyed and washed away. Two-thirds of the stone wall newly built during the dike construction on the southern shore collapsed.

Clean-up and construction of temporary huts began at the same time. All the laborers worked. The women had the tasks of doing the laundry, cooking, and making tea. As late as noon on the island, their joking and happy voices could be heard everywhere. When he passed through those places, Matsuda Gonzo kept on shouting in a voice that sounded like he was yelling into a metal tub.

"A bunch of good-for-nothings," The Red Demon would yell around the male laborers and then say, "It feels good loafing around. Get those rocks, you bums."

If women, he'd say, "You loose witches. You're driven crazy by the scent of a man. I should order you to plunge into the river and wash your asses."

The women fired back. "Well, please do. If it's Matsuda-san, he'll give it a good scrubbing. We're begging you."

Matsuda turned beet red and never shouted back. He knew he had no comeback, acted like he didn't hear them, and left.

Sometimes a man would pretend to lunge at Matsuda but not out of hate or ill feelings. He simply liked Matsuda or loved him like a father.

The watchman Kojima Ryōjirō had the nicest manner and friendly words to others but was hated by most of the laborers. He mysteriously got along well, was never confrontational with the other officials and camp laborers, and communicated a familiarity resembling that between a landlord and a tenant.

"Of course, I noticed," Yohei answered Eiji's question. "I'm sure that's the mood here. Yeah, first of all, the guy who created this camp, Hasegawa Heizō, had the idea that the camp wouldn't be a jail, and the laborers wouldn't be treated like criminals. This was decided by generations of government officials."

"That has continued for a long time until today."

Yohei said, "Some of those officials are rotten. From the magistrate to the police officers, there may be thirty-four or -five men. Right?"

He looked sad as he shook his head.

"I've heard the six hundred sacks of rice and money given each year by government authorities to this place are worth more than 400 ryo. How many officials steal that rice and money or take a cut of the laborers' wages? It would be a first if that sort of thing happened without anyone knowing. They can't stop until they're discovered. This happens anywhere. It's real sad when people give in to greed."

Eiji held his breath like he understood the details of what he was being told and asked, "Money and rice come from the government?"

"That's a special feature of this camp."

Yohei explained that an endless stream of people come to Edo from the countryside. Many of them are vagabonds and thieves because of natural disasters, poverty, or personality.

The official mission of the labor camp was to gather people let out of jail who had no relatives or jobs, teach them a trade, make them save money, and if possible, send them into the city, and allow them to live like ordinary citizens.

"A small gratuity is taken for providing a place to sleep, eat, and work, and medicine if they fall ill. However, the wages they earned are theirs.

"Large amounts of public money and rice had to come from the government. To not misunderstand the objective, the right kind of people had to be chosen for the official posts."

An official must not force anything on the laborers or force them to do anything. In that case, they should not act selfishly and naturally do what they're supposed to do. Their respective duties were determined without pressure.

"You may not have seen it, but think about the old longhouse before it collapsed. The quality of the lumber and the construction were crude but always neat," said Yohei and smiled with pride. "Before I was sent here, I was in the makeshift jail of the Minamimachi magistrate. It was inside the town magistrate's office, but it was so dirty you can't compare it to this place. The food was crude and nasty. I don't know about Tenma-chō, but if it became a prison, I can guess what it's like from what people have said.

"When everyone had a drinking party to celebrate your release from confinement, you remember how many people said they want to spend the rest of their lives on this island."

Eiji didn't answer, he only stared and thought, The number of people who live each day in the lower rungs of society and are easily manipulated by machinations in the world is so large it can't be counted. If those people came here, would they want to return to society a second time?

Sabu is in that group. He's called a dope and a slow man by society and must be driven to work. But there's no ridicule in this place. From eight in the morning until four in the afternoon, all you have to do is your assigned job. By picking a simple chore, a place to sleep and wake up, a bath, and even a doctor are provided. Your earnings are your own, too. That's it, this place would be ideal for Sabu.

Eiji mumbled, "He's kept on the job despite being useless. I've had enough."

Sue visited every five days. Each time Eiji said he couldn't leave his job and didn't see her for a long time. She knew he had a day off every month. On the eleventh of August, he was summoned by Okayasu Kihei. When he entered the usual small sitting room, Sue was not there but Nobu from Sumiyoshi was waiting.

"What do you want?" asked Eiji, still standing. "Aren't you embarrassed to come here?"

Not discouraged, Nobu said, "I thought you say something like that so I held back on coming until today."

"I have nothing to talk about."

"You should sit," said Nobu, gently tapping the tatami. "It's about Sabu-chan."

Eiji looked reluctant but sat.

"Okay, here." Nobu held out something wrapped in paper. "It's a little gift from me."

9.3

Despite himself, Eiji smiled. As usual, she spoke precisely while gesturing. She crisply pronounced "a little gift from me" as Nobu would.

"What happened to Sabu?"

"Of course, you don't know," she said, wiping sweat from her forehead with a folded hand towel. "He left Kobuna-chō."

Eiji looked doubtful. "He was ill and went home to Kasai."

"He was dismissed in June. What's worse, there's only been one letter."

"Who told you?"

"Sabu-chan told me himself," said Nobu, showing her anger as usual, "I received the letter. Sabu-chan said he would immediately go to Kobuna-chō and stop by Sumiyoshi on his way home."

"I heard he's had stomach problems in addition to beriberi."

"That's true. He looked terrible." Nobu frowned. "His face and hands were thinner. His legs were this swollen. He looked like an old man using a cane. If he had been walking slowly with a cane, I truly would not have seen him."

He came although he had severe diarrhea for ten days and should still be in bed. He went to Kobuna-chō but didn't see the proprietor but faced the senior apprentice Gorō.

"Work is slow, so we're letting people go. You seem to be having difficulty recovering from this illness and have no idea when you'll be well again. Therefore, you should resign."

After telling him this, Gorō gave him his amassed wages of one ryo.

"At that time, in the room next door, the proprietress was talking to someone," said Nobu, narrowing her eyes as she spoke. "They were talking loudly and laughing. She never appeared or summoned him."

Eiji was quiet and shook his head.

"They had no reason but said it was because he took time off. Every summer, Sabu stayed behind. How often was he sick and did that? Never. They shouldn't get rid of someone because he's sick. They had no reason."

"I agree. I had many questions I wanted to ask, but Sabu-chan said he couldn't remember."

"Because he's stupid."

Nobu looked angrily at Eiji. "You think so, Ei-san. You believe Sabu-chan said he didn't remember because he's stupid."

Eiji narrowed his eyes and stared at Nobu's face.

She spoke quietly. "Ei-san, you don't know hardship. After the gold broach incident and what happened later, you asked why you had that bitter experience. When you drank heavily at Sumiyoshi, I said I hated that Ei-san. When I heard the reason, I immediately recalled that time. I hated myself a lot for saying terrible things without knowing what happened.

"I flew here right away but not because I said inconsiderate things. Sabu-chan heard the details from Officer Aoki-san and learned about the gold broach in March.

"When Sabu-chan revealed this, I wondered what you were feeling and couldn't contain myself. However, Sabu-chan stopped me and still kept it a secret from Sue-san.

"You got angry and didn't want to see him. If he came now, it would stir up your anger. He said it would be better to come after learning a little more about the circumstances.

"When Sabu-chan fell ill and until he went back to Kasai, his head was always busy thinking about you. He thought about becoming your body and stopped me when I wanted to visit you, and kept everything a secret to keep Sue-san from worrying. Despite doing this," she lowered her voice, "you did that, sat cross-legged, and said Sabu is stupid.

"Despite having a terrible experience, you haven't changed one bit. You were always smart and nice looking but don't know hardship."

Eiji said, "This is not something to praise, but I wasn't saying Sabu is stupid as an insult."

"I know that. I'm your friend and Sabu-chan's. You don't intend to say that sort of thing out of meanness."

"So why are you mad?"

9.4

Nobu stared at Eiji's face again.

"Why was Sabu-chan dismissed from Kobuna-chō? I thought you'd understand right away."

"What do you think, Nobu?"

Looking to be on the verge of tears, Nobu said, "Don't ask me I'm not that bright. But I mostly guessed from what Sabu-chan seemed to be saying. I thought you could guess, too, Ei-san."

Eiji thought while staring at a point on the wall. He muttered to himself, "No, it can't be ..." and turned with a look of surprise to Nobu.

"Oh no, not that."

Nobu slowly nodded. "Yes. That's the real reason."

"Sabu should have been careful. Was he cautious enough to not draw anyone's attention?"

Nobu asked, "If he went out every five days, whatever precautions he took, wouldn't someone notice?

"Not only that, everyone at Kobuna-chō was sensitive about anything having to do with you. Isn't it reasonable someone noticed the naive Sabu-chan quietly going out every five days?"

Eiji kept his mouth shut, folded his arms, and closed his eyes. That's it, he thought. Because he visited me here at the camp, Sabu was let go. He may have tried to be careful not to attract suspicion, but Sabu's not clever enough to pull it off. If they found out he was bringing supplies to a prisoner in this place, naturally, Hōko-dō would never ignore that. The proprietor Hōbei valued nothing more than the name Hōko-dō.

Eiji ground his teeth, visibly moving his jaw.

Nobu said, "Do you know why I came to tell you this? Ei-san, what they did to you is unforgivable. You said when you leave this place, you intend to retaliate to your heart's content."

Eiji said nothing.

"I understand your feelings, but aren't you being too selfish? Listen. Success in getting your revenge would be nice. But your rival isn't carelessly waiting for you. He has money and power. The truth is he sent you here on a false charge. Of course, that isn't as strong as the single-minded human heart, so you may be able to get your revenge. If you succeed, you may feel better but only you," said Nobu, her eyes shining. "But if you do, what will happen to Sabu-chan or Sue-san?"

With his arms still folded, Eiji stayed still for a fairly long time.

"When something is started," he said, and then coughed loudly, unfolded his arms, and rubbed his knee with one hand, "ending it may not be easy."

"Isn't this a situation with no beginning or end? I don't say this easily, but more than revenge being of no consequence, please think about the people who suffered hardships for you and worry about you."

Eiji stood, walked over to the window, and stared outside for a short time. He could see the river stretch to the north. Several nearly blinding white clouds floated in the clear August skies. What looked like garbage tossed before this backdrop was a flight of red dragonflies.

"The pimp Roku died," said Eiji, his back to Nobu. "During the big storm, he drowned when he tried to save an old man who fell off the boat."

"The pimp Roku?"

"He was going by the name of Jirōkichi here," he said and turned around. "It seems he was trying to escape his gang. He didn't get out of Edo but slipped into this camp."

"And he saved a man?"

"He drowned trying to save him. I'm not sure, but several people witnessed it. It was the brute Roku."

Nobu only breathed, watched Eiji, and then she asked, "How did you know it was Roku?"

"I recognized his voice," he said and turned his head toward her, "Sometimes you can't predict what someone is going to do?"

"That's true. If you leave here, perhaps you may make people cry," said Nobu and sighed. "I don't think I know the truth. He was a lowly worm and a man unable to do anything but act in ways that should've gotten him hung a long time ago."

Staring out the window again, Eiji said, "Now, he's in a pauper's grave at the execution grounds in Kozukappara.

"Even if calling him a worm is vicious, in the end, he was unlucky."

Nobu was silent and looked at her lap.

A smart, nice-looking man like Eiji doesn't understand. Nobu's assumption about him was deeply carved into Eiji's brain. By his principles, he thought only about revenge out of frustration and did not think about the people who suffered hardships because of him.

Well, Nobu doesn't know what I don't know about hardship. If she experienced even a quarter of what was done to me, she'd understand the feelings of a person unable to quietly get revenge. Although he resisted, Eiji couldn't erase her words that he was smart and good-looking and didn't know hardship.

"Yeah, that's crap," Eiji grumbled as he carried a board for building a temporary hut, "It looks like the shogunate was persuaded if something was done, I did it."

9.5

"Oh, dammit." Eiji cursed himself. "What are my principles? What does Nobu know? I'm still spouting blood in my chest. Who would understand this pain? Shit. I won't forget her harping."

It took all of August to recover in the aftermath of the storm. The high waves washed away a wide swath of the island's dirt. Sand and dirt had to be brought in from the outside. After the temporary huts where the laborers lived and burn pits were built, and the office building was repaired, soil and terrain were extended. It took more time to rebuild the collapsed stone wall on the southern beach.

On the day off on September 1, Eiji and Seishichi were called to the office and rewarded with one mon each.

On the night of the storm, they were rewarded for two events. They prevented the laborers from collapsing into chaos, evacuated them safely, and convinced more than seventy men to remain behind to save the island.

Eiji turned down his reward. He said, "It was Seishichi's achievement. I was following his lead."

"The magistrate was a witness," gently said Narushima Jiuemon with a smile. "The first success was Seishichi's alone. The wooden hammer Seishichi raised above his head stopped the legs of many who collapsed. If he persuaded them to continue, it went well.

Through only Seishichi's wooden hammer, the many men frightened to death could not be controlled. Power always moves power. The wounded and dead were gone before everyone took refuge."

The magistrate said, "Seishichi's brawn and Eiji's brain kept the commotion from becoming chaos."

Eiji raised his head. "I have a response, but that's what the magistrate thinks not what I think. I simply copied Seishichi, so I refuse to accept the reward."

The magistrate was patient and gently smiled. "You are headstrong. However, as the magistrate, I will not withdraw. What should I do?"

Eiji did not answer.

Narushima said, "The reward is being given with the permission of the town magistrate. Now, there is no reason to cancel it. After careful consideration, what would be best?"

Eiji paused and then said, "I'd like you to give all seventy-plus people who stayed behind on the island a reward."

"Really?" The magistrate nodded. "Very well. There won't be any opposition. One mon for Seishichi and the other mon to seventy other men."

The magistrate stood and went inside. Eiji and Seishichi stood with the officers present. Okayasu Kihei called to stop Eiji.

"I need to talk to you. Come over here."

Seishichi went out to the veranda. The other officers went back to the office. Okayasu turned down the corridor and, as always, entered the small sitting room. He sat facing Eiji.

Like he remembered something, he stood, opened the north-facing window, and returned to his seat where he was silent for a few moments.

Okayasu gestured to the window and said, "Now, the wind has the scent of flowers. Do you understand?"

Eiji sniffed the air three times and then shook his head no.

Okayasu said, "I also enjoy the invigorating, cool taste of the winds of September you're breathing now. Each of the four seasons gives the wind a different scent, taste, and feel. My favorite is the chilly, refreshing winds of autumn. When I taste this wind, I enjoy being alive. Like right now especially, the wind is colored by the fragrance of the flowers of sweet olive trees."

Eiji stared doubtfully at Okayasu's face. He wondered, Why did he stop me? To talk about the smell and feel of the wind. What's going on?

"What do you think?" Okayasu took a deep breath and then quietly asked, "Do you enjoy the feel of autumn and the aromas the flowers send you?"

Eiji did not answer.

"Well, you're still young." Okayasu smiled. "You probably want to say you don't understand old geezers. However, regardless of age, I'm talking about having that feeling or not. You should deeply breathe in the fragrance. This is the aroma of the flowers of the sweet olive."

"Is this what you wanted to see me about?"

"You can't do it?"

"I have no use for flower smells in the wind. If there's nothing else, I'm going back to my room."

It was a reward ceremony, so Okayasu carried a folding fan in his hemp *kamishimo* ceremonial dress. The fan was half open. He closed it with a snap. He didn't seem to hear Eiji and looked toward the window.

Okayasu slowly said, "I'm not interested in you. Autumn winds like those this year are bringing the refreshing scents of flowers.

"But this wind also angers and becomes a storm that blows away houses, twists the waves, and injures and kills people. The July storm turned this island into a mess. Through your labor, it's been nearly rebuilt to its original state. No law punishes the wind, but if people are that violent, laws exist to rule over people."

Eiji quickly asked, "For whose sake? For the strong? For the weak?"

"For the sake of everyone in the world."

"You don't know that."

Okayasu gently said, "I wanted to say that one time. I know a lot about you.

"Your anger is reasonable. What they did at Watabun was

wrong. Your treatment by the private policeman was also horrible. I'll have to think a little more about Hōko-dō and other matters. That's surely what happened, but I do think about one thing, good and bad luck.

"This occurred several years ago. Three men from Tsugaru came to collect gold dust at Ezogashima. In addition to whatever hardships experienced, they collected a large quantity of gold dust worth two *monme*. But when they noticed, their food was gone. The time of the year was September in a land where winter came early. Should they leave? Exchange the gold dust for money and prepare to hole up for the winter? They had to choose one.

"However, a wealth of gold dust was there and to leave it there was disheartening. They decided to hole up for the winter. To buy the needed supplies and food, one man loaded the gold dust onto a horse.

"I don't know the name of the place, but the distance to the hamlet and back took ten days. The other two men collected gold dust while they waited.

"Days five and seven passed, then days ten and twelve. The man who left did not return. Their food ran out. They added wild grasses to a small amount of rice to make gruel and stretch their food.

"Meanwhile, both men thought the man with the gold dust ran away and thought about tracking him down. However, more than half a month passed, and their bodies weakened by the scanty meals made that impossible.

"If the man didn't return, they wouldn't have the supplies and food to survive the winter. They discovered a cave near the river and gathered what looked edible, like birds, fish, grass roots, and tree nuts and berries.

"They did not know what winter was like in that land. They continued to collect dust until winter came. When winter came and they could no longer work, they went to live in the cave.

"The winter's harshness was beyond their imaginations. The fire and food to endure dwindled in no time.

"The two men cursed their partner who fled. Each blamed and hated the other for his leaving. They often heard the howls and movements of wild animals outside the cave. They didn't know if it was a bear or a wolf. It didn't matter. They gave up any hope of being rescued.

"When they were sure they would die, three native people came searching for them and gave them enough supplies and food for the winter. The natives told them their partner obtained these supplies and packed them on a horse but was attacked by a bear on his way back. He asked them to deliver the supplies to this valley and died a short time later.

"The gold dust weighed about eight kilograms. Because the work was hidden from the Matsumae clan, he could not exchange the gold at the regular price. Also, in the inconvenient land that should be called the edge of the country, the prices of things were definitely outside the law.

"If those goods cost less than half of the gold dust he carried, what happened to the rest? The two did not think that. They were saved, no longer worried about dying, hugged each other, and cried.

"Good luck and bad luck are words that you tire of hearing so much they seem like complaints and boring. However, good luck and bad luck exist."

Okayasu sighed slightly.

"What I told you is fairly well known, so you might have heard it. Several instances of good luck and bad luck appeared in the experiences of the three men. The natives of Ezogashima had been tormented by unscrupulous Japanese businessmen for a long time and became sly and ferocious. However, the two men had good luck. Despite being Japanese, they encountered natives who were uncommonly kind and sincere.

"You don't realize this." Okayasu took a breath. "If you quiet your spirit, breathe, and smell the fragrance of sweet olive in the crisp wind, you may also smell the flower's fragrance. Quiet your spirit and think carefully about your good luck and bad luck, and don't forget about Sabu and the young lady Sue."

CHAPTER 10

10.1

Work on the southern dike was nearly finished.

The skies were clear during the first days of September. Mount Fuji was visible from the tidal flat. Mankichi assessed that view to be worth half of 1,000 ryo. A man on the side asked, "Why half?"

"One thousand ryo is the market price. I divided it by two," said Mankichi, showing his generosity.

After the July storm, a calm and friendly temperament never seen before in the camp seemed to be born.

In contrast, Eiji still said few words. He did not engage with anyone who tried to chat. He screamed, "You're boring me," turned around and walked away. He tried to be alone as much as possible.

Sue visited three times that month on her days off, the first, eleventh, and twenty-first. Eiji did not see her.

After that, Okayasu gave up, only delivered the supplies to his room, and did not encourage Eiji to see her. Eiji gave everything to his roommates. He touched nothing and showed no interest in the contents.

On his days off, Eiji went to the southern coast, sat on the grass near the shore, and slept. He usually spent most of the day there.

"Sabu's a dope," he muttered through curled lips. "I didn't ask him to, but he hangs around me. After getting fired from the shop after working there for over ten years, you'd think he'd understand my feelings a little."

"Stop and leave me alone," Eiji said in a quiet shout. "Please leave me alone. I pretty much died at the end of last year. Trying to cajole me won't change anything. Please leave me alone."

He dropped his head and sneered.

"Digging for gold dust is stupid. Was the man who went to exchange the gold dust, attacked by a bear on the way back, and died, the unlucky one? His partners thought he cheated them and cursed him. There's no doubt he was unlucky. What does he have to do with me? I'm not kidding. I'm left out.

"A rich man has the power of money. A hired police officer has the prestige of the government and turns an innocent man into a criminal and half kills him.

"The bear that killed him is a beast. In Edo, I do as I like and don't think about them, but I can't die and leave things like this."

Tears flowed from Eiji's eyes. He pursed his lips, suppressed his tears, and looked far out into the sea while shaking his head.

Someone once told him several dozen boats with large raised sails formed a group that slid on the clear blue sea from Bōshū to Shinagawa. The fishing boats pulled in nets and caught fish near Kisarazu. When they arrived in Shibahama, they filleted the fish, caught more fish, and returned to Bōshū.

"What did they do during July's storm?" Eiji narrowed his eyes and gazed at a group of splendid white sails. He groused, "There are boats that went out to fish. If they went out, boats that couldn't escape sank. What did the men with wives and children feel when they knew they were doomed? How did the wives and children of the dead men grieve? Maybe, they cursed the sea and hated the business of fishing. Yet, men who fish never die out."

To pass time on the southern coast and soothe himself, Eiji

talked constantly to himself, mostly about Sabu and Sue, and ridiculed the officials.

October came. Dike repairs finished around the first or second. Most of the laborers in The Dirt Basket Room were assigned to the outside work of land reclamation. Denshichi the sub-foreman and only seven other men were working at the southern beach site.

That day, winds were strong from the morning. The sea had frighteningly high waves. They had to wait for low tide to drive the piles. The tide was high. Unlike the high tide season, there was only a tidal flat for three hundred feet from the coast. Within seconds, the tide returned to the shore.

"We have five piles to go," said the sub-foremen Denshichi, "If all goes well, we'll finish today."

Large cedar posts were driven in along the exterior of the stone wall to protect the stone wall from raging waves. Fifty-seven logs had been driven in so far. The job was simple. Outside the stone wall, the ground jutted out where the sand was dug out five or six feet. Holes were dug in the ground and cedar logs sharpened on one end were inserted and driven in by a back hammer.

Eiji's job was to dig the hole in the ground. The back hammer had a hammer on the top and three handles attached below. Three men grabbed the handles, placed the hammer on the top of the cedar log, and brought down the hammer. The strengths of the three men were combined as they shouted in unison and raised the hammer. Eiji chose digging, a job he could do alone.

Five logs remained. When he dug the hole for the fourth log, the stone wall collapsed and crushed Eiji underneath. The stones that fell into the sandy hole dug out for five to six feet had irregular shapes. Sand filled in the gaps. Eiji's spine was struck hard and he struggled to breathe.

"Oh shit. Help. Over here." He heard a worker say. "Someone's buried. The stone wall collapsed. A man is trapped under it."

10.2

What hit my spine? Eiji writhed in pain that stopped his breathing. Only his body twisted and turned. His arms and legs weren't moving. The sand and stones with almost no gaps were crushing him.

He heard Denshichi shout "Hey! It's Bushū! Bushū's buried alive. Hey!"

Denshichi called to Eiji. "Bushū, are you okay?"

Eiji heard their emotional shouts and tried to answer but could not. Eventually, his breathing returned to normal. Half of his face was clogged by sand. When he tried to talk, sand poured into his mouth. More frightening was the voice that came out when he spoke.

Each stone weighing from forty to sixty pounds pressed on him from his shoulders, trunk, and hips to his legs. He couldn't feel pain. He had no idea where on his body he felt no sensation like he was numb or how bad it was. If he spoke, he thought he could figure out which bones were broken and which organs were bleeding.

"Everybody. Get over here. Everybody!"

He heard the sub-foreman cry out in a panicked voice.

"First, remove the stones. Those rocks. Stop. Don't do it like that. Careful or more stones will fall."

What condition was he in? The sand gradually swelled and was burying his face. Eiji tried hard not to move other parts of his body as he slowly turned his face to the side.

The tide. The tide is coming in. Eiji realized this and gulped. This'll take more than half an hour. High tide will be here soon. If the tide comes to the shore and my mouth isn't dug out .... He wanted to scream.

Yohei shouted to him. "Try to stay still. The sand must not crumble. Should we dig from both sides?"

"That's no good," shouted the sub-foreman again. "If the sand is dug out, the stones will collapse more. Remove the stones first. Somebody notify the office."

A man answered, "I did."

The sub-foreman Denshichi was older, fifty-five or -six, thin, and wrinkled, and looked like a seventy-year-old. He couldn't lend his full strength. Of the other five, Yohei was weak and useless. But if Bump came, ...

Eiji looked up to see through a space between the heap of stones a part of the grey, slightly cloudy sky looking long and narrow like a rip in fusuma paper. A strong wind moaned faintly at the gap.

Grunts accompanied the removal of a stone. The balance shifted with the removal, and other stones trembled and slipped onto Eiji.

Yohei's crying voice yelled, "Please be careful. Recklessly remove a stone and another falls in. Insert a lever."

Denshichi's raspy voice called through the gap. "Bushū. Please, try to answer. Are you okay? Are you alive?"

"Aaah," said Eiji hesitantly. "I'm okay. Please go slowly."

"We're almost there. Don't give up."

Eiji was about to mention the rising tide but closed his mouth. The instep of his right foot covered by a stone began to feel wet. He first thought it was his blood, but his foot was submerged from his toes to his instep. Seawater crept over and seeped up from beneath the sand.

"It's no good," Eiji whispered to himself, "I'll drown before they dig me out. When one stone is removed, another falls in. Either way, it's over."

Yohei said to insert a lever. One of the cedar logs used as the posts, the lever, was gently inserted in a gap between the stones. It touched Eiji's thigh and went down toward his lower leg.

To alert them, Eiji yelled, "My leg's there. Move it forward or you'll break my leg."

He heard Yohei's tearful voice say, "Look. There's the tide. It's coming. Hurry. Please hurry, everyone. I'm beggin' you."

Eiji thought his whole body froze. The water soaking up to his instep rose to his lower leg. The lever log extending over his thigh seemed to be entangling him.

"You'll break my leg," Eiji shouted, "Move the log to the side."

He heard the sub-foreman say, "We'll start from this stone. Push the lever hard."

The men applied a strong force to the cedar log. Eiji felt like the bone in his lower leg was creaking.

He screamed, "You'll break my leg," and tried to tell them to move the log to the side, but sand flowed into his mouth and blocked his voice. He coughed violently. Although air was blowing in through the gaps between the stones, he heard the sound of approaching waves.

"Save me, Sabu," Eiji said instinctively, "I was wrong."

The log lever added extra weight. Eiji heard the bone in his lower leg snap and fainted.

10.3

If he fainted or preferably died at that time, would that have been better?

Later, Eiji often had this thought. Once he passed out, the pain of saltwater soaking into the wound of his broken lower leg returned him to his senses.

From that moment, the true terror and pain began. He had no idea how long he had been unconscious, but when he came around, he was still under the stones, and the rising tide had reached him.

Water gradually broke down the sand from above and below. Several stones had been taken off him. However, the weight of the stones crushing him from above did not change. He could not move his body from his back to his hip. He managed to breathe in about one-third of the usual volume of air under that pressure. His eyes went dark under the agony that made him want to tear at his chest.

He didn't call it agony. Eiji cursed his inability to die.

"Sabu, help me," he yelled a second time. His voice was unable to shout, but in a red space where he saw nothing, a confused Sabu dimly appeared and disappeared.

Water mixed with sand was submerging his face. The sensation of fear paralyzed him. Although sandy water flowed into his half-open mouth, he could not understand what that meant.

"Please, forgive me. I was wrong," he said in his terror. I'm wrong about pretty much everything. I'm begging all of you to forgive me."

He heard faraway Yohei's sobbing voice and the other men's shouts. But only Yohei's frantic voice seemed to go on and on.

Meanwhile, stone after stone was being taken away. A man from the oil-pressing room came running. He was Seishichi, aka Bump, with his superhuman strength.

"Hold on, Bushū," Seishichi never stopped shouting, "Don't lose hope. Just a little longer. Dammit, don't give up."

Eiji passed out again but for a short time. He threw up water, coughed, came around, and slept facing up. His violent gasps caught his attention.

"Calm down. Calm down," said a voice from the side, "Don't move. Your leg's broken."

It's the doctor. Many thoughts coursed through Eiji's mind. Santetsu-sensei, but he wasn't sure about his family name. The doctor was a middle-aged, slender man with a shrewd-looking face. He didn't seem to be there when the patients were moved during the storm. Also a religious ethics teacher, he heard the doctor was paid nothing. Finally, it has become my turn to help.

The doctor said, "He has a broken leg but no other serious injuries. There's also a lot of bruising, but none of his other bones seems to be broken. I can't be certain until I examine him thoroughly."

Eiji heard Okayasu Kihei say, "Good. That's good. The stones are propped up. I flew here when notified and thought it was hopeless."

"Bushū, are you okay?" asked Seishichi who was peering in.

"That's for later," said the doctor, controlling the excitement. "Don't talk now. Quiet. All of you can return to your rooms."

"Are there men to carry him?"

The doctor ordered them to bring a door panel, attach cords like straps, and spread out a futon.

Eiji's mouth felt gritty inside. He carefully turned his head to the side and spit several times. Each time sharp pain racked his entire body. He had no idea where the pain originated and couldn't get the sand out of his mouth.

His broken lower leg could not be immediately operated on and repaired. The doctor said, "Quickly send a messenger to Nakajima-sensei in Yamashiro-kashi." Okayasu Kihei passed the order to a junior official.

I won't forget this, fellows. Ever, Eiji shouted in his heart. I've been stubborn, unfriendly, inconsiderate to everyone, and didn't get close to anyone.

Although I only thought about myself, everyone, even people who usually didn't get along, combined their powers for my sake and worked hard to save me.

For as long as I live, I'll never forget your voices, shouted the voiceless Eiji.

As if they were my brothers or children, everyone worked as hard as they could. Yohei-san cried for me, and so did Okayasu-san. Until now, I've been difficult and an annoying jerk. But they ran to help me. That's it. Of course, I can't forget Sabu.

10.4

Eiji had no clue what treatment he received. He was told they used medicine compounded by some surgeon, Dr. So-and-So, that eliminated the pain of the operation and helped the healing. Of course, his lower leg was completely immobilized.

While the surgeon called Nakajima was treating him, Eiji could not tell dreams from reality. He alternately saw Sabu and other familiar faces, several superimposed faces, and heard fast-talking voices he couldn't make out.

Oddly, only when he saw Sabu's face, a deep red shade flickered before his eyes.

"Hey, Ei-chan, I'm here. I'm here," Sabu called to him from the deep red. With timid eyes, Sabu watched him and looked worried as a smile rose almost in apology. Because that was so vivid, Eiji shook his head and had to say, "I'm okay. Don't worry. Wipe that weak look from your face."

During his treatment, Eiji threw up three times. The indescribably stinky matter felt like a rotten clump of water of dirt and sand. That smell remained on his tongue forever.

Yohei nearly lived by his bedside. Seishichi always checked in on him. He seemed to be neglecting his work and was scolded by Dr. Santetsu but went home and soon returned to check on him again.

When night came, usually, six or seven men gathered and talked and laughed until Yohei sent them away.

The doctor, Takimoto Naomichi, opened a practice in Uneme-chō in Kyobashi and came every day. No one knew why he was called Santetsu. Takimoto never corrected anyone who called him Santetsu and never introduced himself using his real name.

The surgeon in Yamashiro-kashi was Nakajima Tan'an. He was familiar with Southeast Asian and Dutch medicine and was one of the top five surgeons of his generation.

Nakajima visited three times and explained the prognosis to Takimoto, which was he'll be fine, and left. He never came back.

Finally, Nakajima Tan'an said, "He may be slightly lame. Youth is in his favor. He should not use the leg for fifty days."

He added, "He'll enjoy walking with a slight limp," and smiled.

For two days, he was fed only hot water and then gruel and rice water from the third day. When he was fed watery porridge on the fifth day, Eiji vomited again.

Right after one mouthful of the watery porridge, he threw up everything from what was in his mouth to a substance that contained dead fish, shellfish, rotten garbage, and dried seagrass, and a stench mixed with the smell of seawater.

Later, when he was calm and thought about it, that wasn't the foulest smell. He knew it was the memory of the terror felt when trapped under the stones. The water that flowed into his mouth had a salty taste. However, there was no smell of rotten fish, shellfish, or dried seagrasses. It was the scent of high tide or when the sea forms the tidal flat.

Santetsu-sensei said, "The internal organs might have been deformed by the pressure of the stones and will recover soon."

One night at Eiji's bedside, Kinta said, "Eiji, I know what you're feeling. Well, I may be the only one who knows inside what you were feeling then."

Depending on the situation, five or six men gathered, but on that day, everyone but Yohei was assigned work but not at the site where the stone wall collapsed.

Mankichi shot back, "You always pretend to know where there's five mon. In that kind of situation, no one knows the feelings of another man who's been buried."

"I was buried," said Kinta, "During the big storm, I was trapped under the collapsed longhouse. The tide was coming in and I thought I was gonna drown. Before you fellows came out to save me, I thought I was a goner. I chanted sutras with all my might."

"You know sutras?" a man asked from the side.

"Don't be stupid. I was born and raised in Edo," Kinta replied assertively. "I just don't know 'The Law of the Lotus Sutra.'"

Tomisaburō said, "That's not funny. He's talking about Buddhist invocations or Nichiren Buddhist chants. Sutras are totally different."

"That's funny. Incantations and chants ain't sutras."

"That's right."

"I gotta question. If they ain't sutras, why do they chant sutras at services."

"You're talking about something else."

"Why is it different?"

The inane debate went on and on until everyone was laughing.

Mankichi said to Kinta, "You seem to know what you're talking about. Tonight, you dropped five mon in value."

I don't know what you mean, Eiji kept thinking. Needless to say, since his rescue from beneath the stones, Eiji's bedside became a gathering place. If people were talking, the room was entertained. If things got a little rowdy, Yohei scolded them and one time threw them out.

Apparently, with permission from the office, Yohei did not go to work and looked after Eiji all the time. Once or twice he pushed them aside if he thought they would harm Eiji's recovery.

Eiji often thought, I can't remember what these people did. They worry about me, sympathize, and comfort me, but isn't that on a whim, out of duty, or the same as brothers?

At first, Eiji was not used to that. Before and after the storm, all of their personalities changed. After his accident, the feelings they showed him also changed.

His extraction from a narrow hole was like being confused by a new view of mountains and rivers or being placed before an unfamiliar immense landscape. One day, he recalled what Okayasu Kihei told him.

"Although you are unaware and aren't interested, in this wind, you taste autumn's freshness and smell the aroma of the flowers of sweet olive."

In Eiji's fog, he thought he understood the meaning of those words. Depending on the situation, I may not have honestly seen these people. Like not caring about distinguishing the scents in the wind or the sweet olive, these people in the camp may have had these qualities for a long time.

When these thoughts surfaced in his heart, he felt like his chest expanded and breathing became enjoyable. He also calmed down little by little, he recognized the mountains and rivers in the expansive landscape newly appearing before his eyes.

A day about twenty days after Eiji was hurt, Okayasu Kihei visited. Eiji sat up and spoke his greeting. His leg was wrapped in bleached cotton cloth over a splint, so he was unable to sit properly. Three days earlier, he sat up to eat his meals.

"The young lady Sue may agree to visit. She punctually delivers a package on the decided day, so you should know when she'll come."

Eiji looked down and answered, "Yes."

Okayasu said, "To tell you the truth, I never mentioned your injury to her. I thought it would be pitiful to worry her, but I heard you were getting better, so I gave her the gist."

Eiji opened his eyes and looked at Okayasu who kindly looked into Eiji's eyes.

"Today, instead of Sue, Sabu came and is at the gate. He probably would like to see you."

Eiji was still looking down.

He eventually bowed and answered, "Yes, I'll see him. I'm sorry for the trouble I've caused."

Okayasu stood. Yohei folded the bedding, touched Eiji's back, and fixed his disheveled nightclothes.

Sabu came in hugging the package and randomly bowed his head to the left and right and mumbling like he was giving a greeting or apologizing.

Yohei gestured as he said, "Please come in. Make yourself at home. Relax."

The old man suddenly remembered and brought over two half folding screens from across the room and set them up around Eiji's bed.

Three patients were fairly far away and watched over him. However, Yohei was attentive. Also, while apologizing, Sabu kneeled and edged closer. He placed the package to the side. Eiji timidly raised his eyes like he would see something terrible and smiled.

"Oh, Ei-chan," Sabu stuttered, "you've had a hard time."

As he spoke, Sabu's face twisted loosely. Large tears dropped from his small, round eyes.

10.5

Eiji thought, He's as tense as always. But when he thought that, the words from his mouth were unrelated to his intentions.

"You come here a lot. I'm sorry for making you worry so much." Eiji heard himself say. "I'm doing okay now."

"Good. Good," said Sabu, brushing his palm sideways over his eyes and smiling. "I heard about what happened from Sue-chan. I got scared and wondered if you would see me if I came."

Like he was deflecting, Eiji interrupted, "I'm all right, but how are you? Are you well now?"

"Oh, don't worry about me. Nobu-chan told me about good medicine. It cleared out my stomach. If that's cured, the beriberi will get better, too."

"Do you go to Sumiyoshi?"

Sabu blushed, looked down, and embarrassed said, "Um, well ... If I don't go for three days, I get antsy."

"You're still living in Kasai."

"No, not anymore," Sabu mumbled, "I have something to tell you about that, but I think it's better if you hear it from Sue-chan."

"Why?" Eiji sternly asked.

At a loss for words, Sabu untied the package and lined up six boxes of food. While pushing two toward Eiji, he said, "Nobu made these for you." Somewhat confused, he explained, "They may not be so good, but will give your body energy."

"She said these four are for the men in your room."

"Did you come from Sumiyoshi today?"

"I was with Sue-chan, too."

Eiji nodded like he was restraining himself and then quietly asked, "Did you come with Sue and go with her to Sumiyoshi?"

Sabu kept his mouth shut like he was bewildered and rubbed his right palm over his forehead. He struggled to speak but couldn't find the right words.

Then like he discovered an escape route, he picked up the four food boxes, went outside the screen, handed them to Yohei, and greeted him for too long a time.

Laying back on the futon, Eiji folded his arms and shut his eyes. He thought, He's not telling me something. It looks like something happened. What could it be?

Sabu returned and nervously sat, but Eiji kept his eyes closed.

Sabu said, "Your ... your leg, how is it?"

"It'll be lame."

"Oh no." Sabu caught his breath. "It's that bad. You'll be lame."

"I can show it off," Eiji said then controlled himself, opened his eyes, and smiled. "It's not a sure thing, but the doctor saw it and said I may be crippled."

Sabu's mouth stayed open and without a word, stared at Eiji's face.

"You're too surprised to answer. The exchange was I narrowly escaped death," said Eiji, "Besides, I'll work at home. I was crippled recently, but it won't interfere with my trade."

Sabu quickly dropped his head, pressed his right hand against his eyes, and choked up.

"That's terrible," said Sabu through his sobs, "That's too awful."

"I said it was in exchange for escaping with my life."

"But Ei-chan, you'll be crippled. That doesn't bother you?"

"Stop it. People will hear you," Eiji said softly to calm him, "I didn't decide to be crippled instead of dying. Forget about all of that. Tell me what's going on with you. Yeah, are you still living in Kasai or have you moved? Which is it?"

"You better hear that from Sue-chan. I'm too tongue-tied to explain."

"You can be exasperating."

"It's not that," said Sabu, still sobbing and making noises in his throat. "It's nothing. I say things without thinking. I don't want to make Ei-chan feel bad."

Eiji said nothing, waiting for him to say more.

"I left Kasai at the end of September," said Sabu while wiping his forehead, "My older brother's wife had another baby."

"I read that in your letter."

"You did?" said Sabu apologetically and shrunk his shoulders. "Well, I didn't go back to Kobuna-chō. I talked with Sue-chan. Because you would be released someday, we talked about different things. I ended up renting a house."

Sabu gauged Eiji's expression. He didn't look like he would speak. Sabu stuttered, "If ... if I did, I'm close to Sue-chan's house. It's a backstreet tenement, but I leased it because it's empty and the rent's cheap."

Eiji asked, "It's in Shitaya, Kanasugi?"

Sabu nodded. "I've settled in for now. It may be hard when you come, but that's okay, we'll go somewhere that's not a backstreet tenement."

"You mentioned me a lot," said Eiji, "But I've gone into huge debt in this camp. Since I won't be coming out, you don't need to think about me."

Sabu's mouth dropped open and his round eyes stared at Eiji.

"But Ei-chan." Sabu gulped. "Won't you be with me some day? No, that's not it. Didn't you promise to use the paste I prepared when you have a shop?"

"That was when I lived in the outside world," said Eiji and looked away. "Now, I'm a camp laborer."

CHAPTER 11

11.1

"Hey, are you awake?" asked Seishichi as he came in, "Is it okay for him to walk?"

"No, not yet," said Yohei, "Everyone shouldn't be so pushy. Even without all of you butting in, he's too impatient."

"But wasn't he moved here yesterday? If he left the infirmary, the doctor's done treating him."

Eiji flung out his right leg to sit and ate his meal. His beard had grown scraggly. His face was pale having been away from sunshine for a long time. His muscles seemed flaccid. Over thirty days had passed since his treatment began. The recovery of his body was seen in his eyes and mouth restored to a healthy youthfulness.

"Don't forget the most important thing," said Yohei, "He wasn't sick. His leg was broken. The doctor stopped treating him, but the important phase starts now. Little by little, he'll patiently practice and get used to walking."

"So it's a little too soon."

"What?"

"When I lived in the country," said Seishichi, nervously trying to correct himself, "There was a man with a bad leg named Sakuza. A horse kicked him. Of course, one of his legs went bad, and he walked with a cane. I remembered him and thought I should make one like his."

Seishichi raised a cane to show him.

He made a crutch with a T-shaped crosspiece and polished it to a bright shine.

Waving his hands, Yohei said, "No, no, no. It would be bad if he saw that thing."

Eiji put down his rice bowl and chopsticks.

"Excuse me, Sei-san," said Eiji and turned around to face him. "Thank you. Please let me see."

Seishichi searched Yohei's expression. Eiji hesitated then moved toward the riser at the entrance.

"It may be a little long," said Seishichi as he handed over the crutch. "If it is, I can cut it, okay. Put that part there under your armpit."

"You shouldn't be standing," warned Yohei.

"I've seen this somewhere," said Eiji and sat on the riser. Then he slowly lowered both legs into the dirt room, changed the hand holding the crutch, and placed the crosspiece under his armpit.

"It's good and feels sturdy. What kind of wood is this?"

"Cherry blossom," said Seishichi. "I tried different ones, but they warped or were too heavy. I asked Isuke-san from the Engraving Room. He knows a lot about wood. He said cherry blossom would be best."

"Everyone shouldn't be worrying about me."

"Maybe you shouldn't use it right away," said Seishichi, waving his hand for no reason. "I thought I should be here when you do for the first time."

"Enough already." Yohei stuck out his hand. "I'll keep it until you're ready to use it."

Eiji passed the crutch to him.

"Well, I gotta get back to work," said Seishichi, leaving the crutch behind.

Before Seishichi left, Eiji thanked him again.

As he watched Yohei bring over the bell-hammer-shaped crutch and put it in his cabinet, Eiji took in a long breath and then carefully blew it out. Yohei noticed that breath like he was afraid.

Although Eiji returned to the room from the infirmary almost twenty days ago, Yohei constantly watched over and cared for him. He obtained permission from the office not to go to work but continued to receive wages. Eiji brought that up once, but Yohei laughed and said, "I have eight years of wages in the office, so you don't need to worry about that."

He did everything, from washing Eiji's undergarments and socks to helping him change his clothes. He only left the loincloths in the gift packages and stubbornly threw them out. He washed his face, got his meals, laid out his bedding, and carried him piggyback to and from the bathroom. Giving care with this much compassion would be amazing even from a father.

Yohei said, "You've had enough to eat. If you'd like, I'll make tea."

"Thanks, but I'll take a bath."

The bedding was folded next to the cabinet. When Eiji returned from the riser, he leaned his back against the bedding.

"Yohei-san, I think I'll practice calligraphy. Could you get an ink stone and a brush?"

"No problem. They do the books in the guard room. I'll go and ask," said Yohei as he straightened the tray and looked kindly at Eiji. "It makes me happy you want to do that."

Eiji looked away. "Today is December what?"

"The tenth. Tomorrow's a day off."

"So it's been fifty-five- or -six days."

"Counting the days is a bad idea. A doctor can have a look and easily say when. Even for an illness that lasts a year, if the patient doesn't lose hope, no one can say it'll last more than six months," said Yohei to reassure him. "Don't think about the number of days. Your broken bone had to be grafted, so it may take longer than thirty or even fifty days."

Eiji nodded. "That's why I thought I'd start practicing calligraphy."

"Okay. I see. In that case, it gives me peace of mind."

Yohei's expression reflected his mind sincerely at rest.

It was a cloudy day. The wind wasn't blowing very hard. The building was a temporary hut, so the wind blew between the gaps in the floor and the wall panels. Two fireplaces were cut in the floor. When the laborers were in, both were lit, but only one was lit now. No matter how much charcoal was used, the room never warmed up.

Yohei nearly shouted, "Move closer to the heat."

Eiji didn't move away from the front of the closet. The office was stingy about supplying firewood. Therefore, the laborers took out their sen coins to buy more.

Everyone not only took out coins but also cared for Eiji. Yohei guessed Eiji didn't get closer to the fire because he was thinking about his workmates. However, that wasn't true. Eiji worked hard to validate the change he experienced. He knew sitting beside the fire he would feel much better in the chill of the winds coming through the gaps and shiver less from the cold, but now he didn't want to be in a cozy place.

With arms folded, he muttered, "I'll get an idea of how cold this wind is blowing in through the gaps.

"Since I just ate, I'm not too cold, but when my body starts shivering a little more I'll feel how cold it is."

Until I turned twenty-four this year, I wasn't aware of the cold of invading winds and a shivering body. This is the first time. This means nothing to my body. Not missing that feeling is important.

Huh, have I been influenced by Okayasu-san? He thought for a short time and smiled mockingly but immediately shook his head. No, that's not it. I'm not influenced by Okayasu-san. This was created in my heart. This is important.

Yohei returned after straightening up and suggested Eiji put on a sleeved quilt. He declined. Yohei didn't push him and soon went outside.

"No, I don't need it."

For a short time, Eiji shook off the thoughts that floated into his mind.

"Watabun is over. I'll forget about them."

He said to himself, "But there was only one thing. A gold broach turned my whole life on its head. I'm certain that way of thinking was a mistake. A man's life should not be turned upside down by one gold broach.

"It's strange but during the July storm, I thought this is not going to kill me and keenly felt I would be alive now.

"While lying under the collapsed stone wall and drinking the salty water with sandy clumps, it was so hard I was fine with dying. When I had that thought, I felt I'm alive. I'm alive."

Don't be so quick. Before moving from one thing to the next, please think long and hard about the first thing.

"There is one piece of absolute proof that my feelings have changed."

He shut his eyes and spoke slowly to engrave each word.

"The life of a man should not be turned upside down by one gold broach. That is most important."

He repeated these words in his heart. Now, Eiji could divide his past into two parts and think about them. The first part was until November of last year and being blessed with tranquility. The other part was his body and spirit wounded after the Watabun incident.

These two versions of him are completely different. When he reflected on his experience since becoming a camp laborer until today, he thought, In my life blessed with tranquility, I was somehow small and shallow but could think like an optimistic man.

"That's not it." Eiji's eyes stayed closed. He smiled and said to himself, "The man I am now still can't be said to have matured."

Yohei returned carrying an ink stone case.

11.2

"I'm sorry for not writing," said Sabu as he set the package to the side, "I was worried but couldn't come."

Eiji interrupted. "Forget about it. Who cares you didn't write? Haven't you been visiting me regularly? And you brought more stuff. I have to remind you again to stop."

"You don't have to say it like that. It's a sign of thanks to the men in the room and bleached cotton cut up by Sue-chan."

"I refused it and have nothing to say about this leg."

Sabu looked out of the corners of his small, round eyes. "It's not good, is it?"

"I said don't ask."

"But ..." Sabu started to speak but looked at Eiji's eyes and nodded. "Okay, I won't say anymore."

"Do you go to Sumiyoshi?"

"Once in a while, but recently Nobu-chan said she wanted to come here to see you."

"Were you encouraging her again?"

"No, I wasn't. What stirred her up? Nobu-chan was a little drunk, so maybe she said it in a drunken moment, but a couple of times, she said she wanted to visit soon."

"She got you worked up."

"Worked up over what?"

"You'll never get it. Her ulterior motive is to use me to get you to make up your mind."

Sabu bent his lips and forced a smile like he was about to cry and shook his head indecisively.

"I'm happy you said that. But it's different now. Nobu-chan told me all her feelings."

Eiji kept his mouth shut.

"Ah, I almost forgot. Nobu-chan had her double tooth pulled."

"Why are you changing the subject?"

"Did you forget? Her tooth here."

"I know. I know. When did she get it removed?"

"She said she would do it by the time she was twenty. I'm amazed she did it at exactly nineteen years and ten months."

Eiji stared at Sabu's face.

"Sabu," said Eiji sharply, "Sometimes, you really can't talk."

"Really you say ... what'd I do?"

"What did Nobu say? You said you told her your feelings, so what happened?"

Sabu weakly dropped his head, shrunk his shoulders, and sighed deeply. He looked wretched and hopeless.

Why am I like this? wondered Eiji. I think I'm nicer and considerate when we're apart, but when face to face, I immediately become impatient. My rude mouth kicks in. I'm a rotten guy. Despite these thoughts, Eiji couldn't soften his attitude.

With his head still hanging down, Sabu mumbled, "I've been thinking. Sometimes I think that my falling in love with her was a mistake. From the start, I was never the type to fall for a woman. A dummy like me falling in love with Nobu-chan makes me a joke."

"Tell me straight. Did Nobu laugh at you?"

Sabu shook his head no.

"She didn't laugh. She cried."

Eiji held his tongue again.

"Nobu-chan said she liked Ei-chan from the beginning."

"She was drunk. She can hold her liquor but becomes stubborn when drunk. While insisting it's not in her heart, she'll say the opposite of what she's thinking. Is whatever Nobu says when drunk her true feelings?"

Again Sabu slowly shook his head no.

"Nobu knew I intended to marry Sue. Didn't you know that, too?"

"Nobu-chan also said that," Sabu quietly said. "But she said that's all right and never getting married is okay, and that she'd love Ei-chan her whole life."

Eiji laughed. "That sounds childish. It's drunken babble. Even if she loved me for a lifetime, it's no picture book. Can a flesh and blood human being do that?"

"Not a guy like me ..." Sabu raised his head and weakly smiled. "But I'll never forget her for the rest of my life."

His tone abruptly changed. He pointed behind Eiji and asked, "Did you start practicing calligraphy?"

"Five or six days ago," answered Eiji. "Everybody was surprised by me doing calligraphy. They said they wanted to practice, too. Now, I'm teaching kana to five guys."

"That's great," said Sabu.

Eiji agreed and was relieved from the bottom of his heart.

"That's just like you. No matter where you go, Ei-chan, you always become a leader.

"Do you want to see it?" Eiji crawled backward, retrieved a scroll from the top of the small desk, and passed it to Sabu.

"Look at this one."

Sabu opened the scroll and looked up doubtfully at Eiji. "Isn't this my letter?"

"It's my sample writing. I learned the characters by using yours as models."

"Stop joking. That's ridiculous."

"If you think I'm lying, look on my desk. The scrap papers of my copies are piled there."

"But why are you copying my sloppy handwriting?" said Sabu, confused and floundering, "This is wrong, Ei-chan."

11.3

"No, they're not. These characters are not sloppy," Eiji insisted. "At first, I thought so, too. For a while, I thought the writing was horrible. But when I calmed down and carefully examined the characters, I realized the sloppy parts were genuine characters.

"The boss at Hōko-dō always said he didn't think practicing calligraphy resulted in writing elegant characters. It's a lie to say someone writes elegant characters. The characters reveal a person's true nature.

"No matter how elegantly someone writes, the character means nothing if the person's nature is not revealed. The problem isn't skill or clumsiness. One must not lie and write with honesty."

"You remember, Sabu," said Eiji while taking back the letter. He spread it over his lap and said, "It's hard to say this in front of you, but these characters are the real thing. If we only look at these characters, you are better than me."

Sabu blushed, took out a folded handkerchief from his breast pocket, and wiped his forehead and neck.

"I'm dripping sweat."

"I apologize for sounding so smug," said Eiji as he rolled up the letter. "Anyone has an ability he's not aware of. Since I came here about a year ago, I've observed various people and events.

"The camp is different from the outside world. Vagrants and people freshly pushed out of jail are people, in a word, people pushed out of society. But I've witnessed a lot living with them, fools, dimwits, or men deemed uncontrollably violent all have good points.

'Many of them do fine work that can't be imitated by anyone else. Unless a born scoundrel or crazy, all people are granted skills.

"It's not true that a master carpenter is admirable and a clumsy carpenter has no skill. A street fishmonger may be a person more skilled with a carving knife than a chef at Yaomatsu. I had this thought after living here for a year.

"Sabu, you should not always be humble and take a good look at yourself."

Sabu slowly untied the package, took out a bundle of loin cloths cut from bleached cotton cloth, held three food boxes, and scanned the room. Meanwhile, Yohei had prepared tea and was bringing it over from the hearth.

"Thank you for always making the effort to visit," said Yohei. "I'm sorry the tea's so weak. Please, help yourself."

Sabu thanked him for Eiji and held out the three food boxes. As the tedious mutual thank-yous were about to begin, Eiji turned away.

What an irritating guy, Eiji complained to himself and clicked his tongue. He heard nothing I said. It's like chanting to a rock. I'm tired of talking.

Yohei took the food boxes over to the hearth. As Sabu folded the furoshiki cloth, he said, "Sue's working as a housemaid again."

"The house in Shitaya, Kanasugi is small but the father sells calligraphy brushes and doesn't have a problem making a living," said Sabu. "I thought I'd be apprenticed like at Watabun, but it's not like that. I'm preparing for when you leave this place. I'll get paid more but not much more."

"That again?" said Eiji, not trying to hide his scowl. "I have no idea when I'm getting out of here. Stop thinking about me. Sabu, I'm asking you to speak honestly."

Sabu nodded ambivalently. "Okay, I can talk like that. I can't help but do that."

Eiji acted like he didn't hear.

After Sabu went home, Yohei approached from the side and said, "Ei-san, can I call you that? ... Okayasu-san ordered me to keep my mouth shut."

"Call me whatever you like because the name is like a secret sign."

"This may hurt your feelings." In a stronger tone, Yohei said, "Can't you be a little nicer to that guy Sabu."

Eiji stared at Yohei's face. "Nice, how?"

"You know that fellow uses his free time to visit you often. I don't know how he is related, but can't you be a little gentler? You're smart and may find what I'm saying funny. No matter how wise a man may be, he can't see his own back."

Yohei went away.

11.4

Yohei's last words stuck in Eiji's head.

It was a stupid thing to say and not very wise. With a mirror, anyone can see his back. He had a comeback in his heart but knew Yohei did not mean it that way. In the same sense, you can't see your back without an object like a mirror.

Anyway, he stopped his mind the instant thoughts like this arose. Was Yohei pointing out the way he became annoyed by whatever Sabu said and treated him poorly?

"Yes, I'm a fool," Eiji cursed himself. "Why do I obsess so much over what people say? Is there a point to obsess every time someone says something? Isn't being me all right?"

Eiji told himself, "I must break this habit."

The number of men wanting to learn calligraphy gradually increased. On rainy or snowy days off from work, after dinner, the men facing a desk grew close to ten.

The desks were old ones from the office in storage and made by the men in the Carpentry Room. The ink stones, brushes, and ink were bought through outside couriers.

Paper was expensive, so they also used watercolors. Paper filled with characters was blotted with ink, dried out, and then characters were written on top using water. Of course, the written characters disappeared when they dried, but it was useful for brush stroke practice. A half sheet of paper could be used for a fairly long time.

One day, the watchman Kojima Ryōjirō came and complained that this activity violated camp rules.

"Teaching and practicing calligraphy on your own in the laborers' rooms is not permitted," said Kojima expressly to Eiji without looking at him. "Calligraphy is practiced with a docile attitude. If you intend to do it seriously, you must submit a request.

"Learning calligraphy is not to be done carelessly. Studying under the clueless cannot be undone in the future. Without permission from the office, studying calligraphy is forbidden."

He was referring to Eiji when he said "the clueless."

For ten years, Eiji learned calligraphy at Hōko-dō and was one of the best among his fellow apprentices. He liked Kotaku's and Ryōko's styles and properly learned Chinese and Japanese writing styles.

Eiji thought, If Kojima had an eye, he'd understand. No, that's not it. He immediately shook his head. It may be against the rules. He thought about it again. If protocol demanded permission, he would get it.

To get this permission for the men in the room, Eiji gathered his books of writing samples and had Yohei carry them to the office. A junior officer said he would think about it. However, the next day, Okayasu Kihei came to the room after everyone left for work. Only Eiji and Yohei were there. Okayasu asked Yohei to leave them.

Okayasu began. "Unfortunately, Hakuo practices calligraphy.

"He pointed out only you get special treatment from the office. Someone is always envious. Hakuo somehow got wind of this and sent a complaint to the magistrate without my knowledge."

Hakuo is the religious ethics teacher, Tatematsu Hakuo. He

comes to lecture without pay. He heard a laborer was asked before him to teach calligraphy to the laborers. This seemed to greatly hurt his pride, and he made a strong appeal to the magistrate Narushima Jiemon.

Certain elements are vital when first learning calligraphy. It is not simply learning characters but one's mental attitude is critical. Needless to say, a clean desk by a well-lit window, the brush must be taken to purify the mind and body and be freed of worldly thoughts. He emphasized that in the messy laborers' room, without etiquette and people doing as they please, harm is inevitable.

Okayasu continued, "There's one more reason. The quiet found in the sitting room at the office more than this room would be nice. Don't you think so?"

Eiji answered, "I don't know whether everyone will go. In this room, they easily picked up the brush, but I don't think they'll go all the way to the office to continue learning."

He blew out a puff of air, raised his voice, and laughed. Okayasu looked doubtful and asked, "What's so funny?"

Eiji recalled a lecture Tatematsu Hakuo once gave. Hakuo expertly explored how much the samurai Kimura Shigenaru persevered with his full power and asked how important perseverance was to people. That man was angry. Eiji teaching calligraphy wounded the self-esteem of the experienced ethics teacher who stormed into the magistrate's office. Eiji noticed he exhaled at this realization. Of course, he said nothing to Okayasu.

"When everyone returns, we'll talk." Eiji stopped smiling. "My leg being like this means we're rarely all together. From here on, please leave it to me."

"Don't let this discourage you," said Okayasu Kihei and left.

11.5

All the laborers burst out laughing at the news of calligraphy being taught in the office.

"No, not the fat boy of ethics," said Sanpei. "Maybe, it's his plot to teach lectures. Just the sight of the chubby body of that old man makes me sick. I am truly sorry for anyone who has to be his student."

"Why do you feel sorry?"

"He won't explain things simply," said Sanpei, his fist rubbing his nose. "What do you think? Will you go to the office to learn calligraphy?"

"You're nuts, but why am I the only one who'll show up?"

"Uh, you get burdock tempura, but why does it only come out for me?" said Sanpei and wrinkled the bridge of his nose. "Oh damn, I don't know that tempura-*kinpura* pun."

"Serves you right," said Yoshizo and clapped his hands. "At long last, you solved a pun puzzle with picture clues."

Yohei broke in to calm them. "Wait a minute. I understand everyone's feelings. Nobody will go to the office. Learning one character on your own would be exactly like going to temple school again. That's what it would be like. Okayasu-san is kind enough to worry about us. Because the recommendation comes from the magistrate, I think it's best to go for a month or half a month."

"Yohei-san is right," said the sub-foreman Sōta, "Like someone said, it's too much to ask us to learn calligraphy through tough lectures."

Another said, "I'll go all the way to India to eat green tea over rice."

One day off every month was scheduled for the ethics lecture and calligraphy. Five or six men from The Dirt Basket Room went. Oddly, they did not line their desks up with Eiji. These men always avoided the men who did calligraphy with him.

"I didn't realize it either, but this situation is difficult," said Yohei, "That bunch was jealous. When everyone gathered around Eiji to learn calligraphy, instead of approaching, they stayed back with their friends."

"There's nothing wrong with that," said Eiji. He didn't remember coaxing anyone. He only taught people who asked to be taught and originally intended to work alone. He wanted to learn by copying Sabu's characters. He was annoyed by his disabled body and hoped to distract himself for a few moments.

However, he had to consider sharing the room with more than twenty men. If ten men set up desks with him at the center, what would everyone think? Naturally, people would start talking.

"I had no idea," said Eiji and clicked his tongue.

Snow began falling on the twenty-sixth. Near the end of the day, Nobu visited despite the snow. Work was suspended, and everyone gathered in The Dirt Basket Room.

Usually, they would meet in the small sitting room of the office, but Eiji's leg was too weak to walk there. Yohei spoke with the others and had them go to a corner and surrounded Eiji with half screens.

"Ah, you're better now," said Nobu while wiping the snow off her umbrella at the door. "I'm sorry for taking so long to visit you. It's been chaos since November."

She greeted Yohei and opened the package she brought. She said there weren't many but passed around a rice cake from the package to each man. She carried the other package to Eiji.

"You are looking well."

"You just said that. Relax."

"You're fatter."

"Sorry, but I'm not talking about my leg."

"You have gotten chubby," said Nobu, narrowing her eyes and scanning Eiji's body starting at his head. "Your cheeks look different. Yuck. It doesn't stop there. Your handsome looks have plummeted."

"So you came to chatter on and on. Is there anything else?"

Yohei brought tea. Nobu complimented him and sipped tea to evade Eiji's question.

"Well, at Sumiyoshi, the proprietor died."

"Why?" asked Eiji in shock while staring at Nobu.

"You shouldn't be asking why. Some illness rotted his bones and muscles from his legs to his lower back," said Nobu, frowning. If he had known sooner, he could have been treated, but he talked gibberish to the bumbling doctor in town. He was deceived by an ointment and was treated too late. When he was examined by an elite doctor of something like surgery, there was nothing he could do."

"He had a lousy doctor, too."

As Nobu explained he died eleven days ago, she set down the teacup. "It was just him and his wife. They had no children. His hometown was far away.

"His wife was zapped of strength and began to look ill. I did everything from preparations and cooking to running the shop."

Eiji paused a short time before he asked, "But ... why?"

"The proprietress made me her adopted daughter."

Eiji asked, "Is that a burden on you?"

"It's not easy. The shop Sumiyoshi is small but sells sake and snacks. The late proprietor was a fine cook. If only women work there, I'm sure fewer customers will come."

"That's frustrating." Eiji was irritated. "I hear you but can't do anything about it. You probably have something more important to say."

"Don't be so impatient." Nobu glared. "Sometimes I come to talk, but please calm down a little and listen. Clear your mind and calm down. You need to relax."

"All right. Okay. Say what you like. I'm no match for your strong will."

Nobu stared hard. "What do you mean? You're talking about Sabu-chan."

"You're veering off the topic."

"Well, I'll be clear," Nobu said defiantly. "I told Sabu-chan. No matter what, I would never fall in love with him. I told him, 'Please don't think you'll ever be more than a customer.'"

"Strong-willed women live in this world, too. But there aren't two who when face to face with a man, one she's not in love with, she can speak bluntly."

"I thank that trait for the life I've lived until today," said Nobu and then raised her head. "Without it, like my older sister who died, I would have fallen into the hands of the pimp Roku and been a victim of my parents. If a woman thinks about living respectably, she must first draw clear lines. If anything is even a little uncertain, who knows when that'll become fatal. My older sister is excellent proof of that."

"That's admirable," said Eiji, "Your true motive is not disagreeable. You've become a fine woman."

"Yes, that's my intention," said Nobu and looked away. "I'm not a demon. It's hard when I think about Sabu-chan's hardships. It's as though a knife struck my chest."

"That way is best for Sabu. He won't give up," said Eiji, nodding and then looking at Nobu. "So you have something important to talk about."

Nobu placed her hands on her lap, interlacing and freeing her fingers, and didn't immediately speak.

Eiji asked, "A marriage proposal?"

Nobu gently nodded.

"You're not interested?"

"Yes," she answered in a near whisper. "There's a shop called Tokiwaro over in Ryōgoku."

"I've only heard of it."

A man called Toku-san is the cook. He's thirty-five and seems to be an old acquaintance of the late proprietor of Sumiyoshi. From time to time, he drops in for a drink. The rumor is he'll marry Nobu and run Sumiyoshi.

"He's thirty-five. That's too old," said Nobu. "I sicken at the thought of marrying an old guy like that. What's worse is he's a drinker, full of anger, and gets violent when angry. I'll die. I can't be the wife of that kind of man."

"If you've made your decision, there's no problem."

"It's not that easy. I came to borrow your wisdom, Ei-san."

"How sad," said Eiji and forced a smile. "So he's an old guy of thirty-five?"

"Listen to me. This is serious," said Nobu.

11.6

"I am being serious," said Eiji, "You don't wish a thirty-five-year-old man to be your groom."

"I already said that."

"What's the problem? Like you drew the line with Sabu, shouldn't you be blunt and say what you feel?"

"If I could have ended it like that I wouldn't have come for your advice."

She told him, unfortunately, the man fell for her. If he got drunk and no marriage was arranged, she believed he'd kill her and die himself. It's not empty talk with him, he's capable of doing it. For some time, the proprietress of Sumiyoshi believed in the ability of this man and knew he alone could keep the shop going. She repeatedly begged Nobu in tears.

"Maybe you should run away," said Eiji.

"You'd say something like that."

"Running away is a good idea. The proprietress at Sumiyoshi isn't that old. How old is she compared to him?"

Nobu shook her head. "She's thirty-eight."

"So isn't she in her prime as a woman? The old saying says a man should put on sandals of gold and search for a bride three years older."

"That's dumb," Nobu blurted out and put her hand on her mouth. "It says one year older."

Neither the proprietress nor the man showed any inclination to do this. In the rare chance, it happened, she thought her leaving Sumiyoshi before that would make her the same as a dumb beast.

"I escaped the pimp Roku and didn't become a victim of my parents thanks to everyone at Sumiyoshi.

"You think any other shop is the same. That may be it. Although another shop may be no different, that may not be so. Yes, that's it."

"Nobu, you're a genius at splitting hairs," said Eiji and adjusted the position of his bad leg. "But I want to say Sumiyoshi is not a bad or good shop. Your temperament is key. What you've accomplished until today was not because of the shop. I want to say your won't-lose personality was the reason."

Nobu locked her eyes on Eiji's face and slowly shook her head.

"You don't understand the world," said Nobu with a deep sigh. "No, it's not that." She stopped to think a little. "Not every cloud is good enough to raise a dragon to heaven. Some clouds rise and other clouds can't. Even if a cloud carrying the dragon has the strength to rise to heaven, if there is no cloud to become a stepping stone ... What? Why are you laughing?"

"Okay, enough," said Eiji, waving one hand as he stopped laughing. "I don't understand the world but was surprised at suddenly becoming a dragon."

Nobu shrugged as if to say "I give up" and glared at Eiji as her shoulders drooped.

"Ei-san, I see why you don't understand Sabu-chan's pain," said Nobu then spoke like she was chanting. "If my temperament is to never lose, I'd be safe at any shop. The world is not like that, Ei-san.

"The dragon story might have been too much of an exaggeration, but no matter how smart you are or how skilled you are, I don't think you could become a fine craftsman anywhere. Even now if there were no Hōko-dō, and no Sabu-chan and Sue-chan, you may become a fine craftsman. Of course, Hōko-dō, Sabu-chan, and Sue-chan exist and can't be erased."

Eiji said, "The one rising to heaven this time may be Sabu, and I'll be left behind. Leaving the shop is also a bad idea. If you dislike that man, I don't have a plan."

"That's not true," said Nobu and exhaled a long sigh. "While talking earlier, even I knew this would be hard to discuss with you. I'm sorry I came to bother you with this trifling story."

"It's not a mistake. If my leg wasn't like this, I'd meet that man."

"Thank you. I'm happy hearing you say that," said Nobu, smiling. "How will this turn out? I'll stand firm as much as I can."

"Nothing will defeat you," said Eiji and smiled to encourage her. "But if you have any problems, you can come here."

"Let me ask you one time. What happened to your leg?"

Eiji shrugged and said, "The road is snowy. Be careful not to fall down."

While Nobu stared into Eiji's eyes, she snapped a nod like a girl.

CHAPTER 12

12.1

He could see Sabu's face through a gap in the stones. His face was soggy with tears and so grotesquely distorted it was hard to look at.

"Please don't die, Ei-chan," said Sabu, the fingers of both hands in a powerfully tight grip pressed against his mouth. Sabu made his tearful plea.

"I'm asking you, Ei-chan, to fight. Please don't die. Hold on a little longer. You can't die, Ei-chan. If you die, it's over for me. If you die, I'll die, too."

"Stop crying. I'm fine," Eiji was about to say, but the pain of the weight of the stones crushing his chest stopped his voice.

"Bushū, you can beat this," said Seishichi.

He could see the faces of Yohei, Mankichi, and Kinta. Faces he knew were joined by unknown faces peeking through the gaps in the stones. Voices called to him.

"Don't give up."

"Don't die."

"We'll have you out soon."

Eiji writhed in pain but thought, I'm okay, but my chest is crushed. Please get these stones off me. I can barely move.

"Ei-san." Someone shook his shoulders. "Ei-san, you're having a nightmare. Wake up, Ei-san."

Eiji opened his eyes as he floated up from a deep swamp, feeling a frustrating anguish.

The room brightened with sunlight. He slept on his back in his bed. Yohei's worried face was soon before his eyes.

"You awake? You okay?"

"Yeah." Eiji coughed. "Thanks for waking me up. What a nightmare."

"Here's a towel."

"Thanks," said Eiji. He took the towel and wiped the sweat from his forehead, armpits, and chest.

"Eeyah, it's drenched."

"Do you have another?" asked Yohei.

Eiji shook his head no, folded the towel, and placed it beside his pillow.

"What time is it?"

"About two in the afternoon."

He had slept through nearly half the day.

Yohei said, "You slept so long because you're worn out."

It was January 19, he began to practice walking five or six days earlier. Beginning the morning of that day, he practiced several times during the day with rest. He propped the crutch made by Seishichi under his arm and walked step by step.

He started practicing at the end of the year. However, during his first steps, he couldn't find the center of his body and tottered.

Yohei cautioned him not to rush and never left his side like he was coddling a child. He offered his hand at the slightest sign of danger. Despite feeling annoyed, Eiji let Yohei do as he wished.

"Today's the sixth day," said Yohei. "It would be bad to go for it all at once. It'd be better if you rest for a few days."

Eiji answered, "That sounds good," and shut his eyes.

The impression of his dream was seared into his head with an intense sense of reality. As he cried and asked Eiji not to die, Sabu's pleading face and voice were particularly vivid and brilliant. After he opened his eyes, Eiji found it hard to believe it was a dream.

He thought, That wasn't a dream. It was real. At that moment, Sabu was worrying about me. He's done that for a long time. Sabu's heart and eyes follow me and never leave my side.

Since he was buried under the stones, all his friends in the labor camp worried about him and gathered around to comfort him.

Seishichi made crutches for him. Yohei took better care of him than a parent. They were selfless, but he hadn't thanked any of them.

I'm awful, thought Eiji.

From the time he was rescued from under the stones, he felt deep surprise each time he remembered. When the dream he saw changed into reality, he had no doubt the dream was carved into his heart.

"No, wait, Sabu," he whispered, "I still can't leave. What my friends here have given me is huge. I could never leave this place without giving back to my friends here."

He also thought about the proprietor of Hōko-dō and Wasuke in Asakusa. The incident in December the year before last was unforgivable, but he valued and was grateful for the new world and many people he met as a result.

"The actions of Watabun's proprietor, the boss in that town, and those two private police officers are unforgivable," whispered Eiji, "I'll never forgive those jerks. As long as I live, I can't forget. Just wait."

However, he recognized this in himself.

His feelings of revenge against them lessened over time. He might have suddenly realized a man's life is not determined by a gold broach. Despite recalling every detail of the humiliation and violence visited on him, he could no longer evoke the anger that made him furious.

I'll make them pay.

At one time, this vow sustained Eiji. He was sure if he didn't hold tight to this revenge, he'd die.

He seemed to have replaced revenge with something else.

What would happen if he ended his service with Hōko-dō, opened a shop, married Sue, and lived a peaceful life? When he imagined this, he only thought of his current self as someone marked by unpleasant emptiness.

When he compared today to the four hundred days since he came here, that life had no appeal and felt uninteresting, uneventful, and boring. Something inside of Eiji had been replaced or was being replaced.

Two days later, eight vagrants were sent to the camp on the twenty-first, a day off. Three were moved into The Dirt Basket Room. The Red Demon, Matsuda Gonzo, accompanied the three men; introduced them as Gīchi, Shokichi, and Ryū; told everyone to get along; and left.

Because it was a day off, everyone was in the room. The mature and experienced sub-foreman Denshichi was about to introduce everyone when the young man named Gīchi turned away.

"Who cares?" he said, rolled up his trousers, sat cross-legged, and glared at everyone while his hand tapped his hairy leg.

"Hmph. All I see are a bunch of hicks. I'm in charge and nothing's gonna stop me. From now on, remember I'm Water Snake Gīchi."

Gīchi was twenty-six or -seven; Ryū, eighteen or nineteen; and Shokichi, around thirty. Gīchi's height was average and his build, agile and muscular. His face could be called handsome. This gave an air of menace to his sharp eyes and crisply-spoken caustic words.

What connections did he have in the outside world? Ryū held a deep respect for Gīchi, addressed him like a respected elder, and went overboard to run his errands.

The man Shokichi seemed quirky. His thin face marked by sharp cheekbones topped his small, skinny body. A smirk always floated near his lips. His low, gentle voice said few words but they sounded ominous like a wolf targeting prey. No one approached him. Nevertheless, Shokichi was thorough in completing his work and never challenged the rules. Amid the flickering awful feeling of never knowing when he would show his true nature, he followed the sub-foreman's commands.

Gīchi, however, was the opposite. He didn't go out to work and slept and woke up when he pleased. When awake, he played *hana-fuda* cards and gambled at night.

My spitting image, thought Eiji. Perhaps, I was exactly like him when I first arrived at the camp.

I met the outrageous fate of being falsely accused of a crime. I convinced myself I had special rights and felt I could selfishly fight back somehow.

Gīchi is like that, believes he has the right to the nickname of Water Snake and flaunts that belief to everyone.

I was that way, too. All of them probably thought I was ridiculous.

Whenever these thoughts flickered in Eiji's mind, he broke out in a cold sweat.

Since Gīchi came, he seemed to keep an eye on Eiji, who also did not go out to work, had his food prepared for him, stayed in bed, and practiced calligraphy. Gīchi didn't seem happy because that made Eiji look like a big shot.

When Yohei returned to work, Eiji refused his help other than in preparing meals and washing, but even that seemed to madden Gīchi. Five or six days after he arrived, he demanded his food be brought to him.

"You say it's because he's a gimp, but it should be the same for any other camp laborer."

Gīchi stressed the word *gimp*.

"What's done for anyone should be done for me, too. Who's gonna say I can't?"

"I'll do it," answered Yohei.

"Good. That's how we become good friends," said Gīchi, "And do my washing, too, from now on."

12.2

"Don't get mad. Relax," Yohei whispered to Eiji. "Preparing meals and washing clothes are nothing. That guy's making unreasonable demands on purpose because he was falsely accused."

"Okay." Eiji nodded. "I'm not angry."

Eiji apologized in his heart, Because of me, you're burdened with caring for someone again. I'm sorry.

Since Hakuo started teaching calligraphy at the office, five or six men from this room have gone. They said men from other rooms are learning calligraphy. Now, over twenty attend.

Men still went to the ethics lecture and calligraphy. After January, everyone from The Dirt Basket Room quit. Before he knew it, many more desks surrounded Eiji.

"Hey, anyone for a game?" called out Gīchi as he cut the hanafuda cards again. "The account of wins and losses will be settled at the end of the month."

Then he threw the cards on a rush mat folded in four. He was fairly skilled and cut the cards in an entertaining way. He snapped the cards as he threw them.

Kinta could not resist the lure and was drawn in by the small-stakes gambling. Each time he heard that sound, his entire body seemed possessed.

"Hey, any takers?" Gīchi goaded, "How about you good temple school brats? The word is you camp laborers are crazy, learning calligraphy."

Mankichi, who lined up his desk with Eiji, was about to say something and stand. Eiji quickly reached out and grabbed his arm.

"Stop," he whispered and made him sit.

It happened in an instant but did not escape Gīchi's notice.

"Hey kid," he said and jerked his chin at Mankichi, "Yeah, you over there, next to the gimp, what did you say?"

"My leg's gone numb," answered Eiji, "I'm simply changing my sitting position."

While shouting, "I wasn't asking you. Butt out," Gīchi stood and moved toward Mankichi. "Can't you hear, punk?"

Mankichi paled and looked up to see Yohei running toward them.

"Now, now, this isn't something to get mad about, is it?" said Yohei to soothe Gīchi, "The officials are jammed into the watchman's guardhouse over there. They'll hear you if you start shouting."

"Shut up!" Gīchi screamed and shoved Yohei at full force. "Shut up, you old fart."

Matsuda Gonzo entered and saw Yohei tumble to the dirt floor from the powerful push. Eiji feared being blinded by anger but reached for his crutch propped against the closet behind him. Faster than he could think about what to do, his hand moved. When he saw the sliding door open and The Red Demon enter, Eiji closed his eyes, leaned against the futon, and released a long, deep sigh.

"Ah, it's a beautiful evening. Are things going well?" asked Matsuda and looked at Yohei on the dirt floor, "Yohei, what are you doing down there?"

"What? Oh, I had a spell of night blindness," said Yohei as he brushed dirt off his kimono, "Sometimes I lose my footing at night."

"Well, that's not good for your reputation," said Matsuda, scowling. "Maybe you never heard don't eat the crude food at the labor camp? Do you need to see Dr. Santetsu?"

"There's no need for that."

Yohei gave an uncertain smile as he stepped into the wood-floor room. Matsuda Gonzo directed his attention to the men practicing calligraphy and Gīchi who stood in the way.

"Hey, you, Gīchi," shouted Matsuda. "Are you beginning calligraphy?"

"Hell no," said Gīchi and returned to his place.

"Hey!" yelled Matsuda, "What did you say?"

"Hmm, what did I say?" asked Gīchi and sat in front of the mat. While gathering the hanafuda cards, he answered, "I was talking to myself and don't remember. It's all right. Don't worry about it."

As his nickname says, before everyone's eyes, Matsuda's face bloated and turned dark red. His eyes glittered and seemed to bulge.

"You little shit," Matsuda yelled "Where the hell do you think you are?"

Gīchi fired back, "Ain't this that Ishikawajima work camp?"

Matsuda Gonzo's hands closed into trembling fists.

Eiji's heart filled with sorrow. He's me. I enraged The Red

Demon like this, too. With no mercy, I coldly cast off Matsuda's attempts at kindness. Matsuda wanted to slug me then and, like now, his entire body shook with anger. He pushed down his rage and only said, "Get out!"

He probably hated me and was aggravated by me. I was a rotten bastard.

"If you know that," said Matsuda through clenched teeth, "You shouldn't forget the rules of this work camp. Bring me those cards."

"What are you gonna do?" Gīchi grinned showing his teeth. "If you open a gambling den, I'll deal the cards."

"Gambling is forbidden here. Not even one hanafuda card is allowed. Hand over those cards."

"These are mine. I bought them with my money."

Matsuda bellowed, "Give them to me!"

12.3

Gīchi giggled. When Matsuda yelled to hand over the cards, his rage seemed to hit its peak.

Eiji heard everything and his body froze with shame like he was being yelled at.

Gīchi was mocking Matsuda. By doing that, he would show everyone who he was. I was like that. In reality, my behavior was meaningless. I only made a fool of myself. As Eiji thought this, the smirking Gīchi gathered the cards, stood, and put them in Matsuda's hand.

"I was joking, Matsuda-san," said Gīchi. "Can't you even tell a joke here?"

"You seem to think I'm a fool," said Matsuda through heavy breaths. "The previous warden said this is not a jail. That's surely true, but you'll regret taking this camp lightly."

"I get it," said Gīchi and turned to Ryū behind him. "Remember what this warden said, Ryū. This place is scarier than Tenma-chō. We better behave."

"Is he mad?" asked an amused Ryū. "Are you scared, Gīchi-san?"

Matsuda took long strides out and slammed the sliding door.

Matsuda Gonzo took his hanafuda cards. Everyone saw that. The next day, however, Gīchi was again playing with cards on the mat. In the camp, belongings are thoroughly inspected. Of course, knives, playing cards, and dice are confiscated. Nevertheless, Gīchi easily got his hands on hanafuda cards. Where were they hidden? How were they smuggled into the camp? No one could figure it out.

"You're here because of fighting," Eiji said to Mankichi one day, "Even now, you seem dangerous to challenge and will never provoke anyone."

"But Eiji, I don't think I'll be able to keep holding myself back."

Eiji turned his head. "It's bad. That guy Ryū has a dagger."

"What?" Mankichi stared. "A dagger!"

"He has one and is hiding it from everyone. He took it out of his breast pocket when I was alone. He wiped the blade. Of course, he threatened me. He's at the most dangerous age. If he killed someone, he'd get a reputation. If he had the chance, he'd use it. Do you understand?" Eiji stressed. "No matter what happens, don't challenge him."

"What's gonna happen now?" Mankichi anxiously asked. "I'm worried something's gonna happen."

"Stay away from him," said Eiji.

For about half a month, men were defeated by Gīchi's temptation and began to come out to play hanafuda card games.

First, Kinta sat in front of the mat. Then Sanpei, Take, Tomisaburō, and a few others from the room joined him.

Eiji felt disgust bordering on terror of natural gamblers. Hōko-dō's proprietor hated gambling. When the apprentices bought tea and cakes for the evening, he even forbade using a ladder lottery to decide who would be sent on errands.

He repeatedly said, "The amusements of sake and women will stop at some time, but gambling is a lifetime activity that never stops."

People who gamble were not placed at Hōko-dō. Men so obsessed with gambling they failed in their duties were not hired at the shop although several were there.

The men gathered around Gīchi. Each time those men were so engrossed they hardly breathed. They stared at each of the scattered hanafuda cards and flipped them over. Eiji worried as if he mistook these men for apprentices.

This situation shouldn't continue forever. It should be reported to the office soon, thought Eiji.

He might have thought so, but he knew his thinking was shallow. When Gīchi acted that way, he seemed to have struck a bargain. Whenever the watchman Kojima Ryōjirō approached, the cards quickly disappeared, and the gathered men scattered. After seeing that many times, he knew they were being alerted about the patrol.

"This is bad, Eiji," Mankichi whispered to Eiji, "On the job today, Kinta told me that guy Gīchi is bribing the officials."

"Don't say that."

"So this is okay?" Mankichi whispered in a forceful tone, "They've already noticed. The men in The Dirt Basket Room are divided into three groups: the ones learning calligraphy from you, the gang around Gīchi, and the weaklings who can't do anything like the sub-foreman and Yohei-san. Right?"

Eiji didn't answer.

Mankichi continued. "The gamblers hate us and want our crowd to disappear. Worse than not gambling, we're learning calligraphy.

"Even Kinta looks coldly at us. Haven't you noticed?"

Eiji barely nodded but said nothing.

"Even going to a work site isn't like it was before. Everybody has started to get lazy. It's true." Mankichi took a deep breath. "About half are serious about their work. The rest are pretending. The worst ones do half-ass jobs. Worse than that is the gambling during breaks."

This room is like that, too, Eiji complained to himself. Like Yohei said one time, although only men lived in this room, it was always neat and swept clean. It's no longer so. Everyone only keeps his area clean. Some do sweep without fail, but they're becoming fewer as the days pass. Once in a while, the sub-foreman Denshichi and Yohei will sweep the whole room.

"I can't take this anymore," Mankichi whispered, "I'm gonna complain to the magistrate."

Eiji slowly shook his head. "It's better if you don't. There's no point."

"I'll tell the magistrate myself."

"A government office has a system," said Eiji, then took a breath like he was gathering his thoughts. "People are vulnerable to desire. Who knows how many of the officials Gīchi has bribed? Even if you complained, the desires and reputations of those officials would drive them to carry out some sort of cover-up. Even for the magistrate, the failures of his subordinates become his failures. It's not as easy as you think."

"What should we do? You want us to keep our mouths shut?"

"Calm down," Eiji whispered, "The big storm last year didn't push on for three days. There's no precedent of an inferno that kept burning for a year. Stop." Eiji suddenly turned away his embarrassed face. "You're making me sound like an old man. You're awful."

One evening in the middle of February, Eiji went out alone to the southern coast in search of Seishichi.

For the past five or six days, Eiji had been coming to this place every night and practiced throwing logs. He carried out five unsplit firewood logs about three feet long from the woodshed to throw toward the posts standing near the sea.

He went out after saying he was going to the toilet. Yohei didn't seem to notice. He continued to practice every night except when it was raining. He may never need this, but the time may come when it will be needed.

Eventually, Gīchi, Ryū, and Shokichi would resist physically. On the night he saw a quarrel between Matsuda Gonzo and Gīchi, Eiji deeply felt I'm responsible for that.

What should he do in an emergency? Ryū carries a dagger, and Gīchi is a strong fighter. I don't know how Shokichi could help. I have a bad leg, use a crutch, can't nimbly move my body, and don't have another throwing hand.

Of course, the three logs were inside his folded futon. He

selected them because they're easy to handle and hide. He brought five logs to the coast. He practiced throwing at a post from a distance of around twelve feet.

"Is that you, Ei-san?"

When Seishichi called out, Eiji's heart nearly stopped from shock.

"Aah," answered Eiji in a hoarse voice, "What do you want?"

"It's nice out tonight," said Seishichi as he approached. "What are you doing out here?"

"Just wandering around," said Eiji haltingly, "I'm up to mischief so my body doesn't get antsy."

Then he tossed a log he held toward the post. The sky was partly cloudy. One cloud blurred the moonlight.

A post about twelve feet away didn't look clear even to Eiji's dark-adapted eyes. Nevertheless, the log he tossed hit the post with a loud bang.

"You're good," said Seishichi, "Were you aiming for that post?"

12.4

"Yes," Eiji answered as he thrust his crutch forward and walked. He picked up the logs that dropped around the post. He found four right away but couldn't find the fifth that seemed to have been thrown a distance away.

"You still have the crutch."

"Thanks to you. You don't know what a great help it is. I appreciate this more than anything," said Eiji and stroked the crutch. "Do you want something?"

"Yeah, well ..." Seishichi hesitated. "I got something to ask you. Bushū, no, Ei-san, you'll get tired standing while we talk."

"What? I'm used to it."

"The truth is ..." said Seishichi, then coughed and fingered his earlobe. "The truth is Toyo visited today."

Eiji stared through the hazy white night air at Seishichi's face.

"You know about Toyo, right?"

"Yeah, the handcuffs were hard on you," said Eiji, "What happened?"

"She said she broke up with Shozō and wanted to be with me."

Seishichi spoke like he was wracking his brains, "If I wanted to leave this labor camp, I could. Nothing stands in my way, but my problems would begin after I left. I talked about it earlier. I can only be a construction laborer or a dock worker. Wherever I go, people would make fun of me and work me too hard.

"Even if I went back to the outside world, I can't believe my life will be better. If people are gonna make a fool of me, I'll make mistakes that no one can fix.

"I'll be straight with you. I know I want to be with Toyo. I love her. If I get together with her, I'd worry about what I'd do," said Seishichi and sighed deeply, "When I think about things after going back to society, I don't know what's the best thing to do."

After a few moments of silence, Eiji said, "That's a tough one."

How serious was she? More than anything else, that was essential. While in the labor camp, Toyo had relationships with several men. She made no promises to Seishichi but left here with Shozō and his topknot.

Why did she break up with Shozō? And why did she deliberately come to the labor camp to say she wanted to marry Seishichi?

Eiji felt he didn't understand that much.

"It's hard to say." As he adjusted the crutch under his arm, Eiji said, "It was like that before in the outside world. You've decided it'll be the same this time, too.

"I think you've defended your workmates in The Oil Pressing Room for a long time and haven't advanced. Maybe I'm butting in too much, but I think Toyo's feelings are important."

"I thought about that, too. I wanted to ask Toyo about her feelings," said Seishichi then stressed, "She cries and cries, says she sorry, and makes promises. She said she'd obey me and be a good wife from now on. Her face was smeared by tears."

Did she truly want to marry Seishichi that much? Was she marrying him to escape problems she created? Eiji could not convince himself.

He almost sounded like he was apologizing.

"This seems cold and is hard for me to talk about. What should we do? I think maybe Okayasu-san in the office could share his wisdom."

"I don't need wisdom," said Seishichi shaking his head, "I want to hear what you think."

"And that's the problem."

"Saying a few words like 'Do it' or 'Don't do it' is good," said Seishichi and nearly pleaded, "You're young but have had hard times. Your nature is not to fix things only by reasoning. You seem to guess. Hey Ei-san, a few words are good enough. Please, tell me to 'Do it' or 'Don't do it.'"

Eiji looked up at the sky. It looked like spring but was still the middle of February. The night air was chilly. In the white brightness of the clouds filled with the moon, he felt a secret warmth, like sympathy or comfort for the sadness, grief, and lack of joy among the people on Earth.

"I'm sorry but it's no good," answered Eiji eventually and looked away, "I have nothing more to say."

Seishichi seemed to mull over Eiji's words as he stared at his feet and softly sighed.

"I'm sorry for bringing this up," said Seishichi nearly under his breath, "I'll think more about it. Well, bye."

"See ya," said Eiji and gave a slight bow. As he listened to Seishichi walk away, Eiji's spirit screamed, "Keep away from her. Please stop, Sei-san. It won't go well with that woman. It'll be a disaster for you."

Then Eiji said to himself, "But that's how it goes with people."

If I told him 'Do it' or 'Don't do it,' I couldn't have changed Seishichi's feelings. No matter what I said Seishichi would do whatever he wanted. Living in this world is not a calculation of profit and loss. Life is short. You should live the life you want. Be sensible, Sei-san.

12.5

Eiji rolled open Sabu's letter on a small desk and practiced writing as he studied it. Across the room, five or six men surrounding Gīchi were drinking sake and gambling. Kinta was over there as were Tomisaburō, Nihei, and Isuke from The Engraving Room.

None of them wore dotted work uniforms but striped or plain blue cotton clothes. They sat cross-legged or knelt on one knee. While drinking cold sake, they strained to see the hanafuda cards on the mat.

In addition to Gīchi and Ryū, everyone said they were sick and took off from work. Ryū stood outside the door as the lookout watching for the patrol.

How long is this gonna go on? wondered Eiji while moving the writing brush. Has this place become a proper gambling den? What are the officials up to?

Eiji once said to Mankichi, "Humans are weak in the face of desire."

The officials are human, too, and become weak if there's money to grab. The people who work in the camp for the pittance of a stipend may find it difficult to overcome temptation.

However, everything may not be everything. Where there's smoke there's fire, but it's never the case that no one sees it. What is Okayasu-san doing? For a long time, this has been stuck in his head. For instance, even if the labor camp magistrate was bribed, only the hands of Okayasu Kihei would not be sullied. Maybe, only he can be trusted, and there's a reason.

"Eiji," said Ryū from the door, "You gotta visitor."

"Who?"

"It's not a honey," said Ryū, then paused, "I know, the usual pumpkin."

Ryū chuckled. Eiji opened his mouth and breathed out a gentle puff of air. The pumpkin was Sabu. Since they've been here, Sabu had visited a couple of times. Eiji heard Gīchi and Ryū call him that and laugh.

As Eiji told himself not to get mad, he put down the writing brush, picked up the crutch behind him, and headed to the dirt-floor room.

Sabu held a package wrapped in a furoshiki cloth and looked in from the doorway. Ryū put his body in the way to keep Sabu from coming in.

"I'll be right out," Eiji called, "We'll talk outside."

"Take your time." He heard someone around Gīchi say. Several men snickered. As Eiji hobbled toward the door, Ryū slowly moved to the side to hassle him.

"Did something happen?" Sabu asked as they walked out together.

Eiji shook his head no.

"I wanted to come outside. My leg's better."

"But those fellows ..."

Eiji cut off Sabu. "Ignore them. Let's go to the sea."

Sabu watched with heartbroken eyes the figure of Eiji walking with a crutch. He immediately turned away. Eiji shouted in his heart, "That's it," those eyes. Those eyes had the exact expression he always saw in the space between the stones in his dreams.

The expression in his eyes screamed, "Please, don't die, Ei-chan. That's all I'm asking."

"Do you go to Sumiyoshi?"

"Once in a while," Sabu answered, "Since I asked about Nobu-chan's feelings, it's a strange story, but I feel so relieved. It's weird."

"It's not good to fool yourself."

"I'm not fooling myself. Really," said Sabu. "I like what I like. I won't forget Nobu my whole life, but I'm relieved."

"That's good." Eiji's tone changed. "Nobu came on the evening of the twenty-sixth. She said something was bothering her. Did you know anything about that?"

"A problem? What could it be?" said Sabu and thought a little. "I didn't know anything. I almost forgot to tell you. I rented the house at 2-chome, Sakamoto."

"What house at 2-chome, Sakamoto?"

"Our house. It's an old semi-detached house on a backstreet. A cooper used to live there. The house has a wood-floor room he used as his workshop."

"Look," said Eiji, jerking his chin toward the ocean, "They're already gathering shellfish."

The two came to the southern shore. Not too far away, they could see scattered figures picking up shellfish on the expansive tidal flat at low tide for about two and a half miles.

"We were there once," said Sabu, looking out of the corner of his eyes, dazzled by the light. "During the big tide in March."

"It's near the great teacher in Kawasaki," said Eiji and turned to Sabu. You got the house for you, please don't count on me."

12.6

Looking uncomfortable, Sabu stared at his feet as he adjusted his grip on the package.

"I should have told you earlier," Eiji said, "I can't leave this place until I return the favor for all the care, more than I could ever explain, I received at this camp from everyone."

Sabu paused for a moment and then said, "I was talking to Okayasu-san before."

Eiji stared at Sabu's face.

Sabu said slowly, "Okayasu-san said it would be good for Ei-chan to leave this place. He didn't say anything before, but Aoki-san, the officer of the Kita-chō magistrate, is also worried about you and visits here a lot.

"Once a month, Okayasu-san writes about how you're doing and sends it to Aoki-san who comes to see for himself. Aoki-san also says it'd be better for you to leave the camp."

"Wait a minute," Eiji cut in. He cocked his head, frowning and biting his lower lip.

"You're talking nonsense. If what you're saying is true, it sounds like you're telling me I'm the bastard son of a daimyo."

"Everyone is worrying about you," said Sabu.

"Why?" Eiji shot back. "Why are those people worrying about me? I'm not the only person sent by the town magistrate to the labor camp. How many others have been miserable for much longer and need to be helped? Even so, I'm the only one they worry about. Why? Sabu, what are you hiding?"

Sabu slowly shook his head.

"I'm hiding nothing."

Sabu thought for a while then said, "I don't think anybody knows why."

"Do you believe that?"

"Yeah, that's what I think." Sabu hesitated. "Don't people have their reasons for what they do? Why do people do things for each other? Aren't there times you do things that even you don't know why?"

"You're talking about something else."

"Don't you remember, Ei-chan?" Sabu sighed deeply. "It was winter when we were fifteen. I ran out of the shop to go back home to Kasai. When I crossed Ryōgoku Bridge soaked by the rain, you came running after me."

"Don't dredge up that old story."

"I was stubborn and said I was going back to the country. But you kept following me in the rain and wouldn't give up until I went back to the shop.

"Ei-chan, why did you do that much for me? Why?"

"Because you're my friend."

"You had other friends. Gorō at the shop cared a lot about Ei-chan, so did Sei-chan at the dessert shop in town, and Masa-san at the tatami shop. All of them were your good friends. I'm the biggest dimwit of them all, a worthless apprentice. Why were you so kind to and worried about a dope like me? Why, Ei-chan?"

"Just because," shouted Eiji. "You're my friend. I heard about your situation at your home in Kasai and couldn't let you go."

Sabu asked again like he was searching, "Don't you think Aoki-san and Okayasu-san worrying about you is the same thing, Ei-chan?"

Eiji leaned on his crutch and walked closer to the coast. He was frowning as he watched the people gathering shellfish.

He vividly recalled being rescued from the collapsed stone wall, the aftermath, and the care and consideration that filled everyone's spirit.

So many people flew into action to save me and gathered around to console and encourage me.

"Why do people have these bonds?" he whispered to himself, "A bond connects me to this camp and is not easily broken."

As he walked up, Sabu said, "Okayasu-san was worried. He said some nasty guys live in your room. Those guys may cause some trouble. Ei-chan may keep quiet and not see it, but before that happens, he wants Ei-chan out of here."

Eiji turned to look at Sabu.

"Okayasu-san said that?"

"Yeah. He just told me," said Sabu, nodding

Of course, Okayasu-san knew, but what was he waiting for? Was he waiting for them to get violent? In that case, isn't that right now? Those punks are openly gambling, which is forbidden, buying off a couple of officials, and messing up The Dirt Basket Room. They're already out of control, so what is he waiting for?

Sabu interrupted Eiji's thoughts.

"This isn't about work, but since January I've been getting commissions little by little. I repapered the papered and shoji sliding doors in rental row houses. You know the brush maker Heizō-san, Sue-chan's father? He introduced me to a scroll mounter in Okachimachi in Shitaya, and he's given me jobs. The proprietor's name is Shigesaburo."

"That's great," said Eiji, not paying attention, "You'll do well."

"I talked to the proprietor and told him Ei-chan worked at Hōko-dō. He said if you worked there, you did good work, and he'd hire you."

"I still can't leave. Sabu, this is getting tiresome."

"Maybe so," said Sabu and stroked his forehead with his free hand. "Aoki-san and Okayasu-san both say you can go if a job is lined up and your obligations here are met. Don't you want to leave?"

Eiji didn't answer.

Strangely, Sabu didn't back down. "Maybe you forgot, Ei-chan. I depend on you. I feel like if you're by my side, I can do my job. But by myself, I'd be helpless, irresponsible, and only botch things up."

"Stop, Sabu. We're not children anymore. We're both twenty-five."

"I know how old I am."

"Then stop acting like a spoiled child. If you're twenty-five, you could have one or two children. If I'm not by your side, you're helpless. Do you think you can pass through the world acting like a baby?"

"I just ..." Sabu stuttered pitifully, "I just want to see you out of this place. If I sounded spoiled, then forget it. Ei-chan, I can be second. All I want is for you to get out of this place."

"That's no good. No matter what anybody says. I can't leave."

Sabu set the package down. His round eyes stared at Eiji.

"So I can't even ask for that?"

"I'm sick of going over the same thing again and again," answered Eiji.

Sabu grabbed Eiji's lapel with both hands and while panting, said, "Ei-chan."

In a trembling voice, Sabu screamed, "I'm slow, a dummy with no ability. You think what I say and do are stupid. But Ei-chan, can't you listen to what I'm asking for once in your life? No matter how great someone is, can't he listen to what people say once in his lifetime?"

Eiji looked at Sabu's hands clutching his kimono. The plump, short fingers made rough and gnarled by preparing paste trembled slightly holding his lapels.

Eiji eventually said, "I get it. I'll think about it."

Sabu let go. "Sorry, I was rough."

"You don't need to apologize. I'm the one who should apologize," said Eiji, curling his lips. "I won't speak because I get smug when I say what I'm thinking, but you've cared for me for a long time. Listen to me. I never apologized or thanked you. I don't know if I could repay you even if I had my whole life. The care I received here was the same. My life was saved when I was on the verge of death."

Eiji's words had unnatural pauses. He turned his face away from Sabu and took a few moments to settle his breathing.

"Think about it." Eiji lowered his voice. "I can't say it will be a long time, but I think you can wait for me for the last half of a month or thirty days, or maybe until this time next month. Please be patient and wait until then."

Sabu was silent but moved his body like he was discouraged, and then picked up the package.

CHAPTER 13

13.1

Like viewing a weathered cliff naturally crumbling or the cracks at the edge of a cliff suddenly widening, the eye saw a stingingly hostile atmosphere in The Dirt Basket Room. The men who gathered around Gīchi numbered close to thirty men in March. Its size rose or fell over time but never dropped below fifteen. Games were always tainted with bloodlust. Two or three of the men fired up over a game only wore loincloths.

One time, the elderly sub-foreman Denshichi muttered, "This place is now a real gambling den."

Although Eiji may not have fully understood, he guessed the meaning of his words. Now, two other officials besides Kojima Ryōjirō kept an eye on this room.

One evening while Eiji was tossing logs at the coastline, Mankichi followed and called out from behind. He had watched Eiji for a short time. When he got close, he asked, "What's all this for?"

"Who's that?" said Eiji in a sharp but quiet voice.

"It's me." Mankichi as he walked around to face Eiji. "I needed to talk to you. I was gonna wait until after you left the toilet but saw you here. I wondered what you were doing, so I came over."

"In that case, you can go. I'm training my body."

"Really?" said Mankichi then quickly changed the subject. "Bump from the Oil Pressing Room is gone. Do you know if that's true?"

"I don't. He left?"

"I heard Isuke from The Engraving Room talking in the gambling den," said Mankichi. "He said the woman everyone's been gossiping about visited him a few weeks ago. Bump was in a muddle and went to Isuke for advice. He suggested Bump go with her."

Aaah, Eiji sighed in his heart. I'm a cold-blooded guy. When he asked me what to do, I should have said, "Don't go." Seishichi was confused during those weeks and should not have trusted that woman. At that time, no matter what I said would be useless. Even if I told him not to go, I don't think he could pull back his lingering affection for her. But thinking about it now, I came to that conclusion too fast. I wasn't thinking in my heart about what was best for Seishichi.

I don't have the right to use this crutch. While stroking it, Eiji gazed at the sky's sparkling surface of stars.

Mankichi said, "Isuke has been making fun of this story with his crowd.

"He's saying it won't last fifty days. Before Bump's money runs out, she'll have a few more men."

"You mentioned a gambling den. Where is this gambling den?"

"I'm talking about Bump, now."

"Tell me. Where is this gambling den?"

Mankichi gave a spirited answer.

"Eiji, ask yourself. You're too patient and look the other way. You avoid looking at them, but you constantly light up the eyes of one of them. Even the slightest movement by you quickly focuses the eyes of several men on you. Those guys are reading your feelings."

"What are you saying? That's stupid," said Eiji, looking away. "What's going on in your head?"

"I'll leave it to you, but, Eiji, whatever move you make, it'll be hard to do it alone."

Eiji coldly answered with a question. "When did Seishichi leave?"

"Okay, I'll stop acting like I don't know, but I'll tell you one thing," said Mankichi, then changing to a whisper said, "You don't have to do this alone. We'll join you. I won't say their names, but four men and I are prepared with tools."

"No, you can't," shouted Eiji without realizing it and immediately lowered his voice. "You can't. Those guys have a dagger. I should have told you earlier. I don't think they'll hurt anyone. You four or five men aren't who they want to fight."

"In that case, what are you gonna do?"

"This camp has officials."

"They've been bribed," said Mankichi, "I don't know how many are on the take, but they even bring in sake for those guys."

Eiji shook his head and released a long sigh like he was vomiting a poisonous gas build-up in his chest. He eventually said, "I've thought about it. I've been thinking about it for a long time.

"There's no reason the office doesn't know about what's going on in The Dirt Basket Room. All of the officials haven't been bought off. They must have some reason for staying away. I'm asking you not to do something reckless. Four or five of us can't fix this."

13.2

Mankichi refused to give up and said so.

"I can't take it anymore. We have no reason to stay silent on the sorry state of our Dirt Basket Room. What are they thinking in the office? The Dirt Basket Room is ours. Why shouldn't we fight with all our power to get it back?

"Four men promised to join any action. If you stand up, I think other determined men will step forward. Except for the guys around Gīchi, won't all the others stand up, too?"

"Think about it," Eiji said again. "If we do anything, there must be a plan so it doesn't fail. It's no good without a plan. This situation won't be fixed through brute force. All right?"

Mankichi pointed to a post. "Are you gonna go get that stick?"

"I have others hidden in the room," said Eiji and straightened the position of the post. "Don't be so suspicious. You should go home now."

"Don't stay too long," said Mankichi, then stepped back and walked off. "Bump left the other day."

Eiji went over to the post, searched the ground, picked up the firewood logs, and hid them behind stones on the side.

He muttered, "What should I do? I have no idea."

If I act, so will everyone else. I can't let everyone get mixed up in this. Should I call Gīchi outside? Or challenge him when no one's around?

"But I won't win. With my leg like this, I won't win except by surprise," said Eiji and sighed deeply. "Of course, I have no choice but to talk to Okayasu-san. If he has a reason for doing nothing and even the office won't act, I'll have to re-think this. That comes first."

I didn't want to talk with Okayasu Kihei because doing nothing until now was necessary. But if the situation puts my friends in the room in danger, I must act when I think it's best.

Even if it would only be a conversation, Eiji was determined to talk to Okayasu.

Before walking away, he turned to look at the ocean. The wind barely blew. He occasionally heard the sounds of waves washing the stone wall like gentle whispers. The sea under the starry sky was dark. The lamps of boats night fishing flickered. He smelled the scent of the tide warmed in the air.

Eiji returned to the room and opened the sliding door. When he entered the dirt-floor room while finding his center of gravity on the crutch, Ryū approached and swept away the crutch with his foot. Suddenly, Eiji filled with strength like his bad leg no longer hurt. He tumbled to the side. As he watched Ryū from that position, he slowly pulled back the crutch that never left his hand.

"You missed because you're a cripple," said Ryū with a smirk. "When I don't like something, I turn on it. This ain't your private room."

The room was silent. Tense silence spread like the wind dying the instant before a storm. Nobody seemed to breathe. Right away, someone was walking through the wood-floor room toward them. Three firewood logs were tossed in front of Eiji's eyes. The wood tumbled in with thudding noises. One hit Eiji's shoulder.

"What are you gonna do with this?"

The question came from the wood-floor room. It was Gīchi's voice.

"What are you gonna do with these things?"

Eiji gently rose while protecting his leg and leaned on his crutch.

"I'm so sorry," said Eiji to Ryū, "I've been thoughtless. Forgive me."

Ryū ground his teeth but said nothing. Eiji turned around, bent down, picked up one log, gripped it in his right hand, and showed it to Gīchi.

"I do this. I grip it and exercise my fingers. The doctor recommended this."

"Did you hear that, Ryū?" Gīchi said, never taking his eyes off Eiji. He talked from the corner of his mouth. "A doctor recommended it. This punk thinks we're idiots."

"If you think I'm lying, ask the doctor yourself. I grip and release to strengthen my fingers and build power in my body."

"Get rid of that stick," said Gīchi sneering. "I know that look on your face. Why don't you put down that stick?"

"It's all right, Gīchi," said Ryū, "I'll make him listen."

"Wait." Eiji bent his wobbly body. "That stick is important to me."

"Throw it away," ordered Ryū.

"I'm throwing it away," said Eiji as he watched Ryū's approach from the corner of his eye and put the log in the dirt-floor room. When Eiji raised the crouched upper half of his body and adjusted the crutch, it flew at full force into the thigh of Gīchi standing at the edge of the wood-floor room.

Gīchi looked like he was crippled and had been caught off guard. He stared at Eiji's leg as it quickly flew out. A blow that gathered the strength of Eiji's entire body slammed into Gīchi's shin.

Simultaneous to the sound of the crutch sweeping to the side, the crutch struck Gīchi's shin. He let out a horrific scream and collapsed.

Eiji instantly turned to Ryū. His eyes widened like they were going to fly out. He stood bolt upright with his mouth open.

Eiji saw the fallen Gīchi had taken the dagger out of his pocket. He repositioned his crutch and struck with full force, beating Gīchi from above.

"Please stop," Gīchi shouted again, "I was wrong. Please stop."

Eiji continued to hit him like he had gone mad. The crutch slammed into his head and chest. The dagger flew out of Gīchi's hands. His head and face were covered in blood. For the first time, Ryū moved.

13.3

Eiji's movements were wild, but his mind was serene. His impulsive attack on Gīchi was fury dominated by instinctive anger rather than judgment. However, at the moment of his first blow, he engaged the power of judgment. He didn't waste this chance. If he hadn't acted flat out, the root of the disaster would have remained.

I don't think this is a man. He's evil like a snake. He's a snake. Eiji gave himself orders in his head.

Ryū still stood erect as Gīchi was showered with blows. When blood spouted from Gīchi's head and face, as he paled and trembled, Ryū pulled out a dagger from his pocket and edged toward Eiji.

Not one of the men in the gang of gamblers, the men facing desks and practicing calligraphy, and the older men moved. As if shackled by unseen chains, they were overwhelmed by his ferocity. Mankichi was awakened from a dream by the glint of the blade of the dagger in Ryū's hand when he started to move. He jumped up and shouted, "Eiji, behind you!"

Eiji looked at Ryū. While repositioning his crutch that whacked Gīchi, he turned his back to Mankichi approaching him and shouted, "Stay out of this." Eiji's voice echoed to fill the room. "Go to the office. All of you, stay out of this. This is my job."

Ryū pointed the dagger's tip up. Ryū, breathing so heavily Eiji could hear him, slowly shrunk the distance between them. Eiji glimpsed Gīchi stretched out and not moving. Ryū lunged at each body as he closed in. Eiji swung his crutch from side to side. Ryū stabbed the dagger into Eiji's left shoulder. The crutch smashed into Ryū's head. His body slipped to the side and tumbled to the riser to the wood-floor room.

Not giving him a break, Eiji ran over, swung his crutch, and pummeled him. The crutch hit his head, chest, and his face from the side.

"Please. Help me," said Ryū crumpled on the ground. He shouted while both hands hugged his head, "I'm sorry. I'm sorry. Somebody help me. I'm gonna die."

Eiji would not let up. When he looked at Ryū again, he was covered in blood and no longer moving. Eiji stopped hitting him and looked at Gīchi. He lay prone and groaning, his face soaked in his streaming blood.

"Hey," Eiji called to the gathered gamblers, "Soon they'll get here from the office. Men from the other rooms should leave. Hurry so you don't get caught up in this mess."

More than half of the group of fifteen or sixteen scared-looking men stood and jumped down to the dirt-floor room barefoot, and fled out the door.

Eiji said, "Yohei-san. Did Mankichi go to the office?"

"He went."

Kojima Ryōjirō entered through the door. He looked like he ran there. As he breathed from his shoulders, he scanned the room. His eyes moved from the figures of Gīchi and Ryū laid out on the floor to Eiji.

"I did it," said Eiji, "and notified the office."

Kojima's face stiffened. He opened his mouth to speak but said nothing and drew his sword. Eiji swiftly grabbed and positioned his crutch.

"You better not, Kojima-san," Eiji quietly said. "There are witnesses if you stab me. My bone may break if you cut me."

As Kojima looked more confused, three men carrying objects resembling six-foot-long wooden poles strode in.

"You can't. You can't leave," Eiji shouted as he glared at Kojima. "This is all my doing. Please sit."

Kojima Ryōjirō's eyes steeped with terror quickly scanned the faces of the laborers in the room.

Eiji said, "Please put away the sword. I won't mention you. Officials will be coming from the office. It'll be no good if everyone's in a panic. Put away the sword and go."

Gripping the drawn sword, Kojima stepped back and went out the door.

As Yohei and the two sub-foremen examined Gīchi's and Ryū's injuries, he called for someone to get Dr. Santetsu. Two or three men answered the doctor wasn't there at night.

When Kojima Ryōjirō left, the entire room came back to life. Everyone mulled around without purpose and talked noisily.

When Mankichi returned running and appeared in the doorway, Eiji was exceptionally tired and lethargic like something fell off his body. He sat feebly on the riser to the wood-floor room.

Mankichi said, "Okayasu-san's coming," and pointed back out the door. While wheezing, he said, "He'll be here soon. Eiji, it'll be okay."

Eiji nodded, closed his eyes, and dropped his head.

13.4

"Officials are not as steadfast as the public thinks," said Okayasu, "They are divided into superiors and subordinates, have complex rules and rights in each role, and compete with each other in these roles. If a man wants to rise in the world, he should swindle to gain benefits. Disgusting acts—under-the-table exchanges, taking a cut of the laborers' wages, dishonest transactions with vendors—are not unheard of even here."

A while ago, Eiji was chained with Seishichi as punishment. They were confined in that room for thirty days. The river flowed behind the longhouse. From time to time, he lazily listened to the sounds of waves washing the stone wall and the oars of the boats through an open small bright window.

Okayasu described how the labor camp is one world, and the laborers are also one world. A conflict between good and bad exists in a world molded by people gathered together. There is no uniting only in goodness and engaging only in evil.

In particular, the rule of "this is not a jail" of this camp has many inconsistent and vague points. Confusion abounds over the punishments for people who violate the law. People who discern this and skillfully break the law are unstoppable. They could not exhibit this on the surface but soon understood this themselves.

Okayasu Kihei said, "I knew from the beginning what Gīchi and his gang were up to. This was not the first time. Several times in the past, junior officials were often bribed.

"When we noticed the events in The Dirt Basket Room, we knew Kojima Ryōjirō and two other junior officials had already been seduced by Gīchi's gang.

"I'm a government police official and not directly engaged with the laborers. Based on reports from the watchmen, managers, caretakers of the rooms, and junior managers, they made various judgments. I had no right to ignore them and get involved with the laborers' room.

"It's another story if something became public. If I didn't wait and carelessly interfered, I'd run the risk of strife throughout the camp.

"When their attempts to draw in officials were evident, the true objective was to use the threat of implicating the entire office as a tool."

Finally, Okayasu asked, "Do you understand?"

Eiji seemed dissatisfied but nodded.

Okayasu continued. "To make matters worse, Kojima is a distant relative of the camp magistrate. He's a good man named Narushima but was not comfortable with the camp system and did not have an eye for people. Unfortunately, he bought into Kojima's story without question. That's another reason why I stopped going to the laborers' rooms."

When Gīchi and his gang gradually put their plan into action, even asking to bring in sake, I thought I couldn't keep quiet any longer. However, the arrangements by Kojima Ryōjirō and the junior officials were meticulous, and they appeared to leave no opening.

"I'm telling you these reasons, but they may frustrate you and make you think I'm a coward, and if ..." said Okayasu and took a short breath, and then continued, "if you think so, you should think about yourself. Namely, how should we have treated you when you were sent here? You didn't go to work, were hostile, and didn't follow the rules. How did we handle that situation?"

Eiji seemed to reflect on his words. Eventually, he gently dropped his head.

"Sometimes the problems between people are not promptly resolved. At other times, they wait for the right opportunity," said Okayasu with all his heart. "This time, you ran out of patience, so The Dirt Basket Room could be swept clean more or less. That might not have been the time or might have been the perfect time. We may not know which until a little more time passes. However, this is certainly the end."

Yes, this is the end, thought Eiji.

Without involving anyone else, from the beginning to the end, he did it all alone.

Pulled to the office by Okayasu's hand, thoroughly investigated by the police with magistrate witnesses. Of course, Kojima Ryōjirō and the junior officials kept silent about the gambling.

The police probably knew although the magistrate was oblivious. In response to Eiji's claim of a fight, they were furious about the cruelty of his method and decided to send him to jail.

A briefing was held before the investigation. In a strong defense of Eiji, the police officers said he had two opponents, and both carried prohibited blades. They explained Eiji was only one person and had a disabled leg.

The magistrate didn't accept this, or Narushima Jiemon didn't receive the policemen's defense. The next day, a messenger was sent to the town magistrate who must approve all rewards and punishments carried out in the camp. After that, Eiji was confined to this room.

"It's good you didn't mention Kojima or the names of the junior officials or the gambling," said Okayasu, "If these things were exposed, I don't know what Narushima-san, an opponent of the original labor camp system, would recommend to the town magistrate. The continued existence of this camp may have been threatened.

"I thought I wanted to save and promote this camp. Despite the various defects in the current system, it protects a person with the personality or circumstances that lead him to become a criminal from becoming a criminal, as well as, gives him a trade and wages to return to society.

"This is important. With the increase in population and people's living situations in a sprawling area like Edo, that task becomes more difficult. More important duties will be the priorities in the future.

"All alone, you pushed hard. I want you to know that I've thought hard about this."

"I understand," said Eiji and coughed. "To be honest, I was suspicious about the office being quiet and resented them. I also wondered what Okayasu-san was waiting for. But that's not all. From the beginning, I was thrilled to be on the firing line."

Okayasu Kihei stared at Eiji's face and said, "What do you mean?"

"It's not a reason, but I felt I had to beat up Gīchi and Ryū by myself," stammered Eiji, then clearly said, "The truth is I started talking about this with a roommate called Mankichi. He said he couldn't stand what The Dirt Basket Room had turned into and lost patience."

"Was Mankichi a construction worker?"

"Yes, he boasted about his fighting skills but couldn't fight. Somehow, I got him to stop thinking about that because his rival carried a dagger.

"I didn't know whether Mankichi would do anything, but before he did, I knew I had to act."

Okayasu said, "You didn't talk about that again," then lowered his voice, "Your grudge against those two grew. If you saw a chance earlier, the crime would not have been lessened."

"I don't care about the seriousness of the crime," said Eiji with a smile. "But I never thought about doing that on that night. The moment I went through the door Ryū kicked out my crutch. When I pitifully tumbled into the dirt-floor room, Bastard! I thought but didn't feel like doing anything.

"Then Gīchi came out on the riser. When he laughed at me, my eyes darkened and I acted.

"I didn't think about making the crime less serious. That's the truth."

"It was written the handling was perfect," said Okayasu and nodded. "I didn't know your leg had healed."

"That sounds stupid," said Eiji and smiled again, "But thanks to that, I could make the first move. Those two saw my leg, and their eyes opened."

Okayasu Kihei smiled and said nothing.

"Well," said Eiji, then impatiently asked, "What will be the verdict on me?"

"They'll agree that you can't stay here."

"I'm pretty much prepared for that."

"You crushed one of Gīchi's eyes and broke two ribs," said Okayasu, "Ryū's left arm was broken. His left ear was shredded. However, neither one's life is in danger. They were carrying forbidden weapons. When they heal, they'll be sent to Tenma-chō."

"With me?"

Okayasu shook his head no. "You're being handed back to the Kita-chō magistrate to be re-investigated. I can't tell you anymore."

"I understand," said Eiji, lowering his head. "Looking at it now, I beat them a little too much. I'm sorry about that—"

"No, that's not it," said Okayasu, interrupting Eiji, "Don't apologize to those two, it should be to others."

Eiji shut his mouth. Okayasu Kihei said nothing, watched Eiji, and nodded to say, "You understand, don't you?" then he quietly stood up.

"This may be an impossible request," said Eiji, "but before I leave this place, will I be able to see everyone from my room?"

"That's not up to me, so don't count on it."

"I beg you. I have a debt to everyone I can't explain. Please let me say a few words goodbye. Please."

Eiji thrust both hands forward and repeatedly lowered his head.

"I'll ask the magistrate," said Okayasu, "But he may not give you permission. It'll be better not to get your hopes up. Now, you're a criminal."

13.5

Eiji looked up surprised at Okayasu. He couldn't believe he heard him say, "You're a criminal."

Okayasu's expression appeared to change completely. Only his eyes exuded warmth. His expression was cold and severe. The laborers secretly called this the *official face*. Until that moment, Eiji never saw that look on his face.

Okayasu said, "Your belongings will be brought here from the room.

"I think you'll remain here a few more days. You should use that time to rest."

Again, Eiji thrust both hands forward and lowered his head.

After dinner on the evening of the second day, Yohei appeared without warning. A short time later, two junior officials brought trays with a little food and drink. Their whispers implied this was a small token of their appreciation.

"It's a nice night." Yohei bashfully broke the silence in a quiet voice and looked at Eiji as if searching. "Everyone's worried about you, but you'll be okay."

Eiji said, "The town magistrate intends to investigate again." Holding the sake bottle, he said, "That's not important, so tell everyone not to worry. Let me pour you one."

"I don't drink."

"It's okay. Have one with me. This is my farewell."

"Okay, I'll act like I do," said Yohei and held up the cup. Vinegared miso soup, vegetables in sesame seed oil, small fish, and shellfish boiled in soy sauce were arranged on the trays.

Eiji said, "If I only met you, Yohei-san, it was worth it. Everyone took good care of me, but I owe a debt to you I could never repay in a lifetime."

Waving his hand, Yohei said, "More than anything I did, I can't tell you how grateful we are for what you did this time."

Yohei sipped the last of his sake, put down the cup, and poured for Eiji. He tasted some of the food, still holding his plate, he looked at Yohei .

"Saying this changes nothing, but if I left this place without problems, I wanted to leave with you, Yohei-san, and intended to live with you."

Still holding the sake bottle, Yohei's eyes looked back at Eiji like he'd been threatened.

"In the situation I'm in now that chance has drifted away. If I left jail early and you were still here, Yohei-san, I would welcome you."

"Thank you so much. Thank you," said Yohei and lowered his head. "You saying that means a lot to me."

"I'm alone in this world. After I lost my parents and sister in a fire when I was small, I could live without siblings, but I wanted at least one parent." Eiji paused, grinding his teeth. "Even if that never happened, I could live with you."

"You make me so happy, Ei-san. But aren't you wrong to say you're all alone in the world?" said Yohei, "Your friends in The Dirt Basket Room, of course, Sabu-chan, Sue-chan, and Nobu-san are your family."

Eiji turned to look at Yohei.

"You know that," said Yohei, nodding. "Those three and I know. When was it? When I asked why you aren't nicer to Sabu?"

"I remember," said Eiji and sipped his sake. He sat up straight and said, "This is a farewell, so let's stop talking about this."

"No person ever lives alone," said Yohei, listening to Eiji's words. "This world has smart and not-so-smart people. Even smart people may not fair well in the world. Even by calculating the profits and losses, if there are people with losses, there are people who profit. If you think you owe a debt to us, it's not only us, it'd be wrong to forget Sabu-chan, Nobu-san, and Sue-chan. You are definitely not alone in this world. From now on, you will never be alone in this world."

Eiji stared at the cup in his hand, frowned, took the sake bottle from Yohei, and said, "Just one more." He poured as Yohei reluctantly held the cup and then tasted it like he was drinking poison.

Yohei said, "It's not like me to lecture like this." He spoke while massaging his mouth. "Ei-san, you'll become a first-rate craftsman. You have that personality.

"But you're not alone. Many people are born into this world with the ability to reach the top. However, those people with natural-born talent can't do it alone. To bring out the talent in a person with ability, dozens of untalented people lend their invisible powers. Think about this, Ei-san."

Yohei said with a laugh, "I hate that old age has made me such a windbag."

Sabu, Eiji called in his heart. Oh, Sabu, I want to see you one more time.

CHAPTER 14

14.1

"I want to see you walk again," said Nobu. "Don't be so full of yourself. It's better if I hadn't seen that, but it's okay."

Eiji stopped trying to step up into the small sitting room and walked a few steps into the narrow dirt-floor room.

"My, my, you're absolutely not Taro."

"Who's Taro?"

"Tottering Taro. Don't you know about him?"

Sabu, already in the small sitting room, laughed. Sue covered her mouth and joined him.

"Tottering Taro?" said Eiji, "Watch this."

He demonstrated a few steps. They watched. Although he dragged his right leg a little, few would notice unless it was pointed out.

Nobu watched spellbound and said, "You look kind of stylish. Walking with one leg dragging by that amount looks stylish."

"Is that a compliment?"

"I'm not lying. It's true. Right Sue-chan? Don't you think so?"

"Yes," Sue quickly said in support. Tilting her head a little as if puzzled, she said, "I don't care if he looks stylish, I just want his leg to heal completely."

"Oh no, you already sound like his wife," said Nobu staring at her. "We don't want our men to look stylish to outsiders."

"That's awful. They're our men."

Nobu mimicked, "That's awful. They're our men," and stared at Sue again. "Sue, your cheeks are on fire."

On that day, April 7, Eiji was released after a short stay in Kitachō magistrate's jail. Sabu and Sue came to collect him. Eiji had been jailed for seven days. He was sent back from Ishikawajima for *re-investigation*, but nothing like an investigation occurred. After five days in jail, he heard Officer Aoki Matazaemon had called for him to be released and sent home.

Gensuke, the landlord of 2-chome, Sakamoto in Shitaya, and Sabu came together and asked to take him there. With a rented home to live in and job leads, they asked the magistrate's office whether he could return home there.

Matazaemon told Eiji this, taking care not allowing him to wonder how Sabu knew he worked for the town magistrate. Sabu met the town officer Aoki Kōnoshin when he was searching for Eiji and asked for his help.

Matazaemon was related to Kōnoshin and seemed to be in constant contact with him about Eiji's situation.

Naturally, Sabu was notified immediately about the move from Ishikawajima to the town magistrate.

Nevertheless, despite progress in the re-investigation into the incident at the labor camp and the efforts made on his behalf by Okayasu Kihei, the issue couldn't be swept under the rug because his roommates witnessed the damage done.

Eiji wasn't satisfied and questioned Matazaemon, who lightly shook his head and said, "I forget."

More than one hundred camp laborers petitioned in writing for Eiji's release. After an investigation, it became obvious the facts did not warrant his punishment.

Matazaemon only said, "Now, the important thing to do is

completely forget past incidents. You must return home determined to become a serious craftsman."

Eiji asked for a slight delay to let him go back to jail and spend a day thinking. He thought about Hōko-dō, Watabun, and the contract policemen. Previously, these thoughts alone angered him enough to make his blood boil. But now, his spirit was not moved, and his anger disappeared at the base of his memory, like the small remnant of a fire.

He seemed to recall the same thing many times as if reminding himself. He knew his resolve for the revenge he vowed to take was mostly gone.

He asked himself, Am I sure? I can't say these feelings are absolute because I'm human, but now I'm certain. Maybe, I'll remain calm. Eiji declared this thought to Aoki Matazaemon.

He asked for his clothes stored at the magistrate's office and his wages held by the labor camp. The five ryo, two bun in wages was far more than he expected. He asked for half and the rest to be sent to the labor camp.

The longhouse would be rebuilt soon, and he wanted that money to help cover the costs. After a hard look into Eiji's eyes, Matazaemon gently nodded.

Sabu and Sue came to pick up Eiji. The landlord of the Sakamoto-chō house was not with them. The returned clothes and obi sashes were dirty. Sue brought brand new clothes. He changed into the new clothes from top to bottom. As Sue helped him change, she suggested they go to Sumiyoshi.

"Today is only make-believe," said Nobu as she set down the trays for the three guests, "Now, we'll have a leisurely celebration."

It seemed the proprietress had gone to the bathhouse, and the maid Matsu helped Nobu. The three other maids commuted to work and wouldn't appear until four o'clock. Before preparing the trays, Nobu tucked back her sleeves with a tasuki sash, put on an apron, and sat before the three.

Eiji said, "First, I want to say I haven't expressed my gratitude so please don't congratulate me. I don't want to be congratulated so don't."

Then he lowered his head. Sabu's and Sue's faces were a little strained. To relax them, Nobu picked up the sake bottle and poured a drink for Eiji.

"Ei-san has changed," said Nobu and looked at Sue. "A little while ago, I asked him to let me see him walk again. The old Ei-san would have shouted, 'Stop bothering me.' Instead, he didn't make a disgusted face and walked for me. I couldn't get the old Ei-san to walk on his hands."

"No matter how much I try," said Eiji, "I can't walk on my hands. More importantly, Nobu-san, what about that marriage proposal?"

"We'll talk about that next."

"How will you solve it? Will you tell me about that?"

"All right," said Nobu and set down the sake bottle. She took a razor wrapped in a piece of red silk from her sleeve.

"With this. I'm taking this out to show you."

Sue's teeth chattered and she gasped.

Eiji said, "So that man Toku still hasn't given up."

"It's an endurance contest, and I'm not going to lose," said Nobu and unwrapped the red silk cloth. She took the razor in her right hand.

"I can't do anything if he's not drunk. If he gets drunk and starts a fight, I'll put it to his throat like this. If you try something, you'll die."

"That's dangerous. Stop it," said Eiji. Pointing at the razor, he asked, "Do you think you'll always have your way with that?"

Nobu wrapped the razor in the cloth. As she slipped it into her left sleeve, she said, "Even if I tried to escape my home, I wouldn't be able to escape that man's reach, like my older sister was unable to escape the pimp Roku. Only escaping is the same as defeat, and I won't lose."

"You're strong," said Sue, like she was grieving.

"Thank you," said Nobu and smiled. "You're lucky to have Ei-san. Sue-chan, don't become a woman like me."

"Wait Nobuko," said Eiji, holding the sake bottle, "Let me pour you a drink, just one."

Nobu quickly adjusted her sitting position and properly held up the cup. Both of her hands carefully supported the cup Eiji filled. She closed her eyes, said something to herself, and quietly drank. The other three couldn't hear what she said, but each understood what she meant. For a short time, all three seemed to quiet their breaths.

Sue had not taken time off from her job. She left Sumiyoshi and returned to a mansion in Surugadaishita. Eiji and Sabu headed to Shitaya.

"I'm worried," said Sabu as they started out. "Will Nobu-chan be okay?"

"No, she won't, but there's nothing we can do."

"I think that guy Toku can't do anything."

"How about after I get my situation in order, I'll worry about Nobu?" said Eiji, giving Sabu an encouraging look. "People have a ton of hardships. Nobuko will do what Nobuko will do. From now on, I'll be thinking more about myself."

"Yeah, you're right," said Sabu, nodding but didn't look like he agreed. They took the chance on the way home to visit Shigesaburo, the proprietor of the scroll mounting shop in Okachi-machi. He was a thin man in his fifties and a bit irritable. His head curved a little to the left. As he talked fast, he had the habit of constantly shaking his head.

"So Eiji, they say you have a good eye, a very good eye. I like that," said Shigesaburo restlessly. "I have work, but I'm short-handed. I'm counting on you."

"Thank you for this opportunity," said Eiji and lowered his head.

14.2

The Shitaya house was a two-family house in an alley at 2-chome, Sakamoto. A middle-aged couple named Zōroku lived next door.

The house had two six-mat rooms and an eight-mat wood-floor room. The toilet was attached to the kitchen. The well was right out back, and a built-in wood-burning stove was installed. Buckets, water jugs, pots, and pans were provided.

Sabu opened the closet to show two new futons and said one was made by Sue. The other was wrapped in an oilcloth with an arabesque pattern. Another futon was kept in another place.

"This one's mine," said Sabu, "I haven't touched yours. When Sue-chan comes here, I'll go away."

"Why are you talking about going away?"

"Three people living here would be hard so I'll stay in a row house in Kanasugi-chō."

Eiji was about to say, "Why? There was no point in doing that. Isn't this place enough?" but kept his mouth shut. The inner six-mat room held an oblong brazier, a chest of drawers, a cupboard for tea utensils, a clothes rack, and a hanging mirror. The work tools were in the wood-floor room.

"Did you do this by yourself?"

"Oh, no. Sue-chan helped fix up the inner room."

"This must have cost a lot of money."

Almost apologizing, Sabu said, "You might get mad, but I have something I want to show you."

Eiji sat beside the unlit brazier and restlessly stroked the edge of the brazier and the fireside board. Sabu took out three small sheets of paper folded in half from a drawer of an accessory kit on the chest of drawers, sat in front of Eiji, and passed the papers to him.

Sabu said, "Only these articles were provided by using the money I was holding for you. Sorry I didn't ask you first. I listed the prices exactly. I don't think there are any mistakes. To be sure, will you look at them?"

Eiji looked down at the three papers and didn't intend to peruse them like a balance sheet. He took his wallet out of his breast pocket, put in the papers, and held it out to Sabu.

"You've given me everything. I should be the one apologizing. This wallet contains my wages from Ishikawajima. I'm embarrassed it's so little. I'll get you the rest later."

"What do you mean? Get me the rest?" Sabu looked doubtful.

"Don't worry about it," said Eiji, "Let's have supper. What delicious food do you want to eat?"

Without examining the papers, the money earned by Eiji was

not enough to buy these household goods. He was sure Sabu put in his money.

While Sabu was back home sick with beriberi, he earned his keep at the Kasai home. To buy all these furnishings, Sabu hit the bottom of his wallet. Eiji thought this but avoided this conversation because he wasn't done expressing his gratitude.

After introductions to the landlord Gensuke, the Zōrokus next door, and the three homes across the alley, the two ate dinner. Sabu only cooked rice. They picked up soup, broiled fish, sashimi, and vinegared dishes from a main street caterer called Fish Kiku, and two bottles of sake.

As was their custom, the pair had separate bottles and cups. They didn't pour for the other or drink together.

"This is our shop," said Eiji. After he took the first sip from his cup, he turned and looked around the interior of the house. "We'll start here at this shop, Sabu, we can do this."

"I'll try my best not to hold you back," said Sabu and lowered his head. "Ei-chan, thank you."

Don't say something stupid now, Eiji said to restrain himself. "We'll do this together. I have to thank you, too."

"We finally got here," said Sabu and sipped sake. "We'll have a shop in this house. Whenever I said that to you, Ei-chan, I saw it as a dream, but I didn't think it would happen. I'm happy now but scared, too."

"I feel the same. The world isn't a nice place. Even with this shop, I don't know if it'll go well. When I think about it, I get scared."

Sabu stared fearfully at Eiji.

"Are you afraid?" Sabu turned serious. "Ei-chan, with only your skill, you'll have a good reputation anywhere. Saying you're a little scared is nothing like you."

"Only you think like that about me," said an unsmiling Eiji. "I haven't worked in three years. Will my skills come back? Honestly, I have no idea. But for me now, I'm grateful you're by my side. Don't forget that, Sabu."

"It's not like that. Even now, I'm a dummy with no talent," said

Sabu and looked up. "But I'll do anything if it helps you."

14.3

"Don't get mad," said Eiji with a pained smile. To relax the atmosphere, he picked up his chopsticks and brightly said, "This is our first meal together. Enough of this stressful talk. Let's have fun."

"Should we get another bottle of sake each?"

"That sounds good. I want to drink a bottle but don't intend to until we get job prospects," said Eiji, rubbing his fingers along the side of his forehead like he was embarrassed. "I'm not mad. I can't be. I'm back in the outside world but totally confused."

"You'll settle down soon," said Sabu, then he sounded worried. "It'll be hard for a few days."

The next day, Eiji went with Sabu to 3-chome, Kanasugi to meet Sue's father, a brush maker with a small shop with one apprentice. Her father, Heizō, was a long-time widower. Sue did not share her father's looks or build. He was a man of few words but had a warm personality. He looked elderly, older than fifty, but said he was forty-five.

"Yes, she's my only daughter," said Heizō, smoking without a break. "She's my only daughter but I don't worry. She's the I-do-what-I-do type. As soon as a woman is old enough to marry, she leaves her parents. She can't become a grown woman while she lives with her parents."

When Sue turned thirteen, Heizō called her Sweetie as a way to scold her. His wife was still alive, treasured her only daughter, and raised her to be self-centered. However, he thought when his daughter turned thirteen, she would soon have to be disciplined. Although he forgot why, he gave her a good talking to. When he called her over to chastise her, Sue said, "Yes," stood and came over. The tone of her voice was not the one she had until the day before.

"She never whined or begged me or my wife." Heizō lowered his voice, "How can I say this? In a word, her voice went from a young girl's to a woman's. I remember thinking back then she has already cut ties with us, her parents.

"If that time comes, daughters can prepare to separate from their parents before they realize it. I already didn't think of Sue as 'our daughter.'"

After that, Heizō was silent.

The gathering for congratulations ended. Rain fell from the clear sky after they walked exactly one block from the brush maker's shop. They looked up to see white and gray clouds stacked in the blue sky. One clump of black rain clouds rapidly spread from the south.

Looking at the rain clouds, Eiji said, "An evening shower. Let's hurry."

"I gotta better idea. Let's go to my house."

"Your house?"

"The house I'll move to someday," said Sabu. "It's over there in that alley. Watch out for the boards covering the drainage ditch."

On the right was a rice paddy field, Eiji could see the hills and forests of Ueno. A bridge spanned the narrow flow of water drawn into the field. They crossed the bridge and entered the alley at the corner of a greengrocer. No fires were lit in this area. The eaves of old row houses on both sides touched each other. The eaves and posts leaned. Dirty water flooded from the ditch covered by boards filling the alley with foul air.

What an awful place. As Eiji reflexively scowled, defeated by the downpour, Sabu jumped under the eaves of a row house.

"Are you home, Osei-chan?" He called through the shoji screen and motioned for Eiji to come over. "Osei-chan, it's me. Sabu."

A female voice answered, and the shoji door slid open. The front of the building was flooding and Eiji had to enter a cramped dirt-room floor. A sixteen- or seventeen-year-old girl had opened the door. When she saw Sabu, her eyes widened in astonishment.

"This is amazing," she said in high spirits. "Welcome. Is this your friend?"

Smiling awkwardly, Sabu clumsily said, "Oh, it started raining so I thought we should come here to wait it out."

"Where's your key?" she said and was about to stand but

dropped to her knees. "You can wait here. Close the door. I can smell the mold."

"But it's bad for a sick person."

"Don't worry about my father. I'll make tea." She smiled at Eiji. "You're welcome, too. Please, sit."

Eiji didn't speak but bowed slightly. Osei stood.

Sabu whispered, "We met when I lived here. He used to be a samurai. Her father has been bedridden for a long time. Osei-chan works side jobs at home to support them."

"That makes sense. I thought she had an unusual personality."

While he was speaking, Eiji thought her surprised bright eyes opening wide when she saw Sabu and her happy voice when she spoke reflected her feelings for him.

"She's pretty," whispered Eiji. "How old is she?"

"Uh." Sabu began counting on his fingers. "She's exactly sixteen, still a child."

14.4

Osei said the tea was watery and it was. The tea was brewed hot enough to burn the tongue. Eiji and Sabu sat on the step.

She declined to join them, saying, "I have to finish this," and picked up spread-out needlework."

"And you are," she said, while threading a hair through the needle, looked at Eiji and Sabu and said, "Ei-san?"

"Yes, he is," answered Sabu, "How did you know?"

"A lucky guess. Saburō-san only talked about Ei-san. He bragged about Ei-san to my sleeping father. Right away I wondered, Is that him?"

"Oh, she's dressing up that story," Sabu said and grinned at Eiji. "I never bragged. I didn't do that."

"Sabu has done so much for me," said Eiji to her, "I'm very grateful to him."

"No, he's been so kind to my father and me," she said and stopped sewing. "If Saburō-san wasn't here, we would have been kicked out of our home."

Sabu was astonished. He stuttered, "That's ridiculous. Osei-chan, your stories are a problem." Suddenly aware of his loud voice, his hand rushed to cover his mouth.

Eiji asked, "Has your father been ill a long time?"

Osei kept working as she talked.

Her father's name was Naganuma Togashi. He was fifty-seven. Until her grandfather's generation, they were vassals with small stipends and lived in a small mansion in Honjo.

Her father was the heir. Soon after her grandfather died, men in the Kobunshingumi reserve force of vassals without official appointments were released if they had no post for ten years.

Depending on the circumstances of the Emperor, they received 50 ryo and had to leave the small mansion.

The ronin Togashi married a restaurant waitress and ran a temple elementary school. They moved often.

During this time, his wife gave birth three times, but the first two babies died soon after birth. The third one, Osei, grew up healthy.

She was born somewhere in Fukugawa and then lived in Yanagihara in Kanda. At one time, they also lived in Nihonbashi.

She didn't clearly remember, but when she was five years old and living in a row house called Tasuke-dana on Onari Street in Shitaya, her mother abandoned the family.

Preparing for the rare emergency, Togashi hid the 50 ryo he received when he became a ronin. He dipped into it a little only when necessary. They lived frugally and still had more than 30 ryo. Her mother found the money and took all of it when she left.

Ironically, after the money important to Togashi for emergencies was gone, the rare emergency came.

In the winter of that year, Togashi began to have problems with the joints in his arms and legs and could no longer teach in the temple school. He lay moaning, confined to his bed.

At first, he relied on the students' parents and ate through the compassion of the other residents in the row house. However, that situation could not continue. Before a year passed, he was tactfully driven from the row house.

With no options, my father bore the shame, cried his way into the clan in Naganuma, and we have lived here for the past three years.

The Naganuma clan was a minor shogunal vassal with a small stipend of 200 koku and had an estate in Kōji-machi. The clan was large and life was hard. Her father and she were housed in a place resembling a storage room and treated like beggars. Her father said, "Starving to death would be better."

During the third year, she cried until she convinced her father to get them out of there. The youngest child in the clan, a fifteen-year-old boy, always played tricks on her. If she told her father, it might have brought on some sort of trouble. This was the wisdom of a nine-year-old. She pestered her father without telling him why.

They left the house in Kōji-machi then went from a place called Narihira in Honjo, Sanya in Asakusa, and Shintorigoe, returned to Honjo, and moved to Kiyomizu-chō. Meanwhile, her father experienced temporary relief from his illness. During the two years in Kiyomizu-chō, he was able to expand the temple school although not by much.

"I favor my mother more than my father," she said with a smile, "My father is warm-hearted. I don't remember much about my mother, but from what my father has told me, she was strong-willed, energetic, and had a rather flamboyant personality."

When a temple school was started in Kiyomizu-chō in Honjo, Osei recommended it to her father. After two years there, he fell ill again, but she didn't ask him to quit.

After leaving Kōji-machi, Osei babysat and ran errands everywhere. Sometimes boxes of cheap candies were lined up in the narrow dirt-floor room of the row house.

If she encountered someone skilled at needlework, she pestered them to teach her. People like that are all around town and she could handle silk by the time she was fifteen.

"I'm sorry for going on about myself," she said and laughed. "Soon after Father fell ill again, we moved here. We knew nobody. I hid my age so they wouldn't know. In March of last year, I said I turned eighteen so I could get better jobs and charge for my sewing."

She ducked her head mischievously.

Eiji again asked, "Was your father's illness cured?"

Osei simply said, "Only his pain was relieved a little. There's no treatment." In a frank tone, she added, "It's not that I don't love my father, but if that's how it is, there's nothing I can do."

At last, the rain stopped. Sabu and Eiji expressed their thanks and went outside. Among the traces of the evening rain, puddles formed on the road, gutters overflowed, and water surged down both sides of the road.

Sabu asked Eiji, "Are you tired?"

"She's a well-grounded young woman," said Eiji, ignoring his dragging leg. "The story of her life is not futile. She rises to life's challenges and has a sharp mind."

"Because I moved into that row house in October and rented the house in Sakamoto in December, I've known her for eighty-five or -six days," cooed Sabu, "and have heard the story of her life about ten times."

"What did you do for them?"

"The rent piled up, and they were going to be evicted," said Sabu, lowering his head in embarrassment. "Maybe because I look pretty good-natured and people say I've got nerve, she brought the agent to see me and asked me to pay him. She said, 'This man is my cousin.'"

Eiji's mouth dropped and he looked at Sabu.

"She said, 'Yes, this man is my cousin.'" Sabu laughed lazily. "My mouth didn't work."

He thought he could show the situation there to Eiji who thought she was well-grounded and smart. But that wasn't all, right after she saw Sabu move in, she surely thought to go to him and make this request. This was an instinctive intuition of women that is entirely different from being smart.

For more than ten years from the age of five, she had been knocked around by poverty and the world's callousness. For the first time, she came across a reliable companion.

Her eyes opened wide as if she were surprised by the sight of Sabu. The story she later told explained why. Although he paid her rent, she was not only cunning but also instinctively placing her life into the hands of a good man.

If that hadn't happened, she would have experienced the horror of a man's terror in the Kōji-machi house. Only Sabu would not have seen her audacity.

Sabu said, "Although I heard the story of her life many times, more than her life story being interesting, I'm captured by how she tells it. Yeah, she's still a child. Ei-chan, she's a kid who tells a grown-up story. It's so interesting I can't explain it."

"She'll make a good wife," said Eiji and quickly changed the subject.

"I heard she's sixteen but looks much older."

"Maybe because she's had a hard life."

They walked the short distance from Kanasugi to Sakamoto-chō. After the evening rain, people, pack horses, and palanquins coming and going congested the road. Among them was a married couple selling candy. The woman struck a gong and a *taiko* drum. The man sang a bawdy song and danced in a zigzag down the crowded street.

The slender man was forty-five or -six. The woman looked many times fatter than the man and five or six years older. His face with a receding hairline was painted white. Both cheeks were reddened and plumped up round.

Isn't that Shozō?

That's Shozō who used to make paper cords, thought Eiji and looked hard from the side of his eyes at the man's face. Of course, it wasn't Shozō but looked so much like him that he could be his twin.

"That's a living, too," Sabu said glumly, "What is she feeling?"

"A cab's coming," said Eiji.

When they got back to the house in Sakamoto-chō, the couple next door was arguing. The husband, Zōroku, worked as a head clerk in a kimono fabric shop somewhere. His wife used to be a head maid at the same shop.

From the time Sabu moved in, they fought every day. They weren't very noisy and didn't scream and shout. He heard them cursing each other in low, biting voices. Their fights felt more dreadful than physical fights.

"There are couples like that," said Eiji to Sabu, "I wonder what they're feeling?"

14.5

On April 21, Eiji and Sue married. They chose a day off at the labor camp that allowed four men from Ishikawajima, the sub-foreman Denshichi, Yohei, Mankichi, and Matsuda Gonzo, to attend. These guests provided the gifts of a charcoal scuttle, a fire shovel, a pair of chopsticks for husband and wife, a serving tray box, 1,200 square yards of bleached cotton cloth, and three washed *yukata* summer kimonos.

"These old yukatas are my present," said an angry-sounding Matsuda. "You may think a thing like this is useless. If you think that, you're a stupid, cricket-headed dummy."

He hasn't changed, thought Eiji, smiling, but Sue stared like she was scared. Matsuda faced Sue and gestured for her to come over.

"Young lady, you may not know this," said Matsuda. He sat properly and spoke formally. "New cloth is not used for a newborn's undergarments or diapers. Cotton softened by numerous washings is used. A baby's skin is like freshly pounded *mochi* from the mortar. If your handling is a little rough, you'll immediately rip it to shreds ... Mankichi, why are you laughing? What's so funny?"

"Oh, nothing," said Mankichi, unable to suppress his laughter. "They're still not married, so your lecture about babies may be too soon. Everyone, Sue-san is shrinking her body out of embarrassment."

"You fool! From tonight on, they'll be sleeping together," said Matsuda in a muddle to change the conversation. "Well, uh, we don't know when we'll come again. I thought I'd say it now."

"Thank you, Matsuda-san," said Eiji, while bowing his head. "It's a fine gift. I can't express how grateful I am to each of you. Thank you."

A little confused, Mankichi answered, "You're welcome."

Everyone laughed.

The neighbor Zōroku's wife and the agent's wife came to help with preparing the food trays and sake.

Heizō of Kanasugi seemed to hate this affair. Nearly three households of relatives didn't call. At sunset, one person came.

Sabu suggested Eiji call at least two or three of his brothers, but he refused. Eiji insisted Yohei-san stood in for his parents, Sabu for his relatives, and never acknowledged the matchmaker even as a formality.

Eiji said, "Anyway, if you know there was a matchmaker.... Somehow we met each other and decided to marry. I'd never trick you about a proper matchmaker."

"That may be so and is a part of society," said Sabu and sighed. "Wherever you go, I think it's good someone stands in as a go-between."

"Aren't you here?" asked Eiji, pointing to Sabu. "To me and Sue, having a confidante named Sabu is enough."

Heizō wore hakama trousers bearing his family crest and made the sake dealer carry in two half-gallon *tsunotaru* sake barrels.

Sue dressed as usual in a thick obi sash over her striped, pongee silk kimono and no socks. Eiji also wore a workman's obi over his striped cotton kimono.

Eiji introduced each of the people from the labor camp as his benefactors to Heizō, who thanked them and properly greeted them. Even after hearing they were from the labor camp, he showed no disgust and said few words but his greetings were very ordinary.

It was called a wedding but was brief. The bride and groom sat side by side. Instead of placing a small offering on the box tray gift they received, they only sipped sake from the nuptial cups three times. The cups were unglazed earthenware carried in by Yohei. The sake came from a sake-warming bottle. When they finished, Sue stood to serve. Eiji stepped down and sat.

"Thanks to you. We are exchanging these nuptial cups of sake and committing to marriage. Thank you," said Eiji, as he thrust forward his hands pressed together. "As you see, we lack the money to repay you even in celebration. The three of us, Sabu, Sue, and I, are broke and will get to work. Sue understands that it's not going to be easy, but I learned patience at the labor camp. I'll endure being treated coldly even if it lasts five or ten years. I am determined to have an ordinary shop."

When he said what he needed to say, he shut his mouth tight.

Mankichi, his face red from drinking, said, "I'm gonna give you a gift. Matsuda-san, you can help, too? We'll sing *Takasagoya* for the happy couple."

Matsudo Gonzo's eyes widened. "What? Are you that bold?"

"A little performance won't hurt."

Yohei said, "Please sing and bring tonight's celebration to an end."

Mankichi began singing.

14.6

Mankichi had a good voice, a fine one, both melodic and resonant, for workmen's chants. This was no surprise given he was originally a construction worker. When he came to the line about sailing out in a boat under the moon, he broke out in laughter, tapping his forehead several times as his body convulsed from laughing.

Matsuda yelled, "You're laughing. What is wrong with you? You're a fool.

"You make a joke out of the part where one settles into a serene place."

Eiji said, "No, that's not it, Matsuda-san. I'm very grateful to my friends for being here to celebrate and their compassion although clumsy. Man-san, thank you."

"Please, Matsuda-san." Yohei picked up the sake bottle to pour him a cup. "Tonight is special. Sometimes you gotta relax, take off your *kamishimo*, and get drunk."

"Kamishimo you say?" said Matsuda, opening his eyes wide again.

"That's your kamishimo, Matsuda-san," said Denshichi while eating. "You hide your kind nature by working your surly mouth. We know that so don't strain yourself."

"Don't look down on people," Matsuda yelled, "You assholes know how I feel?"

His face became blood red, an omen foretelling the start of the customary abuse. This time, however, he cast down his eyes and held his tongue. He seemed overwhelmed and continued drinking nervously.

Even a labor camp has time limits. Special permission was received for today. When Yohei heard it was seven, he said, "It's time to call it a night," and put down his cup.

Eiji talked to Yohei but never said, "Come here when you get out of the camp and we'll live like father and son."

Eiji thought he'd visit the camp later and speak to him alone.

Eventually, the four stood and so did Heizō. When Heizō stood, they looked at him a little surprised. He neither spoke nor laughed, and they had forgotten all about him.

Eiji, Sue, and Sabu saw everyone off at the street.

"Now, be happy," said Matsuda when he left. "Sue-san, you're this guy's wife. If he's unfaithful, it's all right to bring your complaint to me. If you do, I'll set him straight on the spot."

Matsuda Gonzo spilled sloppy tears as he told them to be happy again.

"Hey, what's going on?" said Mankichi, "It's gotta be a lie, tears in the demon's eyes."

"What did you say? You bum. A demon is a demon but not a simple demon. I'm The Red Demon," said Matsuda as he wiped tears and snot to the side and leaned on Mankichi's shoulder. "Ah, I'm drunk. Lend me your shoulder, you ugly bastard."

By then, Heizō and Yohei were already gone.

When back at home, Sue tidied up, helped by the neighbor's wife and the landlord's wife. Eiji and Sabu sat facing each other, collected the sake bottles not yet empty, and started drinking. Neither was a strong drinker. Sabu seemed to drink the most but, as always, didn't get drunk.

"I only got to say thank you once," said Eiji, digging his hands into his lap and bowing. "Thank you, Sabu. Thank you so much."

Sabu waved his hand near his head but didn't speak.

"The two of us are a team," said Eiji and dropped his head. "I'll do my best."

Sabu wanted to say something but couldn't find the words. He shook his head and mumbled, "I, uh ... I think I'll call it a night soon."

"Don't be stupid. Didn't you decide to stay overnight? Come on, drink."

"Oh, yeah. Then I'll have one more after this."

Sue saw off the women who came to help and sat beside Eiji while wiping off her hands.

"Sue-san, I apologize," said Sabu. Tongue-tied, he bowed and then said, "I thought I would leave earlier but at this rate, I'm gonna become a burden to you."

Eiji said to Sue, "I'll be drinking for the rest of the night. You can go to bed if you're tired."

"But Ei-san ..."

"It'll be good for the guys to be alone," said Eiji and gave her a knowing look, "There's tomorrow for you. If you're sleepy, go to sleep."

After Sue signaled she understood what Eiji said with her eyes, she said a few words to Sabu.

"You said you're going to drink all night, but that's no good because Eiji already smells of sake. Sabu, you drink and don't get drunk, but now you're completely drunk. Your body is wobbly, and your speech is slurring.

"Are you asleep, Sabu?" Eiji eventually asked. "You looked pained when you woke up."

While speaking, he turned and could see Sue changing clothes in the adjacent six-mat room through the half-open paper sliding door. She took off her kimono and slipped into her nightclothes. He was almost surprised by his feeling of being seduced by her smooth but tense, narrow shoulders and naked slender profile.

"I'm no good," said Sabu and turned to the side, "My whole life is foolish."

CHAPTER 15

15.1

Eiji began as a helper on Sabu's jobs. He often did interior sliding screens, mostly papering the thick paper used in row houses. Sometimes he repapered the shoji screens at businesses on the main streets or in the homes of mistresses. He thought his dulled skills idle for three years would be restored starting with these minor jobs.

"This sort of work is good," said Sabu like a cliché, "but Ei-chan deserves more. I'll fix this."

"It's okay," said Eiji, always sounding annoyed. "Don't worry about it."

Sabu moved to the Kanasugi house. He came at eight every morning. On days he worked late into the night, he went home after eating dinner. The workload was not heavy, but he had to work nights. The scroll mounter in Okachi-machi had almost no work. When a request came early on to mount a very wide, obscene picture, he understood Eiji's reason for turning down the work, claiming he was still rusty and couldn't mount it. He seemed proud of his association with the name Hōko-dō. The work passed on to Sabu diminished.

"It's all right. Don't worry," said Sabu again. "Kobuna-chō is on its summer break. Isn't it like this every year? We'll get busy when the cool breezes come."

"I'm not worried," said Eiji and smiled. "How do I say this? It wasn't going to be smooth sailing from the beginning. You're the worrywart."

Eiji thought, Under these circumstances, the labor camp is best maybe even far better. You don't have to worry about eating. There's always work and you get paid. If you get sick, you're treated for free. It's only natural not a few people don't want to leave the camp.

Looking at their lives, he was earning money but not being put to useful work. Now, he had a wife and a shop, although small. When he bumped into crippling hardships every day of his life, he gained a new understanding of the meanings of words he heard in the camp.

Eiji thought, Here, one job must be stolen by several dozen people. I will not limit myself to particular jobs and must have skills so that others won't defeat me in winning a job. Even a little slip allows the job to be snatched from the side. This is exactly like a pack of wolves stealing prey.

He willingly took jobs with the lowest pay regardless of the job. When there were no orders, he made the thick patterned paper for row houses or sold goods. When August came, even the minuscule savings he held were drained.

Once Sabu whispered, "It's almost inhuman to say this, but I'd be a little relieved if there was a big fire."

"If there was a fire," said Eiji, "this house would burn down first. That's how good and bad luck goes. More than thinking strange thoughts, please focus on preparing paste."

Sue did well. From the beginning, she was never in a great mood or excited about the new household. If she had free time, she would immediately go to the workshop and dedicate herself to helping Eiji.

After Watabun and before being a live-in maid, she was the head maid in a large business at 2-chome, Nihonbashi Dōri. Her hands were slender and pretty but suddenly became rough and swollen at the finger joints.

In only fifty days, her hair was always tied back because she had neither the money nor time for the hairstyle of a new bride. Of course, she no longer wore makeup.

Eiji thought about saying, "You've quickly turned into a housewife," but the words never came out after watching his wife's busy days.

Breakfast was at nine in the morning and dinner, at six in the evening. The three ate both meals together. From around the middle of August, however, Sue disappeared. Eventually, Sabu no longer came for dinner.

Supposedly, Osei at the Kanasugi house prepared his meals and waited for him. Sue said she would eat alone later and appeared to be tidying up the cramped kitchen.

Eiji suspected nothing, but Sabu was eating cheap meals of some food poured over rice at a stall in Kanasugi. Sue stretched the leftovers by adding them to rice gruel or porridge. The side dishes were plain miso soup or licking salt. In a word, the family finances were so tight they were forced to eat these meals.

To regain his skills as a picture mounter, Eiji lingered at his work every night. Sue stayed by his side to light the mosquito repellant, fan the sweating Eiji, and bring damp towels to cool him.

One evening, Eiji said to Sue, "There's a young woman named Osei at Sabu's row house. She's sixteen and seems to be in love with him."

Sue said, "So that's her. She makes his dinner and waits for him."

Eiji nodded.

"Sabu thinks of her as a child and doesn't seem to notice at all. But that girl is already a fine adult. Her life has been hard since she was five years old. Even now, she cares for her bedridden father. You should meet her sometime."

"Me? Why?"

Eiji smiled. "Because I think she'd be the perfect wife for Sabu."

15.2

September came. A short time after most people were wearing lined kimonos, Eiji noticed Sue was still wearing an unlined one. She was not wearing a yukata but the delicate cotton kimono she wore all summer.

"It's not an unlined kimono, it's lined," Sue said absentmindedly and turned the hem over to show him. "See, there's a lining. I like this design so I altered it."

"You had the lined kimono with the fish-scale pattern. I like that one, too."

"I gave that to our neighbor Bun-san."

"Our neighbor Bun-san?"

"The neighbor's wife," said Sue softly. "The shop where her husband Zōroku-san worked as the clerk failed. He has been peddling dry goods ever since."

After hearing his work was not going well, Bun started taking in piecework to keep going. The couple sold off or pawned all their belongings and couldn't have one lined kimono made. After hearing that, Sue gave Bun the fish-scale kimono.

"She asked a favor of me, but you may get mad."

"Wait, push that end a little," said Eiji. While smoothing paste onto his brush. "Press hard. That's good."

As Sue pressed one end of the paper with both hands as instructed, she glanced up at Eiji.

"You'll get mad."

"What is it?"

"She wants me to help with her sewing," said Sue nonchalantly. "Bun-san has a lot of orders now and can't keep up. If she turns them down, she said work may not come in the future, so she must finish these orders."

"Why should you help?"

"So you won't let me?"

"I may be cruel, but you shouldn't." As Eiji moved the brush, he said, "You're busy with our work. You work nonstop from morning to night and don't have time to sleep. You realize that, don't you?"

"That's awful. Am I working that much? It's too enjoyable." Then for the first time, she spoke in a babyish nasally voice. "Hey, it's all right. I'll be sure not to slack off in my work at home."

"You're serious about this. If you want to do this," said Eiji, staring at his hands, "it's okay if you don't overdo it. Hey, the oil in the lamp is low."

"I'll get more oil," said Sue. "I'll tell her first thing tomorrow. Bun-san will be so happy."

Eiji knew nothing about the situation in the neighbor's home. What was the name of the shop where Zōroku worked? How did the shop fail? Was he truly working as a peddler? Sue's explanation was the first time he was hearing about these things.

The world is usually in hard times. Even in the large wholesalers in Nihonbashi, not a few stories talked of bankrupt stores. When walking around town, he noticed *Store Closing Clearance Sale* or *Building For Sale* pasted to the large doors of shuttered shops.

Several alleys around their home were tightly packed with old row houses. Most of the residents were day laborers. Once children reached seven or eight years old, they had to work to help with the family finances.

One time, Sue was washing at the well out back. A girl around eight carrying a baby on her back came up to her side and wrung out the clothes Sue washed. She was surprised by the girl, thanked her, and wrapped up candy for her. The girl said she didn't need candy, asked for money, and stuck out her hand. The same thing happened many times.

"This sort of life exists in this world," said Sue and sighed.

When Sue said she wanted to help the neighbor's wife with sewing, Eiji immediately wondered, "Is this what we've come to?"

He had few orders. The thirty fusuma sliding screens and paper sliding doors for sale were propped in a corner covered in dust.

He had high hopes for the season of cool breezes, but it was already here, and nothing more than mostly darkness lay ahead.

No matter how bad things get, a man is finished when his wife has to earn money. The proprietor Hōbei often said that when Eiji worked at Hōko-dō. Eiji believed that was so.

Around him now in Kobuna-chō, several houses had wives who worked hard and husbands who loafed around. While they seemed to be doing well, they decided to fly away in the night.

Eiji thought, It's wrong to make Sue do piecework. If I can't use my skill to get through this, my work will never be genuine.

However, he knew money for tomorrow's food would be a problem and clenched his teeth to endure.

A little earlier, Sabu began a job somewhere as a helper. Although Eiji asked where and what kind of job it was, Sabu was evasive and never said.

After a few days, he secretly passed a little money to Sue. Eiji wasn't sure whether it was money or goods. He thought it was money but, never having seen it, he wasn't sure.

"An attack on the front or back gate," muttered Eiji. "I don't know if it's an attack on both sides. This is suffocating."

The two weathered this emergency so that Eiji wouldn't notice. Although they tried to protect him, their concern was more a great burden than a benefit to him.

One day in October, Eiji went out to the public bathhouse. He didn't return home but walked out carrying a folded damp towel. With no destination in mind, he went around the back, down the streets in 2-chome, turned corner after corner, and came out at a road in the paddy fields of Iriya.

Most of the fields were harvested. Stubble arrayed on the black dirt and spread out to the left and right of narrow paths. Black birds he thought were crows danced around or swiftly took flight.

He talked to himself as he walked. "I'd be laughed at if I called for Grandpa. If I called on a substitute parent, it would cause hardship even for Yohei-san."

The wintry skies were clear. When he reached Asakusa with its many temples, the mud walls and white plaster walls were so bright they dazzled in the sunlight. Their brightness only darkened Eiji's suspicions.

"I have to go home. Sue's probably worried, but I don't want to."

The voices of two men talking came from behind.

One said, "He's a mystery man, an illusion. Without fail, he thinks he has to do something and remembers something else he had to do earlier."

"That guy's a busy man."

The first man said, "An ink stone is set up in the center of the room. When he was about to wash the ink stone, he realized he had to split firewood. He put down the ink stone there and went to the wood splitter. When he finished splitting the wood, he remembered another job. A service or a purification, something like that. There are various ones to do.

"Guests of a family supporting the temple or visitors to the main temple arrived. Several times he was about to wash the ink stone, but each time, he remembered a more urgent errand."

His companion said, "I've never seen a man that busy."

The first man said, "Meanwhile, the ink stone is in the middle of the room. It's starting to look like it belongs there. If it does, I can't make him move it and will use another ink stone. What else can I do but leave it there?"

Eiji looked at the men as they passed him from behind. Both were middle-aged monks. They were easygoing and lived without the slightest knowledge of life's hardships.

He listened to them for a short time but knew they embodied the proverb, Killing an ant is the same as killing one thousand monks. In other words, a monk produces nothing, which means they're parasites. These words were filled with the anger of poor people. At that moment, Eiji thought that, too.

"Where should I go now?" he asked himself. "I'll go deep into the mountains where no one will find me and die by the side of the road.

A man shouted, "Watch out! Horse coming through!"

Eiji looked as he jumped out of the way, nearly getting hit by a horse carrying a load. His face felt wrapped in the horse's breath and the strong scent of the beast. He wiped his face and the back of his neck with the towel. His temper flared. More than being yelled at by the horseman, he got angry at himself for mulling over the same thoughts so much he was nearly run over by a horse while walking.

"This wasn't my hope," Eiji said without realizing it. "Hey, Eiji, this isn't what you hoped for. You hesitate like a woman and only sigh. What's wrong with you? Where did the old Eiji go?"

A woman called from behind.

"Is that you, Ei-san? Where are you going?"

He turned to see a twenty-four- or -five-year-old woman hugging a package. She was smiling as she approached. He could not recall where he had seen her before.

She bowed and said, "It's been a while. Have you been doing well since then?"

"I'm sorry, but have we met?"

"Oh no, you've forgotten me," said the woman, glaring with an alluring look.

"It's me, Okame. I'm Okame from Sumiyoshi."

15.3

Eiji was having a drink at Sumiyoshi. He was not in his usual place in the small sitting room but sat in the dirt-floor room. Nobu placed dried foods baked earlier and stew before him and then sat across from him.

Nobu asked, "What is Okame-chan doing now?"

"I didn't ask," said Eiji, narrowing his eyes, "She looks like she's doing well, like a respectable wife."

Nobu said, "If that's true, I didn't expect that."

Nobu explained the situation when Okame left the shop and about her male suitor. Eiji was not listening. He hadn't had a drink in a long time and got tipsy after two drinks. The stiffness in his chest, feeling as if it were filled with lead, relaxed as if the wind were blowing across it. The tension he had forgotten about seemed to overflow from his chest.

He said, "Just to let you know, I don't have any money on me."

"I already guessed that."

"I don't have even one mon."

"Why are you telling me this?" asked Nobu, pouring him a drink and looking mischievously at him. "I know. You had a fight with your wife and ran out."

"Can you quarrel with your spouse when you're about to hang yourself?"

"Why would you say that?"

"I don't have any work." Eiji was surprised when these words slid out of his mouth. "After opening the shop, no real work came. I know the economy is in the dumps, but what are we supposed to do? I want to hang myself."

"Oh, you're being dramatic," said Nobu, staring at Eiji's face. "It's been only six months since you opened the shop. Why are you so anxious?"

"Sue has been taking in piecework. Sabu is taking day jobs wherever."

Eiji sipped his drink and then spoke. He didn't sound desperate or hopeless but stressed.

"I don't know where he goes or what he does. Where does he get his day's earnings? He secretly passes some money to Sue. Being who she is, while Sue says she's helping a neighbor, she sews from morning to night whenever she has time."

"Oh, stop being so proud," said Nobu and poured him a drink. "When the husband's job is not going well, it's normal for the wife to do side jobs. Look at the world. That story happens all the time."

"Listen to me," said Eiji and took a sip. He seemed to be gathering his thoughts and was quiet for a short time, then he said, "I'm devoted to regaining my skills and have done all sorts of jobs Sabu drums up, but I'm also driven by improving myself."

"That's what you wanted to do from the beginning."

"If I get back my skills, I think I'll be doing the jobs I mostly do now."

"But you said you don't have any work."

"It's not just that," said Eiji and then raised one eyebrow. "They say if the wife makes money, the man is finished. I've not only heard that from others. I've seen things several times with my eyes. When the wife makes money, the man is already done."

"You are full of yourself."

Eiji looked with surprise at Nobu. Her voice chilled to a sarcastic tone.

"It's good you hate losing, Ei-san, but I hate your self-centeredness," said Nobu, glaring at Eiji. "Aren't a husband and wife one mind and body? The thought that the man earns and feeds the woman is selfish. When the husband fails to get work, why is the wife earning money a bad thing? Aren't the man and the woman both human beings? In this world, men aren't the only remarkable people."

"Nobu-san, you're missing the point."

"I need a drink," said Nobu and stood.

A customer entered. The maid Matsu said, "Welcome back," and guided the guest to a seat.

Nobu returned with a cup for herself and a sake-warming bottle. When she saw the guest, she smiled brightly and said, "Oh, welcome back." Then she winked at Eiji and went over to the guest.

"She's angry," said Eiji and poured himself a drink and drank alone. "A man works to feed the woman, but I know that's not true."

He thought, Saying that may be conceited. Both Sue and Sabu work to tide all three of us over in bad times. It may be arrogant to think I'm living off my wife's earnings.

"That's funny," said Eiji, so drunk he strongly shook his addled head like he was trying to wake himself up. "I shouldn't be the least bit proud. That's ridiculous. I think I owe apologies to Sabu and Sue."

"Excuse me."

Eiji raised his head to see Nobu and the guest had come over. He was fifty-five or -six and closed his haori jacket on his lined kimono of Yuki silk with a deep navy blue Hakata obi sash, and wore hemp-soled sandals with white-tanned leather ties.

Nobu introduced him. "This is our customer, Sanukiya-san.

"He said he'd like to come over to speak with you about something."

Eiji didn't answer yes or no but gestured for him to come closer and said, "Please, have a seat."

"I'm sorry for being so pushy." The man's words were colored by a regional accent. He sat across from Eiji and said, "My name is Sanukiya Ihei. Pleased to meet you."

15.4

Eiji gazed lazily at the five koban coins on the paper as he sipped water from the teacup.

"Sanukiya Ihei, so his story's true."

"It's in Sōshu on Enoshima island," said Nobu, "It's not close."

"It's 244 miles away. I shouldn't be surprised, but this came out of nowhere. I still can't believe it's true."

"Even if it's a surprise to Ei-san, Sanukiya-san has been searching for five days."

Every bit of the story was true. Sanukiya was a restaurant with twelve guest rooms located in Sōshu on Enoshima island. He searched from there to Edo for a craftsman to repaper its entire interior.

The craftsman had to be capable of redoing three sitting rooms with fusuma sliding screens with pictures and mounting pictures. The work in the other sitting rooms ranged from picture framing to backing paper. The order was lucrative.

The work was serious and demanded skill. After so long, Eiji was excited and explained in exacting detail his opinion of the order. Ihei seemed interested in Eiji's view, asked him to conduct a preliminary inspection, and said he would put down a deposit of five ryo.

Ihei said he visited seven or eight picture framers and scroll mounters, including Hōko-dō, but couldn't settle on a price. Every shop estimated the need for at least five skilled craftsmen able to handle the work. Also, they were unable to send craftsmen to Enoshima this season. If they could, the materials would be separate from the time and labor of the craftsmen. They requested a sum three times more costly than Ihei's calculation. With a deadline of New Year's, Eiji thought he and Sabu could do this job. More than the wages, more than anything, he wanted the work. Because this was a proper job, if asked, he wanted to do it.

"I'm drunk," said Eiji. "Because I'm drunk, I talked so smoothly. Thinking about it now, it was like a dream."

Nobu said, "There's money in this. Ei-san, don't you dare say what just happened isn't good."

"Did I sound like I was saying that?"

"I forgot something," said Nobu and stood. She went to get her cup, asked Matsu to pour the sake, and sat facing Eiji. "Earlier, I thought I was going to drink to complain, but now I'll drink to celebrate."

"Is the proprietress okay with that?"

"I haven't been home since last night. I'll tell you about that later," said Nobu, poured herself a drink, and drank. "Sanukiya-san came five days ago and has been staying at an inn called Yoshidaya across the canal.

"When he first told me about the job, I thought about you but didn't say anything, so he didn't know about you until today. If I didn't mention you didn't have work, I couldn't say anything about you to him. Anyway, Enoshima is farther away than Mount Hakone."

"What? It's farther away than Mount Hakone?"

"Please pour me another," she said and thrust out her cup, but she immediately stuck out her tongue. "Ah, is that bad? Not pouring drinks for each other?"

"I'll pour you a drink. Thanks to you, I got a job."

"So you remembered."

Matsu came with warm sake. The other two maids appeared and said, "Good morning."

Barely noticing them, Nobu kept on drinking, became serious, and lashed out at Eiji.

"Ei-san, you were talking earlier about Sabu-chan doing day labor and your wife taking in work."

"Stop. It's too early to pick a fight."

"This is my third round, isn't it? You can't say I'm drunk. Not at all," said Nobu. "Hey, Ei-san probably had the best skills at Hōko-dō. Even if this doesn't work out, in time you will become a leading craftsman.

"You said it's no good for a man when his wife has to make money. The world says something different than you. It wasn't that way originally. You're carried by your wife's earnings and look like you're fooling around. But that's not you, Ei-san. You wanted but didn't have work. When there was no work, the mythical Hidari Jingorō worked as a beggar."

"I've never heard of Hidari Jingorō."

"Don't change the subject. From now on, this is the issue," said Nobu and continued pouring and drinking. "Ei-san, earlier you said you're making Sue-san work for money. I said you were being very proud. You understand that, Ei-san?"

Eiji vaguely shook his head.

"Please, don't get mad. I believe this," said Nobu. "This is what I feel about you making Sue-san work. When your work does well, by working, you feed everyone."

Eiji asked, "Isn't it obvious the man earns to support his wife and children?"

Nobu gently shook her head. "That's ridiculous. You're joking. People nurture people. You have ridiculous pride. As a craftsman, Ei-san will lead, but several or dozens of people will lend their powers from the shadows.

"Sabu-chan often said, 'I have no talent and am slow.' But without the paste he'll prepare, you couldn't do your work well."

"Sabu's paste compares favorably to anyone's. Even at Hōko-dō, no one was better."

"You've said that a lot."

Two men, who looked like regulars and lived nearby, entered. Nobu greeted them and called the maids. She signaled Eiji with her eyes, placed the sake-warming bottle, bowls, and small plates in front of him on the tray, and stood. She whispered, "Go over there," like an order. Eiji stood and moved to the small inner sitting room.

It was already getting dark. The interior of the sitting room was in shadows. Nobu told Matsu to bring lanterns.

"I have a few more things I'd like you to hear," Nobu said, quickly set up the table, and began talking the moment she sat.

"It's no lie when you say nobody is better at preparing the paste than Sabu-chan. If you use his paste to do your work on hanging scrolls and folding screens, it will be done well, and you will be praised. They'll say your finishing touches are superb and you have great skill.

"Maybe people will praise the paste. I think they will praise the paste used for the hanging scrolls and the fine finish it produces, Ei-san."

"Now for Sue-san," said Nobu then her tone changed, "Ei-san's shop will prosper. Even if her piecework going away is a good thing, there's no reason she'll be happier. I don't think hardships much worse than piecework will ever end for Sue so she can manage your home so her husband can do good work."

Eiji said nothing. He picked up his teacup and sipped water. Nobu poured and downed two drinks.

"I've served customers for a long time and believe that," said Nobu and sighed deeply. People who stand up to others in this world, like older brothers and parents, have several people like Sabu-chan by their sides. It's true, Ei-san."

"I know. Believe me, I know."

He recalled while in the labor camp, Yohei said the same thing. He said something like, "You know, you're not alone. At least, Sabu-chan, Sue-san, and Nobu-san are there for you." No matter the situation, no one is completely alone.

Eiji was stung by Nobu's words about all people respected in the world secretly having people like Sabu.

Matsu brought in the lit lantern and two sake-warming bottles.

Nobu said, "You understand what I'm saying," and poured a drink from the new bottle. "Your eyes say you do."

As she spoke, she stared at Eiji's face. Tears instantly flowed from her eyes.

"Why wouldn't you marry me?" she asked, still staring at Eiji and crying. "I love you so much. I would show everyone what a good wife I would be. To earn money, I would happily sell my body for your sake."

Sounding like he heard nothing, Eiji mimicked a narrator introducing a kabuki play, "The pale yellow curtain falls to reveal a domestic scene.

"I must not worry my wife. I shall return home. Thank you."

"No, you can't go yet," said Nobu and snatched his hand. "My wish for my life is for you to stay a little longer."

Eiji took a package of money from his breast pocket to show her.

"I shouldn't forget this."

Nobu saw the package and was excited as if she fell from a cliff. While smoothing back her limp stray hairs, she grinned.

"I'm sorry, I'm drunk," she said and stuck out her tongue a little and shrugged. "Sue-san must be worried. Go home now. Hurry."

"Nobu-san, are you all right?"

"No," she said and tapped the front of her obi sash. "I think this doesn't need to be said, but I can be your wife here."

Nobu stuck up her right thumb, the sign for a man.

"Who do you think it is?"

Eiji read Nobu's expression and said, "As always, the cook Toku-san?"

"I no longer carry a razor, but there's one mystery," said Nobu and shrugged. "If he has a wife, I have a hunch this time I'll get my man. Women are strange creatures."

15.5

When Eiji returned to 2-chome, Sakamoto, he didn't give Sue a chance to say anything and talked about what happened at Sumiyoshi. He sounded like a criminal defending himself. Maybe he was ashamed, but Sue's cheerful face lit up.

"That's great. It's wonderful," she excitedly said, "I will never forget Nobu-san's kindness for as long as I live."

"If you even hint at this, Nobu-san will fly into a rage."

Of course, she loves you, Sue said only in her heart.

"When are you going to do the preliminary inspection?"

"Tomorrow. I'll leave while it's dark tomorrow."

"Isn't Enoshima far?"

"I don't know. I've never been there, but I know it's closer than Hakone."

Sue hopped up. "I'll make dinner."

Eiji asked, "How was Sabu, today?"

"Oh, that reminds me." She turned around. "I met Osei-chan. She's like you said. She's a pretty, levelheaded, nice girl."

"Did they come here?"

"I went there. You went to the bath. It was late, and you hadn't come home. I thought you had gone to see Sabu-chan, so I went to Kanasugi."

"I'm sorry." Eiji looked away like a bright light blinded his eyes.

As she entered the kitchen, Sue said, "You were right. She will make the perfect wife for Sabu-chan.

"We only chatted while standing, but Osei's love of Sabu was obvious in her words and facial expressions. Sabu is so quiet, Osei's clear-eyed personality will be helpful. When the time comes, those two should be together." Sue's voice coming from the kitchen sounded high-pitched.

Eiji asked, "Was Sabu there?"

Sue said, "No, he was working. If he doesn't come over tonight, he'll come tomorrow.

"Are you taking Sabu-chan with you to Enoshima?"

"I can do that alone. I'd like him to buy supplies while I'm gone. Our stock is no good. We'll have to buy new underlayer paper, too. We may not get them on time if we don't order the supplies right away."

"You'll be very busy," said Sue and went over to him. While setting up the tray, she said, "We've waited so long for this night but have nothing special. Shall we have a drink after such a long time?"

Eiji's hand brushed aside that notion. "I've had enough sake. I have to straighten up and prepare for tomorrow."

During the meal, a smile filled Sue's flushed face as she rambled nonstop. Eiji was about to tell her it was too soon to be so happy and that she should wait until after the job is done. However, he thought her happiness would turn into anxiety and didn't want to pour water over her joy.

Right after dinner, Eiji wrote down the order. He needed several types of backing paper for picture sliding screens; he used silk canvas for calligraphy or pictures on paper; and paper having properties matched to different surfaces, like Mino paper and Gampi paper, facing, middle liner, and extra liner. Of course, he needed handmade paper, coarse and fine, thin and thick, even for Mino. An important condition was spotless paper.

He didn't have much experience selecting paper and was a little unsure about Sabu but the work had to begin immediately after receiving the order. For now, Eiji's only option was to rely on him.

He finished writing the order and showed it to Sue.

"When Sabu comes tomorrow, tell him to take this to Yamatoya in Hongoku-chō and tell them to have the order ready within ten days."

"Yamatoya in Hongoku-chō," she repeated.

"The paper maker is Yamatoya Saburōbei at 4-chome, Hongoku-chō," Eiji stressed. "Sabu goes to Haibara because Hōkodō has used them for many years. However, I'm using Yamatoya. Don't forget."

"I won't," she said and nodded.

"I have five ryo." Eiji opened the package and took out the money. "I'll keep two to travel by palanquin to and from Enoshima. I think one ryo is more than enough but want to make sure I have enough because this will be an express journey. Give the other three ryo to Sabu and tell him to deposit it in my account at Yamatoya.

"I'm sorry I don't have one mon to give you."

"Do you want to see something?" asked a smiling Sue and went over to the bureau and brought back a wallet she took out of a small accessory box. She shook out the contents onto her lap.

"Please, count it. There's two bun and one shu, but I'll be fine."

Eiji stared at Sue's lap. Like a weight was lifted from his shoulders, he released a long sigh as his body relaxed.

"I have to get to bed soon," he said, then his voice changed like something was caught in his throat. "I'll have to see about brushes, too."

CHAPTER 16

16.1

Eiji returned from his trip on the evening of the third day. As after any express trip, he was worn out but in high spirits and carried on a brisk conversation as he changed out of his traveling clothes.

"Sue, we'll both go," Eiji said first, "The scenery is gorgeous, you won't believe it. I could see Mount Fuji. The immense sea was all around. The white waves rushed the beach nonstop. I thought the sweet winds came out for me."

"Shouldn't you take a bath?" asked a smiling Sue, "You're covered in dust."

"The water at the bathhouse is grimy around this time. I'll boil water at home and wipe down," said Eiji, while tying his obi sash, "Like I said earlier, you're coming with me on this job."

"Enoshima. I'm a little scared to go so far," said Sue, moving his discarded clothes to the side. "I'll go boil the water."

From the kitchen, she said, "You're tired. Lie down for a while."

"This job is first class like I thought," said Eiji, as he listened to Sue's words.

"If this were in Tokyo, I'd gain instant fame, but either way is good for my name. This is my first job standing alone. I was lucky to chance upon this job. "The funny thing is the proprietor of Sanukiya said he'll pay me fifty percent more than my entire estimate. He said, 'I'm worried about your estimate. Don't worry if the costs exceed the estimate.' You don't find customers like him these days."

Eiji realized he was talking too much and stopped.

He was wondering how things went for Sabu when he heard the front lattice open and Sabu's voice.

"Come in," said Eiji and watched him step up. He was wearing a striped cotton haori half-coat over a plain blue cotton kimono. His hair was tied back.

"Please sit," said Eiji like nothing caught his eye. "The Enoshima job is ours."

Eiji took out his money belt from the bureau and pushed it to Sabu.

"Thirty-five ryo is half the total. Because I received a five ryo deposit, this is the remaining thirty ryo."

"So ..." Sabu licked his lips, "So the job is worth seventy ryo?"

"When done, the amount will be fifty percent higher, but let's not go that high."

"That's amazing, but I'd expect it with Ei-chan," stuttered Sabu. "Of course, the levels of men with and without skill are different."

Eiji was quick to say, "It's thanks to you, Sabu. Thanks to you and Sue. I've never said this, but when I finish this job, I'll thank you again."

Sabu waved his hands, like he was trying to dodge Eiji's words, and broke in, "That's crazy. Stop it."

Paying no mind, Eiji changed the topic.

"Did you order the paper?"

"Yeah," said Sabu and licked his lips again. "I gave the order form and deposit to Yamatoya."

"Will it be ready soon?"

"They said it would," said Sabu then looked nervously at Eiji. "Is this a rush job?"

He sounded afraid. Eiji took note and observed Sabu's face.

"I promised to be finished by New Year's. Why?"

"Nothing really," said Sabu timidly and looked down. "But I heard from my family in Kasai. My mother is sick. They may send for me in a day or two."

Indignant, Eiji urged him, "And?"

"And uh if my mother ... Kasai isn't that far."

"Don't get upset," said Eiji, without realizing it, his tone hardened. "You want to go to Kasai. Did you forget what you went through when you went to Kasai?"

"Hearing that from you bothers me."

"What else can I say? You got sick, and it took a lot for you to recover. You lost a lot of weight. Your legs swelled to twice their size. You were tossed into a shed. They forced you to work hard. Would this family that shares your blood treat a stranger like that? Isn't your mother one of them? You say she's ill. You shouldn't feel any obligation to that mother."

"Oh, welcome," said Sue when she came in from the kitchen. "Eiji, the water is boiling."

16.2

Eiji went to the kitchen.

"Tonight, I'll buy sake, and we'll eat delicious food," Eiji said and left. Sue brought out tea for Sabu.

"What happened?" Sue whispered, "I heard raised voices."

Sabu explained the situation and said, "I want to travel by night to Kasai."

She said, "That's a problem, isn't it?"

"Ei-chan is mad at me," Sabu quietly said. "I was treated badly. Ei-chan has hated Kasai for a long time and says they're not parents or siblings. It's true my family is a pretty awful bunch."

Sue nodded and hesitated before going back to the kitchen.

Sabu said, nearly whispering, "But this is what I think. My family hurt me, but I don't blame them."

"No one in this family is mad at you," said Sue and blushed. At first, she seemed embarrassed when she said "no one in this family."

"Do you think someone blames you?"

"It's not that. No, no, it's not that," said Sabu, shaking his head in frustration. "What can I say? I stumble over my words and don't say what I think. I mean no matter how badly they treat me, my mother is my mother. It's different if I blamed her. If I don't, I think it's not a bad thing to be at my mother's deathbed."

"There's nothing bad about that at all," said Sue, seeming not to understand the meaning of the words she heard. Like she was cheering him up, she said, "Eiji understands that much."

While wiping the back of his ears with a damp towel, Eiji returned.

"Bring the sake cups, please."

"Welcome back. Coming right up," said Sue, signaling Sabu with her eyes as she stood. Eiji sat beside the oblong brazier and asked, "When are you leaving?"

Sabu sat properly for no reason.

"You're going to Kasai, right?"

"Will you still use me?"

"You're a sorry fellow. A man like you ..." said Eiji, "but I already told you. If the materials are ready, I'll leave Edo immediately. I intend to bring Sue, who'll be a great help. Being too lax would be a problem."

"Thank you. Ei-chan, I'm indebted to you," said Sabu and bowed. "They only said to come but didn't say if she was dying. If she's not, I'll come back immediately."

"Just in case, I have some questions about the paste."

"Now?" asked Sabu. Eiji nodded. The two stood and went to the workshop.

Sabu lit a candle and opened the cooker lid in a corner of the workshop and showed five jars under the edge. The lower half of an object a little smaller than a water jar was buried in the ground. Three of the five jars had dates inscribed on the sealed lids.

Sabu described the objects as he pointed from the edge. Eiji nodded and said he understood. When he closed the cooker lid, Sabu looked doubtfully at Eiji as he blew out the candles.

He meekly asked, "Maybe, I should stay."

Eiji said, "Do what you want," and went to the kitchen to hang the wet towel on a rack. He returned to the workshop and sat.

"This job may decide our lives. It's now or never."

"I understand. It'll be all right," said Sabu then almost apologetically asked, "So is it okay for me to go?"

"This is a small celebration. Let's eat together and then you can go by palanquin."

"By palanquin?" Sabu gaped.

"So you can finish this quickly. This is a part of work," said Eiji and drew close his money belt. He took out only one koban. "This is an advance on your pay. Don't worry, take it."

Sabu started to speak, but Eiji broke in.

"It's okay. Take it."

Saying no more, he closed the string of the money belt.

"Sabu, it has to be this way given your personality. This is your money. I may sound heartless but don't spend it on your people in Kasai.

"You know, Sabu, depending on how the work goes, you will marry Osei-chan. If you show your generosity with money in Kasai, you will make Osei-chan cry because of your family."

"Wa ... Wait," stuttered Sabu. "If you say everything at once, I get confused. Ei-chan, what are you saying I'm supposed to do with Osei-chan?"

Eiji waved his hand like he was brushing him off.

"Forget it. We'll talk after you get back."

"But if you expect me and Osei-chan to get married, you have the wrong idea."

"I know you say she's still a child. Okay, but we'll talk later."

16.3

The next day, a strong north wind blew. The cold was biting. Soon after breakfast, Eiji went to Yamatoya at 4-chome, Hongoku-chō to check on the order.

As requested, the items would be ready within five days. The proprietor of Yamatoya said future prices would get better if their business relationship developed.

Usually, papermakers were a proud lot. This appears to be the origin of their temperament distinct from that of other merchants. Regardless of the distance to the region where the paper was produced, a lot of money and a discerning eye were critical requirements for the supply of a large quantity of high-quality paper. More than anything, the paper was a precious article.

However, Yamatoya was different. All the ordered items were reasonably priced, even the finest quality papers. Also, the process of placing orders may have agreed with Eiji's personality. Especially, the proprietor Saburōbei was personable, told Eiji not to worry about the bill, and spoke of future orders.

"Hey," called Saburōbei when he saw Eiji stand, "What happened to your leg?"

"Oh, I hurt it last summer in the big storm," said Eiji, rubbing his leg. "I was a klutz and sprained it, but nothing was damaged. Is it an eyesore?"

Saburōbei shook his head no. "My second son has a bad leg. Well, please be careful."

Eiji said nothing and lowered his head.

When he left the shop, the strong winds were stirring up dust on the road. Eiji thought about a quick visit to Ishikawajima.

He thought they might have heard about his leg but wanted to share his good luck in getting this job with Okayasu Kihei and Yohei.

He felt the chance meeting of the Yamatoya proprietor to be an endorsement of that good luck.

After being sent to the labor camp, bad things kept happening. His experience was bad luck did not come alone but often in clusters. However, good luck may be the same. If that's the case, thought Eiji, I have to grab onto this and make it work for us.

He hailed a street palanquin at the corner and rode to the ferry going to the island at the riverbank in Funamatsu-chō. Eiji went to the guardhouse when he arrived at the island and asked to see Okayasu Kihei.

"If it isn't Bushū," said the surprised elderly watchman. "You're the last man I expected to see. How are things going? How's your leg? Please have a seat. Wait here."

A middle-aged watchman returned to tell him Okayasu would be right over to see him. While the elderly watchman smoked a cigarette, he wanted to talk about the big storm, but Eiji demurred and apologized again saying he stopped by on his way home.

A lower-ranking official going to the office escorted Eiji to the reception area.

Okayasu Kihei appeared a few moments later. He wore black hakama trousers full of wrinkles. The collar of his undergarment was exposed at his chest. His clothes were rumpled as though he'd been brawling.

Something caught Eiji's eyes. Okayasu noticed and patted his trousers. While fixing his collar, he sat.

He muttered a new arrival was an incorrigible thug and then stared uneasily at Eiji's face.

"And you," whispered Okayasu like a spy, "What fix are you in now?"

Eiji was moved. Looking at Okayasu's expression, he asked that question from his heart out of concern. As Eiji felt burning in the backs of his eyes, he shook his head no and extended both hands in greeting.

"The truth is I finally landed a job. I thought you'd be happy so I dropped by to tell you," said Eiji, raising his head. "But it's not in Edo. It's work requested by a customer in the countryside. If it goes well, I think I can get a foothold in running a shop."

"That's great. Wonderful," said Okayasu, his tense expression relaxed in relief. "That is excellent news. I heard from Matsuda that congratulations are in order for your having found a fine wife."

Okayasu Kihei suddenly seemed inattentive and wasn't politely listening to Eiji. Needless to say, his concern was directed toward the newly-arrived laborer. If Eiji came with some problem, he would have spent time talking it out. But Eiji left the labor camp and found work. It's good he knew that, and now Eiji no longer needed his care.

Okayasu Kihei was preoccupied with a new laborer, specifically, the unruly thug. While Eiji was thinking this, he asked about Yohei and heard about Seishichi, aka Bump. Every man in The Dirt Basket Room was off the island at work. Of course, Yohei was with them. Everyone he knew was absent. There's been no news about Seishichi, not even where he was living.

"He was with Toyo, that woman," said Okayasu, the area of his eyebrows clouded over. "He moved three times with her. The third time they moved to 1-chome, Kobiki-chō, but after that, Seishichi disappeared."

"How do you know that?"

"People who leave here are monitored by the police of the town magistrate for a year. Of course, neither he nor his neighbors are aware of this."

"So ..." Eiji lowered his voice, "Am I being watched, too?"

Okayasu smiled. "You didn't notice, but of course, you're monitored, too. This prevents a mistake from becoming, in the rare event, a crime."

Eiji bowed his head deeply.

"The woman Toyo still lives in a house in a backstreet of 1-chome, Kobiki-chō," said Okayasu. "Her new man is a packhorse driver and seems to be five years younger than she is."

Okayasu said, "Seishichi may have gone back to the country."

16.4

Eiji thought, He has no reason to go home to the countryside. He's so in love with Toyo, I can't believe he'd leave her.

Seishichi disappeared after moving to Kobiki-chō. The monitor following him said, "He vanished," and wondered if something unusual happened to him. Thoughts of the packhorse driver, who succeeded Seishichi and was five years Toyo's junior, created a heaviness in Eiji's chest like a dark, ominous shadow.

"What happened, Sei-san," Eiji softly pleaded in the palanquin on his return to Sakamoto-chō. "Where are you?"

Eiji whispered almost in prayer, If you're somewhere safe, it'd be better to go back to the camp. On the island, people could no longer torment you.

Sabu hadn't come back. Yamatoya delivered the paper. Eiji matched them to the measurements notebook and absorbed himself in cutting the paper. He burned with anger when he thought about Sabu, so his mind concentrated on nothing other than his task of cutting the paper according to the measurements.

After dinner, he drank sake to distract himself. Even Sue never mentioned Sabu's name; she understood Eiji's rage. Like touching the tip of a wild rose's thorn, it always pricked a nerve.

On the evening of the eighth day after Sabu left, while drinking sake after dinner, Eiji suddenly slammed down the cup.

"Sue, have you finished preparing?"

Sue nodded uneasily. "Yes, I'm ready."

"Good. Then we'll leave tomorrow," said Eiji and stood. "I'll have a look. Please bring me the light."

He asked bluntly like his patience was gone. Sue couldn't say a word.

Eiji entered the workshop and opened the cooker lid in the corner like he couldn't feel the chill in the wood-floor room.

When Sue followed with a paper-covered standing lamp, he said, "Give me the paste barrel."

Sue took down a lidded bucket from the shelves built on one side of the workshop and thoroughly wiped the inside with a dry cloth.

Eiji peeled off the seal of the first bottle and took off the wooden lid tightly inserted.

The scent of the cold dirt floor and the smell of the aged paste enveloped his head. He turned the lid from the bin upside down, placed it in the wood-floor room, and stared at whatever was written on the underside of the lid.

He wrote the date affixed to the prepared paste on the front. Eiji wondered what was written on the back and drew the lamp closer. It was certainly Sabu's writing. As he read, Eiji's face stiffened, and he seemed to instantly sober up.

"Sue," he said, his voice sounding hoarse. "Bring the sake. Cold is okay."

"Bring it here?"

"Yes, here," he said feebly. "Please bring two or three bottles and a cup."

Sue started to speak but brought the sake without questioning him because of his odd behavior.

Eiji sat cross-legged directly in front of the wood-floor room beside the lantern. As he stared at the underside of the lid, he drank cold sake from the teacup.

Sue carried in a tray with a snack, she said because it was cold. He didn't hear her at all and said nothing. He didn't pick up the chopsticks, riveted by the characters on the back of the lid. She looked at the sake bottles, two were empty.

In a calming voice, Sue said, "If we're leaving tomorrow, maybe you shouldn't drink so much."

"It was him," said Eiji, "Sabu did it."

"Did what?"

"Stole the gold broach at Watabun," said Eiji. He scowled. "Read this," he said, pointing at the back of the paste lid.

Sue peeked and read the characters written there, then she looked fearfully at Eiji.

"You see?" said Eiji.

Sue shook her head.

"It's written here," said Eiji, tracing the characters with his fingertip while he read and made her listen.

"I was bad. Ei-chan being sent to the island because of that broach was my crime. Even if it takes my whole life, I must make up for this crime."

16.5

Eiji sat up properly and scrutinized Sue's face. He picked up the third sake bottle, filled his cup, and downed it in one gulp.

"This didn't make sense to me for a long time," said Eiji, continuing to glare at the ceiling. "Sabu and I have been friends since we were apprentices. But after being sent to the island for three years, naturally, he did things for me. What was he thinking? He went too far.

"Not only did he take time off from work to search for me. That wasn't normal. I never spoke my name or mentioned my love of Hōko-dō. I was sent to the island as a vagrant.

"Locating anyone in this vast Edo could be said to be an impossible task for a human. Not only did he find me, but later he also did other things for me. Sabu often took time off from Hōko-dō to visit me on the island."

"Please wait a moment."

"You wait," said Eiji. He poured sake into his cup and took a sip. "During each break from work or vacation day, he brought gifts, even for the men in my room. Why? Eventually, the proprietor of Hōko-dō heard about it and fired Sabu from his shop. For what? Was it because we were friends since being apprentices and good friends?"

"Yes, I think that's so," said Sue. She nodded, her face pale and tense. "I heard when at Watabun that Sabu-chan had been your friend since you both were small, and he would depend on you his whole life. If Ei-chan weren't there, he'd probably become a construction laborer or a street peddler. I heard this from Sabu-chan."

"Yeah." Eiji sipped the sake and slowly shook his head like he was sneering. "You were about to say, 'Don't you remember?'"

"What are you remembering?"

Eiji gently shook his head again as an action to erase the scene at Ryōgoku Bridge in the rain evoked in the backs of his eyes.

"This is what I think," Sue said, "When the golden broach mishap happened, Sabu-chan was working with you and didn't know the broach was placed in your tool bag.

"He was by your side and wasn't aware of that serious incident. He couldn't prevent the calamity of the man he thought he'd rely on for his whole life while by his side.

"It would be natural for Sabu-chan to think it was his crime and to pay for it somehow. Sabu or anyone else would think so. Sabu-chan certainly thought this."

Eiji stared at Sue's face. "You're shaking."

"Sabu-chan did extraordinary things for your sake. It's not like you to suspect a man like him."

"If so, what am I supposed to do about what's written here?"

Sue turned up her hardened face. "Will you drink water?" she asked and stood.

Eiji poured sake into the cup and held it up to his mouth. He scowled and didn't drink. His hand brought the cup down to his knee. Sue returned and sat.

"I have to apologize to you," she said, staring at her knees. In a near whisper, she said, "Although I intended never to mention this for my whole life, you suspect Sabu-chan. If your friendship falls apart, you will never recover. So I'll tell you."

Eiji said nothing and stared at Sue.

"I'm sorry. Please forgive me," she said, raising both hands to the wood-floor room. "The person who put the gold broach in your tool bag was me."

"Stop it." Eiji broke in. "If you're trying to smooth things over for Sabu, pitiful lies like that won't work."

"It's not a lie. It's the truth."

Sue returned her hands to her knees. Eiji stared with widened eyes.

"I wanted to become your wife. I would do anything to make you mine."

Eiji shook his head in disbelief, calmed his eyes, and looked at Sue's expression. He leaped up, left the workshop, and shut the front door. To digest the meaning of her words, he had to clear his mind.

"Tell me," said Eiji when he returned to his seat. "What are you saying?"

"You were popular at Watabun," said Sue. "More than being a visiting workman, you got along well with both daughters, Kimi-san and Sono-san, like a sibling. The rumor was someday one of them would become Ei-san's wife."

"Stop saying Ei-san."

"I heard that rumor," continued Sue. "Each time I heard that rumor I'd get a knot in my stomach and couldn't eat."

"You should have known how I felt," said Eiji.

Sue nodded. "I know. I know, but doesn't a woman have petty feelings? I thought the rumors I heard were true. It was awful. I was a maid. My rivals were the Watabun daughters. In that situation, my dream would never come true. At some time, you'd be taken. I fretted over what I should do and what I could do. I didn't sleep for nights."

"I understand," said Eiji, "If that's true, you can stop."

"No, please let me speak. There's one more thing," she said. wiping away tears with her fingers. "So that the daughters couldn't take you away, you couldn't be allowed to work at Watabun. I was obsessed with that one thought.

"Later, I wondered how could I make this happen. You may not know this, but I knew the Watabun proprietor valued that broach and lost my head."

"Enough," said Eiji, "I know. I don't have to hear anymore."

"I'm sorry."

"Don't cry," said Eiji, slid closer on his knees, and hugged Sue's body with both arms.

"I'm so sorry. Forgive me," said Sue, clinging to Eiji's chest and groaning. "I wanted to become your wife. This filled my head. I couldn't think about anything else."

"All right. It's okay." Eiji put strength into his hug. "Look, aren't we married? This is good proof."

"Please forgive me," said Sue in a broken voice while sobbing. She buried her face into Eiji's chest. "Don't send me away. I'm begging you. Please don't drive me out."

Sue's moans grew louder, and she cried out. Eiji kept hugging Sue with his left arm while stroking her back with his right hand and pressing his cheek to hers.

"You are my wife," he whispered. "I told you at the beginning. My wife in this world is you. Did you forget?"

Sue's crying voice got louder. He held her tighter in both arms.

"This may sound funny, but please listen and don't laugh," Eiji said softly. "I think being sent to the island was a good thing. I learned many things during my three years at the labor camp and ran head-on into events I never faced in the ordinary world. I learned about connections among people, phony and true feelings, and life's pains and hardships. I learned these things directly with my body I could never learn from books or talking."

Sue stopped crying but still heaved with sobs.

"The three years at the camp were worth more than ten years in the outside world. That's how I feel. Don't think I was lying. Now, I want to thank you."

Suddenly, Sue hugged Eiji's neck with both arms and shouted, "Oh, Eiji."

He kissed Sue's lips, her cheeks, her eyes, and her soft neck as he embraced her with all his might.

Tapping sounds came from the front rain shutter.

A voice passed in from outside. "Ei-chan. Are you there, Ei-chan? I'm back."

"It's Sabu," said Eiji.

Again he heard, "Please forgive me, Ei-chan. I stayed until today when my mother took her last breath and then I left. I was wrong, Ei-chan. I'm sorry. Please open the door. It's me, Sabu."

衣食住之内家職幼絵解之図

CREDITS

Japanese Text
Yamamoto, Shūgorō. "Sabu" (in Japanese). *Shūkan Asahi* (January 4 to July 5, 1963).
Aozora Bunko file accessed June 14, 2019.
Input by: Harukaze Non-Profit Organization
Revised by: Sunaba Kiyotaka
https://www.aozora.gr.jp/cards/001869/files/57624_69967.html

Cover Image
Ichiryūsai Hiroshige. "Tōkyō Meisho Nihonbashi Shinkei Narabini Uoichi Zenzu," Tsutaya Kichizō, National Diet Library Digital Collections. (Accessed November 9, 2022.)
https://dl.ndl.go.jp/pid/1302537

Calligraphy and Picture Shop
Utagawa Hiroshige. "Edo Meisho Gasan," 2, National Diet Library Digital Collections (Accessed November 9, 2022.)
https://dl.ndl.go.jp/pid/1287444/1/30

Paper Craftsmen Woodblock Print
Utagawa Kuniteru II. *Ishokujū Shoshoku Etoki Nishikie*. Tokyo: Monbushō Seihonjo, 1870.
National Diet Library Digital Collections. (Accessed April 9, 2023.) https://dl.ndl.go.jp/ja/pid/2542939/1/8

Paper Craftsmen Painting
Kuwagata Keisai. *Shokunin Zukushi Ekotoba*. Scroll 2 (Original), Wada Otogorō, 1000.
National Diet Library Digital Collections. (Accessed April 9, 2023.) https://dl.ndl.go.jp/pid/11536005/1/14

ABOUT THE AUTHOR

Yamamoto Shūgorō was a Japanese novelist, essayist, and playwright. He was born Shimizu Satomu, the oldest child of Shimizu Itsutarō and Toku, on June 22, 1903 in Hatsukari-mura, Yamanashi Prefecture, Japan, and died February 14, 1967 in Yokohama, Kanagawa Prefecture, Japan. After graduating from school, he became a live-in apprentice at Yamamoto Shūgorō, a pawnbroker's shop that closed in the wake of The Great Kantō Earthquake in 1923.

In 1924, he joined the clerical section of Teikoku Koshinjo, a credit agency, and later became an editor at the employee magazine *Nipponkon* of a subsidiary company.

His debut literary work *Suma-dera Fukin* was published in the April 1926 edition of *Bungei Shunjū*. The magazine misunderstood his address at Yamamoto Shūgorō Shimizu 36, resulting in his pen name.

In 1943, he declined the 17th Naoki Prize for his work *Nihon Fudōki*. He published over twenty novels over forty years. Many of his stories were adapted to film and television.

From the Japanese Wikipedia page about Yamamoto Shūgorō. (Accessed March 26, 2023.)

https://ja.wikipedia.org/wiki/%E5%B1%B1%E6%9C%AC%E5%91%A8%E4%BA%94%E9%83%8E

Printed in Poland
by Amazon Fulfillment
Poland Sp. z o.o., Wrocław

43716161R00156